SCANDAL
AT THE
ALPHORN
FACTORY

ALSO BY GARY BARWIN

FICTION

Nothing the Same, Everything Haunted: The Ballad of Motl the Cowboy
Yiddish for Pirates
I, Dr. Greenblatt, Orthodontist, 251-1457
Doctor Weep and Other Strange Teeth
Big Red Baby
The Mud Game (with Stuart Ross)

POETRY

duck eats yeast, quacks, explodes; man loses eye (with Lillian Nećakov)
For It Is a Pleasure and a Surprise to Breathe: New and Selected Poems
A Cemetery for Holes (with Tom Prime)
No TV for Woodpeckers
The Wild and Unfathomable Always
Moon Baboon Canoe
Franzlations: the imaginary Kafka parables (with Craig Conley &
Hugh Thomas)
The Obvious Flap (with Gregory Betts)
The Porcupinity of the Stars
frogments from the frag pool (with derek beaulieu)
Raising Eyebrows
Outside the Hat
Cruelty to Fabulous Animals

NON-FICTION

Imagining Imagining: Essays on Language, Identity, and Infinity

EDITOR

Sonosyntactics: Selected and New Poetry of Paul Dutton

SCANDAL
AT THE
ALPHORN
FACTORY

NEW AND SELECTED
SHORT FICTION, 2024–1984

GARY BARWIN

Assembly Press
Prince Edward County, Ontario

Grateful acknowledgement to the original publishers and editors of the books from which these stories have been selected. Stories from *I, Dr. Greenblatt, Orthodontist, 251-1457* appear with the permission of Anvil Press.

Library and Archives Canada Cataloguing in Publication

Title: Scandal at the alphorn factory : new and selected short fiction, 2024-1984 / Gary Barwin.
Names: Barwin, Gary, author
Identifiers: Canadiana (print) 20240417224 | Canadiana (ebook) 20240417267 | ISBN 9781738009886 (softcover) | ISBN 9781738009893 (EPUB)
Subjects: LCGFT: Short stories.
Classification: LCC PS8553.A783 S23 2024 | DDC C813/.54—dc23

Cover and interior design by Greg Tabor
Printed and bound in Canada

Published by Assembly Press
assemblypress.ca

TABLE OF CONTENTS

The alphorn factory is vast beyond belief

Rudi puts his lips to the mysterious
by the time it arrives at the other side
there is no other side

✦

LEDERHOSEN, COMPASSION, AND NEAR-DEATH

Eight years old in a Northern Ireland school, late-afternoon sun slanting across the ink-stained, initial-scratched desks. An old man is telling us Irish fairy stories. I was never a Knight of the Times Table (something eluded me about jousting with sevens), never understood cricket—was stuck in the outfield, under the trees, gazing up at the leaves, daydreaming, while other boys worried about wickets and bowlers, the crease and the perfect bowl—but I feel the sound of this storyteller's voice, the tropes of story, the space-time everywhere and nowhere of folktales. The made-up but already there. Words but not words. Like individual pieces of glass, they are also part of a larger pattern, each pattern part of an even larger mosaic.

What does it mean to be fictional for forty years? My friend Mark Gormley and I imagine the headmaster's daughter on the third floor and we become some kind of coal-grimy *Water-Babies* chimney-sweep children fallen into the hearth beside her all-white four-poster while she in Victorian lace is a girl version of *Chitty Chitty Bang Bang*'s Truly Scrumptious. But we are also the near-naked slaves prostrate before the ageless queen in H. Rider Haggard's *She*, which I'd seen as a movie on the telly. We tell each other these stories on the gym floor before chapel, where a graduate plays harp and others hit each other on the head with hymn books they slide expertly back into school blazer pockets before being caught by the masters.

I tell another friend I am part of a secret organization. I have a small leather-bound book and point to an engraving of a bearded man in the front of the book—our leader. Charles Dickens, who stood for my identification with the perception of mystery, what language was, what story could be. And, of course, this was itself a story. A story always tells the story of itself. The self-defining fiction of its own fiction. The two Escher hands drawing each other.

NINETEEN-SEVENTIES CANADA. MY first published story: "Cosmic Herbert and the Pencil Forest." My dad's medical resident thought I'd written "Penis Forest." "The penis mightier than the sword," a friend would later quip. I wrote, illustrated, photocopied, and bound copies to sell for the Grade 5 White Elephant Sale at Graham Park Public School—we loved when the first L fell off that school's sign. Cosmic Herbert looked something like a cartoon of Mel Brooks's 2,000 Year Old Man in a wizard hat, but he was also a writer.

Next memory: A villanelle about "my wonderful tuba made of bread." Repeated revisions, each annotated, then retyped, a feeling that if I were to make or discover a new part of the world, it had to be perfect, even in its ridiculousness.

As an adult, I go to a massage therapist and share the selected stories of my body. A car accident at sixteen. Back surgery in my early thirties. Forty-year-old father leaps with his kids off a cliff into a Honduran river. Toe broken on a tree root while wearing Birkenstocks in the woods, listening to a podcast about Tolkien, the nerdiest injury ever.

What does it mean to have a career's worth of short fiction gathered in *Scandal at the Alphorn Factory*? That the fiction isn't long? That there are themes or approaches that recur? Perhaps an explanation of the title might serve as an answer.

I'm attracted to images that, like the alphorn, are both simple real-world objects and yet also uncanny and magical. Alphorns are very basic wooden horns, but at the same time, they're twelve feet long and used to signal from Swiss mountaintops. To me, the alphorn reveals the wonder and strangeness of the world and the human imagination. Their doleful high-altitude bleating speaks to tenderness and uncertainty, and to the bewildering and marvellous situation of being alive.

But the title also mentions both a scandal and a factory. What kind of narrative might connect the two? Could it involve lederhosen, compassion, and near death? Astronomers? Plumbers? History? Is this us, never more ourselves than feeling sad or happy in the parking lot of an alphorn factory, looking in the windows and trying to understand, to remember, to recognize? I'm moved by the juxtaposition of natural spaces (alpine meadows) and urban human spaces (factories), of the poetic and the absurd, and how we creatively navigate between them as individuals and as a culture.

This book gathers forty years of individual works of short fiction. One story leads to another, another iteration of story, just as each year I am a particular iteration of myself, a different iteration of the possible me.

Same hat, different rabbit.

Same rabbi, different hat.

Each individual piece of fiction reads as continuous with the others, yet, at the same time, as a reinvention. A reimagining, a recontextualizing. In Italo Calvino's *If on a Winter's Night a Traveler*, a novelist ruminates in his journal that he'd like to find a way to experience "it writes" the way one can experience "it rains." This resonates with me: the idea that the writing is "out there" and my role as writer is to find it, to draw from it, to frame a small piece of it—perhaps as the landscape artist only represents one scene of the larger surrounding world. It's not the world per se that I'm gathering but the writing that's out there. Writing surrounds us. The world is writing that has some relation to our experience in and of the world. In this sense, it feels most certainly larger than my rational, ego-bound mind.

Since I began writing, I've worked hard to incorporate broader experiences, expand my technical resources, try new things, and uncover a deeper understanding of, well, everything. I feel tender and excited about the writing of the twenty-year-old me who sometimes stumbled into things that forty years later are still fresh, energetic, and open. And, to be honest, I feel tender and excited about the writing of the other me's too, including this most recent, sixty-year-old me, though I know all too well his hopes and shortcomings.

Here I am near the end of this introduction and I'm feeling emotional about collecting all this work together in one book. I'm grateful to have a chance to share it. Life is many things—bewildering, strange, beautiful, painful, absurd, inspiring, breathtaking, surprising, funny—and braided throughout with the paradox of language, space-time, and story. I hope some of that has found its way in here too.

NEW AND PREVIOUSLY
UNCOLLECTED STORIES

GOLEMSON

"There is love in me the likes of which you've never seen."
—Kenneth Branagh's *Frankenstein*

Night. I was waiting on a bench. On the sidewalk. In the fog. Toronto: Eglinton, near Dufferin. Outside a music store, its window filled with accordions, lurid red plastic trumpets, and a *Que Sera, Sera* LP leaning against some maracas. It was a fitting theme song for the students who passed through the little backroom, taking lessons with Pasquale, at least in terms of the uncertain melodies they produced with their nervous, ill-prepared fingers. But kids—who knew what those fingers were capable of now? The future's not ours to see, after all. It may possibly be filled with skilled accordionists.

Night and fog. The music store mute. I watched him walk down the street, moving between clouds of lamplit luminosity and obscurity. Wearing a dark suit and a bowler hat, like Magritte or the men in his paintings. Like me.

Kidding. In a bowler hat, I'd look more like an aging droog. He moved toward me with no expression on his face, but I saw he was a form of regret made manifest. One of my many regrets. Usually, they're not so dapper.

My golem.

I hadn't seen him for years. We'd lost touch and, in a way, I was surprised I recognized him. Surprised he was still alive. I didn't think golems could live so long.

We had been close once. Twins. Lovers of a kind, even.

No. We never were. I know nothing of his viscera. I do not know if golems can love. Or if they can make love. With another golem. With anything. All that clay. Might gum up the works.

It's said that, like Adam, we're all born as golems. Guileless mammal-forms. That misfortune shapes us into the complex humans we are. But I've met breadboxes more capable of love than many of the misfortune-moulded walking Freud couches I've encountered.

"My dreidel," I said to the Golem. "I made you out of clay."

But how do you make a golem? I didn't know, so I googled it. It is said that you harvest a bathtub's worth of clay exhumed from a grave by a riverbed, enough to fill a body bag. You take it home and form a colossal, three-dimensional gingerbread man with your mortal hands. You are tender and stern. You do this at night while weeping, praying, while drunk.

Then you write the name for God on the skin of a woman who has died in childbirth, skin the span of a baby's chest. Or you ask for and are given a hymen on which you write *Elohim*. You write *Shem*, a name of God, and a magic formula on a piece of parchment, a slip of paper—even a Post-it note—and place in it it in the golem's mouth. You write אמת, *emet*, the Hebrew word for truth, on its forehead. When you wish to undo the life of the creature, the creature who was only a certain kind of alive, you erase the first letter, aleph, leaving מת, *met*, the Hebrew word for dead. If you do not know Hebrew, you write something else. You freewrite. You edit. You take the name of God from its mouth. The creature returns to being earth only, can be used to make pots, or coffee mugs, or terracotta tiles.

How had I made the golem?

Clay. Amphetamines. The Hebrew I remembered from my bar mitzvah.

A kit ordered from the internet.

It was a mess the first time. The second time also.

I threw the clay over the fence.

HE'D COME TO me in the night. I woke, and before I opened my eyes and saw him, I knew he was there, standing silently by our bed, a massive presence, a dark shadow in the dark. As always, wearing a dark suit and a bowler. A nice touch, I'd thought.

Mary was in the bed beside me. We'd been married for six years, though we'd been together for thirteen, having met at university when we both lived in the Annex, on Brunswick, just off Bloor. We tried to have children, but eventually our doctor determined that, in terms of procreation, I was a Peter Pan, a feeble warbler in a choir of perpetual boys. The few swimmers I had were dog-paddling splutterers.

"Will I ever be able to have a child of my own?" I asked.

"Unlikely," the doctor said.

We tried anyway. Each month a ritual of waiting, hoping, praying, of temperature-appointed times, of reassurances. Of discussions of options.

There was a month when we thought Mary was pregnant. Hoping against hope. Mary was late and she had a feeling, a murmuration behind her ribs. Blood cells turning in a slow sarabande, or maybe it was too much smoked meat, too much coffee, an anxiety-hope blend. We'd been trying for so long. We'd made tomato sauce and soups together, made bread and family meals, as if through ritual we could transubstantiate our relationship into a living thing, a viable zygote that would divide and divide and divide into our child, Zeno's paradox: the arrow finds its mark,

GARY BARWIN

the rabbit overtakes. We would make more cells in the world and the world would come into greater focus, a kind of higher-resolution pixelation. Our story would become more vibrant, luminous. Moving. Happy.

But as we worried and hoped, I was increasingly turning into clay myself. My cells merging, not dividing, into large simple shapes. Cellular goons. At one point, I gave sperm to the doctor to be centrifuged, boiled down like maple syrup, syringed.

Syringe. I remembered when I was a child in an Irish hospital ward. Rows of starched white sheets, metal-framed beds. A large needle stuck into my upper thigh. The needle still in, the blue-uniformed nurse replaced the syringe with another and again emptied it into my muscle. I'd thought of the stamps I'd been given commemorating John Millington Synge, his shaggy-dog moustache and expressionless face. I thought it said John Millington *Syringe*.

"Are you happy?" my wife began asking. It was then that the golem appeared beside my bed, silent, shadowy, dapper.

My golem. I made you out of clay.

Was the golem happy?

Because of him, I ill-advisedly quit my teaching job without telling my wife, even though we had no real savings. I imagined myself a sad sack in a Tom Waits song, heading west with a suitcase and a back seat full of bourbon, looking for cheap hotels in which to write a mixture of despair and out-of-focus faith. But really, after I quit my job, I just stayed home, became silent. I slept all day. My marriage ended. My grandfather used to say, "Der oylem iz a goylem"—"People are fools." And I was people.

For years after my marriage ended, I thought I saw my golem walking down streets, in a booth at a restaurant, in a passing lane beside me on the highway. I kept watching for him, waiting. And then I got an email. It was from the golem. All caps. Of course.

I didn't take it for internet shouting but as an ironic dig at the simple preschool sensibility of the average golem. My wife— my ex-wife—had a child. Unto her a son was born. Apparently, the child was his. I imagined their late-night coupling as if it were a folktale. In rain and fog, in a graveyard, they had come together, an elemental and preternatural force, as if it had to be so. The cracking open of gravestones and of things as they were. I saw her thin hands reach around the incredible clay hulk of the golem's shoulders, leaving scalloped impressions, like a child's fingers squeezing a kindergarten craft project. The golem swaying like an old tree. His face wasn't peaceful—rather, I'd say, unperturbed. A character in a legend following the story he knows to be written for him with quiet resolution and little emotion.

But it wasn't like that.

I MADE THE CHILD, his email read.

It was an opaque night. A story.

Under the crow limbs of a dark tree, he did agitate his fertile horn until his seed was free. Lightning strikes the oak, in a Jekyll-and-Hyde moment, the instant of the golem's grounding. Glass vials like vacuum tubes hide under the black wing of his cloak. And then he rides to town, a headless horseman, his satchel full of jism.

I assumed that Mary hadn't planned on being the mother of the golem's child. I thought of that creepy yet surprisingly beloved kids' story where the mother slinks across town, sneaks into her grown son's bedroom to hold him and sing of her love. I imagined the golem silently crushing the screen door handle in his fist to let himself in the back door to Mary's kitchen. Mary stretched out on the living room couch, her nightgown hiked high in the summer heat, a bottle of her customary sleeping pills beside her. Stalwart, silent, unblinking, the golem solemnly approaches. The golem has a syringe. A turkey baster.

But then my story fades. This was not the story in his email. Yes, he arrived and stood before her in the summer heat. He touched his big fingers to her slim face. The golem large as an armoire. She smiled. He leaned down, a hummock come to life. He kissed her forehead. She felt the cool coils of his lips, the low rush of his breath. His eyes filled with desire. To be human. To be tender. To love.

He would lie with Mary, would be the lithe Romeo to her delicate Juliet. But almost-human that he was, he could not. Yet Mary would lie beside him after, butterfly fluttering through the great forest of his body. They would join. Would share life. Would create it as the golem was created from the unpromising mud of earth. Life would be created by sharing life. Their life. His forehead presses against hers, imprinting it with the word. *Emet.* Truth. Met, death, always there within the word, and now marked on Mary's skin, its mirror image.

The golem and Mary, from his sample, did join gametes, both male and female, and so did cause the spring. And I, distant, absent, my words telling another story.

The child, the golem wrote, was named after me. Kidding, he said. It wasn't. They named it René, after Mary's father.

When I'd finished reading his email, I'd responded immediately. *Golem*, I wrote. *Congratulations. To all of you. And—since you seem to have some experience in this sort of thing—grant me, if you would, this kindness.*

All the golems, from those in the Bible to those in Reb Loew's Prague, were Claymation palookas with no more wit than a brick. But they had life. Sometimes a golem is created out of longing, ambition, failure, and a need to know that you are somehow real, that your ministrations and hope may affect the world. But sometimes too, in time, a son can create his own father, and a golem can create the writing that created him. A kind of pearl writing the clam into being. As I wrote my golem into life, or at least wished it, so he would write me.

And so we met at the hour and location he suggested. Midnight at the bench. Outside the closed music store. In the Toronto fog.

My golem carried a small box, a green dented-metal cooler, held to his chest in an embrace. Protecting it, as in a mother-and-child painting. I was both disturbed and relieved by what was likely inside.

"I have it," he said.

"Don't spend this all in one place." I handed him an envelope. "Really," I said. "Don't."

He handed me the box without another word, and then he continued down the sidewalk, past the 7-Eleven, the library, the mattress store. Into the night. What was in the box? A corned beef sandwich? A donated heart? A taxidermy squirrel dressed as Napoleon, little tricorn hat pinned between its ears? Did I trust him?

I opened the box with apprehension. I felt a cloud of cold on the back of my hand. Inside, an envelope. I pulled out the slip of paper with a sense of inevitability and dread.

אמת.

✦

WESTERN

Because my desk is a horse, the world is my office. Yes, these mountains are inbox and out, the sky a glass ceiling. I receive emails from the dust, poorly written spam from desperate tumbleweed. This all happened so long ago it might well be the future, for I was a young man, just a girl, a flash of lightning from the midnight tinderbox, my world the edge of the world. I'd left both future and past, stole a palomino, rode out beyond the horizon into the short corridor of the present. Buzzards and vultures circled the cooler, hankering for my weak nerves to expire. Instead, I throbbed like a sorrowful thing while the sun sent memos direct to my temples, boiled my spine.

"Hey, good lookin'," I said to the cracked river, but it had gone to lunch. By late night, I played mouth harp as doggies burned and constellations got to howling. I reckoned somewheres along the way, I'd got a sidekick: my own brain. It didn't always listen but spoke short and laconic and was sometimes eager. What do we hope out here beyond pavement, where coyotes are known to invest in diversified lamentation?

"Well, Brain," I said. "We're here to set up shop as heroes and now it's time for cold calls to the helpless. Civilization's stelliferous veneer is thin, and happenstance can grit like sandpaper. We've travelled this moving dirt sidewalk to be shellac on hard times." My brain said nothing back, but nodded as I nodded and raised my hat to possibility. It was all around us, hiding in plain view. The world was on hold, and we'd find its flashing button.

Rabbit arrived first. We shot and skinned him and ate his warm breath. "Rabbit," I said. "You and I, and, of course, my brain, are one, and in my human canyon, you are fire. Look around, for I have eaten your eyes, and with this dinner of flesh there's possibility everywhere. We'll not starve before we have saved."

"Now, Brain," I said, "we are well fortified for adventure. Let us find some." Brain said nothing but steeled as I steeled myself and scanned for what was to be. We looked beyond inbox and out and past the great boss's hallway, but there was nothing. We looked again; there remained nothing.

We were visited then by many dry days and weeks of desiccated impossibility. Insides became as boot leather. My gut was a black rock rolling in place like dry thunder. Bones ached dry thunder also. Great doubt came upon us, and we heard the muttering of despair in the next room. "Keep it down," I said. "We're trying to work here. We aim to be heroes before our mortal end."

It was a ghost that found us second, all the vapours of what we wished would be. "Ride further," it said. "Find more days in your weak bones." It wasn't lost on Brain that this goading spirit was but voice and no bones, advice but no meat. I remembered Father calling me to his knee and opining, "When there's no fish and no river, cast down your rod and ride to the next valley with a gun." Ah, gun, my handshake of fire. I breathed in the ghost's tobacco guts as if they coiled from a pipe, closed my eyes, and began to think of the respite that awaits at the end of days. But Brain spurred on my weak horse, my soft hands and weak will, and we travelled slow into the next day, which was a pink folder of opportunity. Or perhaps I should state that there were many people looking like work to be done. "We have rode far beyond the previous end of our own story to rescue you from yours, which is possibly grievous or sorry," I said. "We hope to relieve pain or misfortune, to allow the waters of ease and comfort to flow once more through the difficult rivers of your life."

When we awoke, we found our body tied to the wheel of a large wagon and the sun slumped russet over the edge of day. Brain was suffering contusions of his perception, and I felt as a carpet must surely feel after a sound dusting. Our senses, except for those supplementary to suffering, were in great disarray. Finally, I remembered my hand, intending next to discover my gun. I learned then that I was birth-naked, and Brain, without hat, was covered only by skull.

I became aware of a great muttering. "We are planning something of a fricassee," one of the mutterers explained. "Our intended meat is to be yours."

If fear and low feeling could have lubricated my beef-jerky eyes, I would have wept, but instead my lids burned and I cried out, "We have come to this place because our business is in proffering aid to those in despair. We entreat you to spare our sorry flesh and choose another for this meal."

There was some chuckling, which I later learned had its source in a traveller named Theodora. "We intend not to dine upon you, but to offer you sup of flesh for your maintenance. Surveying you now, we see you are but gristle, despair, and starvation. Once you find hope and attain some worthy steak, we shall feed you to our God, who lives in that cave." She pointed to a black stain among glowering hills.

They fed me then, great red gobs of fat-ripe bone and muscle. I was as one gasping for air who had previously been under considerable water. "We thank you, Theodora," I said. "We have returned from a dark and hungering place." Brain awoke then, buoyed by vitamins and joy, and commenced his crafty calisthenics. Still affixed to the wheel, Brain and I concocted the notion to feign sleep, gnaw our restraints in silence, then ride away by moonlight. It was then we understood we had eaten our horse. "Sorrow not," I told Brain. "Our blood runs with gallop." We lay still as if carrion, awaiting the sleep of our captors. In darkness we gnawed and with stealth we crept beyond the circle of wagons and toward freedom.

The moon in its office of stars was the third thing that found us, alone on the plain, uncertain of our direction but charged with the vocation to seek the correct path. "Moon, memo to what must be, advise us of the way forward. Outline with your incisive silver our tasks and responsibilities, our role in the structure of this world."

The moon shone over the buttes that were as overturned chairs but said nothing. Its bright light searched our soul and we remembered and sorrowed for our lost steed, the desk of our ambition, the outcomes projected and wished for. And then we felt as much as understood that we toiled within the vast office of the possible. There was work to be done and we would attend to it, shaking down deadlines both personal and metaphysical. We would be known as heroes, for it was heroic to have such courage, to wish for such toil. And we would remain in the world, if we must, long beyond closing, far into the moonlit night, our sleeves rolled, our coffee cups grown cold, the world quiet, a brain and a body in the emptiness straining toward a destiny of our own making.

RADIAL

His mathematician father was dying, the father who would say that the body was an elaborate tube beginning with eating and breathing, ending with exhalation and excretion. A tube surrounded by the decorative hoo-ha of heart and lungs, brain, feet, flesh.

And now here he was, filled with love for a body that had always been his father. The fear of what the body had become. Would become.

Thank you for loving me, his father had said, speaking into the phone held against his onion skin, his worn snail ear. And so he had flown across the country to sit beside his father's thinning body, a lesser hillock rising from a hospital bed.

The small father, the tall son, each with the digits of π tattooed on their body. Round and round, the looping digits, the initial number 3 over the heart, then decimal point and numbers running across the chest, the nipple, the ribs, back to the shoulder bone, spine, shoulder bone, the ribs, then around front again to chest, the other nipple, then below the heart and around again, spiralling down and down and down, and then like a Gordian snake twisting up, over and under, intertwining with itself, a Möbius strip, a cat's cradle, quipu, math text. $2\pi r$ and $2\pi r$ and $2\pi r$, completed circles rising to the shoulders. π the never-ending, the not-repeating.

If you know the area, the radius is. If you know the

circumference, the radius is. If you know the span of your father, the radius is. And the tattoo of π: From 44137 in his thirties. From 31854 in his forties. The last numbers from 52563, ringing the throat. As he aged and his skin sagged, more surface, more room for numbers, and numbers were added. How many? Ten thousand? Eleven thousand? His favourite joke, something once announced on the PA at a math conference: "Will the mathematicians please move to the smaller half of the room."

He was ringed in beauty, elegance, practicality. Infinitude. How to measure the spokes for an ox cart's wheel. How to calculate the dimensions of a basilica's dome. What were the odds he'd found his grandfather's camp number somewhere in the sequence of π. A late-night discovery from a little-explored region far into π. But the tattoos weren't intended to obscure the original body. His father, huffing small sips of air, his vein-rivened eyelids blue, the back of his hand pierced to receive morphine. Several days of this; he waited and his father weakened. Was there time to say what needed to be said? What did they need to say? His father recounting the story of the cottage broken into by a bear that then found its way into the kitchen, everyone hiding in the toilet, unsure what happened next. When his father met his mother and later she died as another car crossed the line and only father and son remained. When his father then began the tattoo. Three. Mother, father, son. Then 3.145 and on and on.

The son thought the body a stand for the brain. A camera on a tripod. Keep it high and out of water, away from the ground. Walk it around. Keep it fuelled. Keep it safe. Make sure it was safe. He was a math professor like his sober father. He'd been drunk when he started the tattoo. "Begin like my dad's, a three on my chest." Once begun, then continued. Always it felt incomplete, a song commenced and unfinished. 25906 94912 93313 67702 89891, this in his late twenties around his lower back.

A steady beeping, the sound waves of his father's heart, their small mountains and below-the-line reflections, mountain inverted by a lake. Like during airplane flight, time in hospital felt suspended. The beginning forgotten, the end uncertain, provisional. He didn't hold his father's hand, but he touched the edge of the bed, the starchy sheets, the wide-weave blanket. Watched his father, he himself breathing slowly, reading the numbers visible through gaps in the gown, above the covers. 41354 73573 95231. 13427. Patterns like small waves rising in a numerical ocean without shores. As π approaches the horizon, the horizon shifts, a world if not with an infinite circumference, then, as always, with π, infinite and unchanging.

His father's body, not his father's mind. The mind had disappeared. The same thinking, but now its conclusions made little sense. Sometimes the body wept. It trembled. Mostly it slept. He waited. His father shrinking into the body, into the brain. His mind shrinking, perhaps, not smaller but bound by a smaller new world.

As the son felt also. Bound by a smaller, less brave world.

But thank you, Father, in your own way, for loving me too.

✦

CARES OF A FAMILY MAN

We found it upstairs in the attic, huddled against the eaves. It was frightened and alone. A sad little squirrel, or a little lost mouse, how could it have got in? Perhaps when the weather turned cold, it had squeezed through a hole in the roof. The soffit or fascia, though we didn't remember what those were, exactly, likely needed repair. It was an old house. It was all we could do to cover the basics: work, cook, shovel the walk, feed the dog.

We approached cautiously. It was small, but it was scared, and we knew fear could cause it to try to hurt us. My wife suggested a broom, just in case, but I thought that might make things worse.

"Let me talk to it," I said. "My voice is reassuring."

"Right," she said.

"Hey," I said softly. "Hey there. Don't be scared." It moved slightly, curling in on itself. I could see it quivering.

"Maybe we should offer it food," my wife said.

"Sure. What?"

We didn't know. We tried cheese, pieces of bread, nuts. Then I remembered the leftover sausage—bratwurst—wrapped in brown paper at the back of the fridge. We'd been saving it for the dog. I tore it into bite-size chunks and rolled them over.

"Here," I said. "You'll like this." There was some uncertain rustling and then it edged slowly forward. It nuzzled against the sausage as if proximity gave it comfort. Bratwurst, my familiar, my own.

"Shh," I said. "Everything's okay." My wife and I crouched beneath the roof's slope, trying to be quiet and still. I could hear breathing.

"Give it time," I said. "It's scared." After about ten minutes it moved further into the room, pressing close and nervously against the next piece of sausage.

"There you are," my wife said. "See? It's alright."

"There's lots of sausage," I said. "You're safe here."

While my wife kept watch and offered reassurance, I went downstairs to find a shoebox and tissue paper. I punched holes in the lid—I remembered grade school. The things we found: injured birds, baby rabbits, worms, a broken toy soldier, an escaped hamster.

We weren't sure if we should touch it, but finally, my wife slipped the lid of the shoebox underneath it, then tipped it into the nest of tissue paper waiting in the box. She secured the lid.

"What is it?" I asked.

"Not sure," she said. "I have ideas. I've seen things."

I carried it carefully downstairs in the box and put it on the desk beside the computer. My wife sat down and began typing.

"I thought so," she said. "I knew it."

I had my own ideas but I didn't trust them. They seemed too unlikely. "What?"

"It's a moustache," she said. "That we know. And look. It's Hitler's moustache." She pointed at an image on the screen. The edges, the little bristles, the shape. It wasn't the same colour, but it had been many years. We read about how it had gone missing after Hitler married Eva Braun in the bunker and before they committed suicide. It was mentioned in a few accounts. There was a note from Martin Bormann, and a sentence or two among Göring's papers. Eva and Adolph were surprised when it disappeared, that it escaped the notice of the guards outside the Führerbunker and then at the door of the Vorbunker, which led to the Reich Chancellery stairs. But the moustache was small and dark, and perhaps in those last intense days of the war, with a sense of looming dread and madness upon all of them, they had been distracted. Hitler fulminated about many things as he lost his grip and raved about, then fell silent, despondent, and hopeless. And then suicide on the couch in their private room. Cyanide for Eva, gun to the head for Adolf. An opportunity to disappear.

Where had the moustache been all these years? Certainly there had been a network of supporters, from Argentina to Canada, many places for the moustache to hide, to begin a new life, to assume a new name. Pictures of the moustache at a London men's club, trimmed and brushed. A snapshot of the moustache on a boat in the Adriatic, holidaying with a sheik and an industry titan. The moustache, waxed into curls, at the wedding of its grand-daughter in Rio. It had been a happy life, a life of conviviality and friendship. One, it seemed, with few regrets. But who knew the moustache's private moments, the middle-of-the-night awak-enings, the early-morning beach walks, the trembling, the rage. Had the moustache changed? Was that even possible? Was its escape simply self-preservation, a Himmler- or Göring-like loss of confidence and desire for surrender or a new regime? Or was it more? What had the moustache been thinking, all those years under Hitler's nose, spackled with saliva as his lip convulsed with apoplexy and mania?

"What do we do now?" I asked.

"Now?" my wife said.

"I mean, what next? Should we speak to the authorities?"

Instead we got some food, plopped down on the couch, and turned on the TV. The moustache was tucked between us, a bowl of popcorn on top of the box's lid. We scanned the channels. Sports. News. History. Nature. Movies. A few seconds on each, a tiny cross-section of complete scenes: bodies moving, trees swaying, a train crash.

"Wait." I went back to the history channel. Charcoal bombers flickered through a pockmarked grey sky. A documentary about the Battle of Britain. "Maybe it'll recognize something," I said. "Maybe it'll react and…"

"And what?" my wife said.

"Give a clue."

"About what we should do next?"

"Yes," I said.

The expected drone of engines, the indistinct cityscape, pale citizens navigating rubble, the stentorian voice of the narrator detailing the devastation, the losses, the gumption, the heroism. I listened carefully to the box. A few times the moustache read-justed its position with an indistinct scratching.

"Nothing," I said.

"What were you expecting?"

"Not sure."

Weeping, an admission, denunciations, apology, prayer? I wasn't sure what I'd anticipated. I had thought the sounds of battle might cause the moustache to respond. Had it no regrets? Did it live in a self-contained world of certainty, self-congratulation, and delusion? Or was it simply too old, frightened, lonely, or hard of hearing?

I muted the TV. I lifted the lid a few inches. The moustache had balled up the tissue paper into a corner and was mostly hidden underneath. Cautiously, I rested my upturned finger on the floor at the other end of the box.

"Don't be scared," I whispered. "Don't be scared."

The moustache pulled itself completely under the tissue paper.

"I'm not here to judge you," I said. As we waited, my wife began scanning through the channels on the muted TV.

After a while, some of the moustache appeared from beneath the paper. It was green and blue in the screen's undulating light. The moustache crept carefully across the box and then, after a moment's hesitation, settled against my finger. I could feel the warm bristles trembling. I held still. Then the moustache climbed onto my finger, circled carefully around, and lay down. I didn't risk moving. My wife had stopped looking through channels. The screen glowed an aquatic blue-white. I could hear my wife breathing beside me, my own breathing, the low electric hum of the muted television.

"What now?" she whispered.

We waited. Then I moved the lid aside and raised my hand as smoothly and slowly as I could. I brought the moustache closer and closer. I bent my head down.

The moustache and I. We were inches away. I touched the moustache to my lip and it held on as if it were my own.

"It's a new life," I said.

THE FORGIVENESS OF SCISSORS

There once was a woman who wrapped herself in paper. She had many children. The children did not recognize her surrounded by the petals of a cocoon, surrounded by the wings of a flower. She seemed like a soldier, her head wrapped because of a grievous wound.

There once was a woman who wrapped herself in bandages. A wound like the petals of a red flower. The setting sun like the petals of a red flower. A wound the golden hour of the body, a honey-coloured time before night or forgiveness.

We wrap ourselves in stories. We wrap ourselves in flowers. We use scissors to try to escape. We use scissors to turn our stories into petals, into leaves, into the wings of a book.

Our stories are scissors. Our stories are made of the many cuts scissors make. Our stories are cuts in larger stories, cuts in bandages holding the army together. The story of the army is told in the pages of a book. The soldiers are made of many cuts. Our children are wounds. The woman cut the pages of the book.

There once was a woman who used scissors to cut herself out of a book. She used scissors to cut the sheets of the bed into ribbons. She cut a path to her children. She sliced her bandages to escape from her ancestors. To escape from the soldiers. She had no wounds. She was in no war. She could return home to her children.

There once was a woman who cut herself from the cocoon that surrounded her. She used scissors to cut her bones into pieces and so escape forgiveness. She used scissors to cut the army into ribbons. She used scissors to cut the light into a thousand bees.

There once was a woman who was not a flower, yet used flowers to escape. There once was a woman who disguised herself. There once was a woman who cut herself from her disguise.

Scissors are a gun. A bayonet. A bomb. The woman used scissors to escape. "Children," she said. "I am home. My wounds are the petals of a flower, the red sun falling over the horizon. The honey-gold light filled with a thousand bees."

There once was a woman who cut herself out of the story. The woman cut herself out of her wings as if escaping from forgiveness. She cut forgiveness into ribbons. There were soldiers all around her, there were the bones of the army. She held the scissors and made hundreds of cuts. There were her eyes. There was her mouth. She looked at her ancestors and she spoke to her children. "Children," she said. "Children, I am home."

✦

THE MRS. SANTA STORIES

Mrs. Santa, Jupiter, and Saturn

Mrs. Santa was in my kitchen drinking again. "Listen, Elaine," I said, "I would have left Santa too, after the kickbacks from Walmart and that thing with the elf. Again. But look at the snow, look at the people of the world—at least the Christian ones—with their little hearts lit up like that reindeer's nose, just melting all the bullshit and finding joy and spiritual contentment in commodities. The world is one big fire, and even Jupiter and Saturn are disappointed by the fogginess of the conjunction. And Jesus— Jesus remembers being born, he's always hoped to recreate that cozy feeling in the manger by making everyone else feel cozy too, especially the meek and those people with guns who choose not to use them, at least not on other people. Everything's like marzipan, Elaine, there's sweet snow everywhere. Let me get you some toast. I'll butter it right to the edges, and you take my bed, I'll sleep on the couch tonight."

Mrs. Santa and the International Jewish Monetary Conspiracy

Mrs. Santa sat down and wrote another letter to the leaders of the Jewish international monetary conspiracy. Of course she didn't— even if Santa believes they are a thing and always complains about them: "Bezos is secretly in their pocket, and where does the Vatican hide its money?" But Mrs. Santa did write a letter to John Coltrane to thank him for the saxophone lessons. Of course, John Coltrane is dead, but long dim days in the woodshop with her tenor playing *Ascension* were one of the things that helped Mrs. Santa get through the desolations of winter. Even though it was cold, Mrs. Santa would open a window and send reedy and plaintive tones out into the emptiness. Sure, Santa made it round the world in one day, but Mrs. Santa imagined *Ascension* flying like a cloud around the world too. *Thank you, John,* she wrote. *You've taught me things I never knew.*

Mrs. Santa Has a Coffee

Out Santa's window, there's nothing. The North Pole: imaginary, featureless, disappearing into the always twilight. Mrs. Santa, a cup of coffee held to her chest, remembers the small bright sun, low on the horizon, undefeatable. The day of her marriage and her travel here. Of course, it wasn't as if Santa actually existed. All rosy-cheeked in Mrs. Santa's bed, he was always the sentimental love child of advertising campaigns and folktales. Didn't stop his attempts at merriment with what he irritatingly called his "elf." There's a reason he was able to travel around the world so quickly. She'd begged him to do the inevitable and sell to Old Jeff Bezos, so she could gather the elves around her, the real elves, each with their small childlike brightness, and, dressed in warm reindeer skins, set out into the tundra, the real tundra, and find the winter sun.

Mrs. Santa Sings

Mrs. Santa sees the northern lights. O Sargasso Sea of the night sky. Eels of the cosmos. Santa is tied up in the basement, O festive ropes, and the little elves throwing tinsel. Santa, tell me your routes, and I'll bring real peace and justice to the world instead of wrapping paper. Let's sing. O knots and duct tape and chairs in the dark. Santa's bladder can't wait and he wets himself. Now is the time for true compassion, for sending the sled through the world with its message of non-hierarchical, non-capitalistic celebration. The remarkable star above us all signifies possibility and how humans may fall to their knees and love the world, love all the species of the world, each rock and sea cucumber, each glimmer and fog, each slug and individual beneath the rock of a mortgage. Northern lights, you remind me of frog spawn, of bioluminescent sea muck, O Mrs. Santa so loves the world that she looks around and sings and she didn't really tie Santa up, except for role play.

Mrs. Santa Is Prepared

Everyone says she should be happy because of the elves. They are "her children." Okay, by "everyone," I mean Santa. The elves aren't children, they're just sweatshop workers or, let's say, Amazon employees, except with little green hammers and hats. Mrs. Santa keeps her children in a shed behind the house. After midnight, when everyone is sleeping, she sneaks out and opens the shed door. There's a gleam in the dark. It's Jesus and an old bicycle. Jesus sits on the seat while Mrs. Santa stands and pedals. They bike big loops around the North Pole. "Oh Elaine," I say, "how wonderful!" Because of course I'm there. I'm Jesus. We all are. Just like we're all Mrs. Santa and the gun that she keeps out in the shed too. Just in case.

Mrs. Santa and the Opposite of Grief

Santa working late, down at the workshop, Mrs. Santa reading Sherlock Holmes, her feet on the ottoman near the fire. He tamps his pipe; Mrs. Santa tamps her pipe too. Her special blend. Sherlock would know it by the distinctive ash that flutters down onto her nightgown. And here she is, slippers, nightgown, enormous cup of steaming tea, reading about the Colonel's murder in Aldershot, Watson disturbed late at night, Holmes silent in front of the fire, mulling things over, finally recounting the facts as he knows them. Mrs. Santa now knows them too.

Mrs. Santa and the Big Picture

Mrs. Santa eats another candy cane and wonders what it all means. *Who would I kill to save us?* she thinks. She remembers Santa telling her, "The trees are proud of the axe, because 'it's not the handle that does the cutting.'" She puts another log on the fire. When it flames, she wonders at the light, releasing energy from so far away.

Mrs. Santa Remembers Her Boy

In Mrs. Santa's room, an old typewriter sits on a shelf at the back of the closet. Black, worn, heavy. It belonged to her son, Floyd. T T T, Floyd would type when he was small. "No, dear," Mrs. Santa would say, "F is for Floyd. It's F F F." T T T, Floyd would type. "Okay, dear," Mrs. Santa would say. "That's close." Later, he would type other things. F L O Y T or M U M. And Mrs. Santa would make him little notes to discover on the platen. C O O K I E S   U N D E R   P I L L O W or S P E C I A L   B O Y. They would write stories together, M O M A N D   F L O Y D   R U N O U T I N   T H E   S U N. T H E Y   L A U G H. T H E Y F A L L   D O W N. T H E Y   H A V E   C O O K I E S. Mrs. Santa wrote all this down on the typewriter, made up these small tales when the afternoons felt long, and then she'd put the typewriter back on the shelf and return to her needlepoint. "Like a hurricane, there is a quiet place within the heart," one needlepoint read. "Rain can destroy any palace if you're patient," read another. "Fuck everything and all its reindeer," read a third, beautifully decorated with pretty yellow flowers.

THE DARK REDACTED

for Donna Szöke

Dust plumes the facade of a falling house, a redaction transparent as twilight, transparent because the moment, redacted, falls around us.

The way to become invisible is to let light travel through you.

The language of attention/intention, memory.

Walking through a dusk of smoke, invisible in a dark suit. The falling house, our pre-set catastrophe.

Dusk or dust when the house falls. Pockets of twilight. The future tense when the ocean rises over trees. We fall asleep in deep water without ever leaving home.

Light is redacted dark. Grammar herds windows. A suit fills with smoke. Time in the hands of the clock, just before the house falls.

Babies in bassinets of smoke, invisible to nurses, mothers, fathers.

An open window. Light from the sun lands on the babies. They shine and cry, invisible. Small dark windows in the house of the night.

Blindfolded is not the same as invisible. Now we turn to the small trash can in the nursery, filled with discarded papers, smoke from a typewriter, open doors in forgotten words.

Hold on to a clock and time does not move. We shine and cry. We make things happen out the open window and time travels through us.

When we remove ellipses, we replace them with exact copies of themselves. Vast clouds like the Dark Horse of the Milky Way. Is the shadow of a shadow the object itself? Outside, everything is smoke.

The phone rings. You look at it. It rings again. The phone rings. Smoke like twilight. A meandering animal in a dark suit.

Here: the previously irretrievable, the inexplicably present. The ordinary and magic. "Hello?" you ask.

A phone call from another time. An ordinary place far from here. A phone call from another time and place.

We're quiet, we hear the invisible. "Shh," I say, and it sounds like the wind. "Shh," I say, and it sounds like the sea.

The heart is fist-sized, unborn, invisible, like the hand of a swimmer. Sometimes it beats against the rib cage as if against a baby's crib.

What isn't dark might be memory. The heart takes in blood, sends it out to sea. "Shh," I say, and it sounds like wind. "Shh," I say, and it sounds like sea.

The sounds of sleeping babies, the shh of their small mouths.

A flock of birds made of nothing, only light and air. Invisible, the darkness of night drawn narrow.

This is where we used to live. Invisible, we remember you.

A pile of snow becomes leaves. Day hides in leaves and twigs, branches, fences, hydro poles, and buildings.

Night is the sky filled with the absence of day. This is your country. A shaft into the earth, the cool air rising, breath the memory of a name.

The small hairs of your neck, your arms, rise with memory. Invisible, we remember.

Tiny creature, soft as breath, small chest rising and falling. Hush, little moon, dearest one, curl around the night.

Daylight like snow, breath like snowfall. A moon that rises.

A hole like a bullet hole in the heart, or rather, the heart forming around this emptiness.

This open mouth.

A breath finding its way out. Mouth upon mouth upon mouth. Night sky, invisible river of scars. Joy.

Our son small, hiding by closing his eyes. In his bedroom, the ghosts of his own small clothing. How much breath can you pack in a suitcase?

It's not unusual to get a phone call in the middle of night.

Smoke, shadow, air, light, memory, invisible, past.

You answer, sleepy, rolling onto your side. "Hello?" you say. "Hello?"

A braid of smoke, the invisible, dimensionless. Echoes, signals, song.

✦

THE BLIND POODLE'S EYE

A Viking, playing cards at our kitchen table, is smoulder-
ing. His indistinct shape is engulfed in a leather-scented
fog. He shuffles the deck, places the ace of spades over
our blind poodle's left eye, and laughs darkly. The moon catches
fire and destroys a small European country. Vikings never much
cared for Monaco.

The phone rings. The Viking has not completed his homework,
did not properly shade his fjords, and besides, it is against school
rules to pillage the principal's office. He will not be allowed to
traverse the whale road with the crest riders, will have to keep
one eye closed during the film strip about bathing decorum in
Valhalla's winter pools.

Smoke detector, cloud-siren, wisps of Viking curl through the
ground floor, cause our family to wake. Our driveway—car hoarder,
unwanted flyer bed—is filled with the keening of firefighters, their
hands like birds. The fire chief, his beard itself a grey-curled cloud,
followed by a flock of other firefighters, climbs a ladder, shatters
glass, and climbs into the Viking's bedroom, darkens the lights,
obscuring the baseball pennants, the posters of girls and guitar gods.
Our poodle begins to howl from beneath the ace, Grandma, awake
since dawn, from beneath a shampoo-conditioner blend.

I have a sweatshirt halfway over my head and I bump my knee
on the radio.

"Take an alternate route to the highway while you still can," the announcer says. "Remember flowers for your mother." The poodle knocks my wife into our wedding picture, and there's confetti just like in the photo, but this time it's glass.

"Daddy, I smell axes, broadswords, and serpents of blood," my daughter calls, breaking through her door with a stump of Barbie torso. We gather in the hallway, crouch beneath a portrait of the god Odin, try to remember our fire safety plan, the route to outside.

"Where's Grandma?" we ask because she has disappeared, but then we see her chanting by the side of the swimming pool, remembering the old songs. Then the fire chief is upon us, his beard bright with shrieking thunder, his eyes dark with the rumble of lightning, the stairs shaking, white stucco falling from the ceiling above. My son brandishes his geography textbook, the corners of *An Introduction to Physical Geography* sharp and battle ready.

"For Monaco!" he shouts, and dives at the chief. The chief's hands swoop down. The knives of smoke are cruel and our blood keen. My daughter brains the chief with her Barbie camper van.

In a thousand years, where will I find the teeth of my ancestors? Will there be the marks of a bright spade on my poodle's grave, the same stars shining through the window of my family's den?

The firefighters climb backward through the window, retract the ladder.

I worry for Monaco and for Vikings of smoke. The world will have changed beyond description, beyond what even *An Introduction to Physical Geography* can explain. Will I see the principal behind his golden desk, surrounded by fjords properly coloured by students who have yet to be born?

The emergency vehicles retreat dolefully down our street. The Viking, now only a cloud of berserker, waves glumly by the door.

Will I see the firefighters' bird hands stroking the undulating necks of their puppies, the fire chief's donated organs in the bodies of small children?

I worry for this and for the driveways—those long tongues of our sighing city—the pink limbs of Barbies lost in the hedges, the capes of action figures misplaced in the grass. Yet I sleep, hoping that on a bright day far in the future, my children will repay my blood money, my golf membership, my subscription to *Monaco Today,* and then they—my beautiful, brave, slightly scorched children—will make a doghouse for time's blind poodle from a new deck of cards and will each hold their breath, lest it fall.

THE BEARD OF THE TIME TRAVELLER

with Michael Sikkema

birds acknowledge I have a song in my heart but ask that it stay there indefinitely

Do not trim the beard of the time traveller. Do not step in the same river once. Do not animate puppets, it's ugly and obscene. Do not assume you are the same species as your body. Do not name villains after insects. Do not dial that body part. Do not assume birds are not poisonous. Or venomous. Do not doubt the flying snakes. Do not make the plane joke. Do not use the blanket for such purposes. Do not lick the suit. Don't make moss of me.

*

Do not cut the first runner. Do not put his foot in the river. Don't ride on donkeys, they are ugly and also rivers. Don't think your size is the same as your body. Donkeys should not be attached to inches. Don't talk about that part of the body. Don't think that birds are poisonous. Or medicine. Don't argue at height. Don't laugh at the plane. Do not use buckets for such purposes. No offence, don't get over it.

*

Do not operate heavy medicine. Do not think venomous birds, crows or otherwise. Do not think the same body, no river. Do not body the river. Do not stop. Do not shiver in the gaps. Do not answer the offence. Do not laugh in the plane crash. Do not donkey the air. Do not blanket. Do not.

*

No, really. Do not use harsh Meso-American quinine. A poisonous bird, a raven, you think nothing: the body is not inane, it is not a river. Not part of the river. Don't worry about gaps. Do not respond to losses. Do not laugh at the plane crash. Do not evaluate addictive downloads. No carpeting.

*

The donkey is not carpeted. Raving the same. Losses accumulate, do not question. The river parts ways, weighs less upstream. The gaps don't worry. The poisonous laugh loads the cartridge, releases the bots. *BAM!* goes the satellite question.

*

The donkey is not covered with stars. Anxiety is one thing. The loss is huge. Do not ask. The rivers are bright. Diversity is not a problem. A poisonous smile carries a gun. Disruption is a problem with sartorial ham.

*

Scientists have been isolating river problems. Do not advance the owl. The stars uncover the donkey's anxiety quick as problems.

The bots refuse. Venomous disruptions hypnotize the Saturday. Once without asking, shame on Steve. Upstream guns question the older bots. A stirring.

*

The river feels isolated from its water. Inside an owl is still owl. There's a region of the donkey that is all donkey. When I was a bot, I was and-less. Line up the days of the week like thumbs. Don't feel bad, Steve. Feel Steve's outside. I licensed my unlit gums in a smile.

*

Inside Steve is all owls. More owls outside Steve. Also, time travellers during the stirring. Don't donkey. Don't do keys. Isolating river water is endlessly bots. A game of inches talks about body travel, rigs the animal crackers. Don't. Just really. Reel me in an ugly ugly. I'm all thumbs, no buttons.

*

Endless owlessness is opposed to owlful Steve. His arms and head. His memories muling song from old river water. The work of boots is never done. Instead of tarot cards, the baby read her future in biscuits and spoke by making her mouth into a fish. If the world were a button accordion, dusk would be the bellows.

*

Nine button owls do not snake a horizon. Endless Steve bowls owls over all summer and we get stuck with the accordion light, the mule body monkeying around with the fish spokes. What started off as advice ended up as vice. Don't inch away from the game ray. Don't name a dog Biscuit without expecting an early gravy.

*

From a certain angle, an owl is a snake the way the horizon can be a dark bird. Where are Steve's limits? It's as if there were a day so long there weren't weeks. By mule light. By monkey lamp. By fish speech. Like the shaggy energy of a dog, immortal yet in a doghouse only as large as the life of that one particular dog.

THE GOSPEL ACCORDING TO JUDAS

The sky is luminous yellow and we're all at the table with potatoes and wine. Everyone's arguing and why won't Jesus overthrow the state? We don't need heaven on earth but better civil society. I kiss Him and an otter enters into me and does flips. It's like an orgasm 24/7 in there. This is the secret. There's an otter inside everyone and it makes them come 24/7 just like the sun, moon, stars, and all those unexpected holy rivers.

✦

BABIES

There is war and so I plant babies. The babies grow slowly but eventually burst from the ground. "Why grow babies when there is a war?" everyone asks. But soon everywhere is filled with babies. Or baby-coloured light. And there's no room for war. A soldier tries to lift a gun, but a baby is in the way. A tank tries to enter the city, but there are babies in the way. It rains, but the rain falls between the babies and only falls on the soldiers. It dissolves their uniforms and the soldiers become baby juice, which runs through the streets and into the ocean. When winter comes, the baby juice freezes, and we all skate on it. The baby juice is a story, a lie, and my sister spins and spins and spins on its slippery surface. But the babies are true. The babies stand and leap and leave shadows all over forever. The first time someone said a word, no one knew it was a word. The first time someone died, everyone knew it wasn't the first time.

✦

BUXTEHUDE

for Marika Fischer Hoyt

One of those typical mornings with music, reading, friends' messages. They send earnest pictures: small men, all in fake beards. A dozen Jewish kindergarten students celebrating Purim in Baghdad in 1927. Kermit the Frog singing with Choir!Choir!Choir!

How is it we connected over Buxtehude after all these years? *Dieterich Buxtehude, organist and composer of the Baroque period, whose works are typical of the North German organ school.* At a school reunion, I said "Buxtehude deniers" in a poem, and then, for me, you programmed him on your radio show.

This morning, I learned you'd died. There was your beautiful picture, you as always, with viola. The huskier, more earnest violin.

That Roethke "Elegy for Jane," his student thrown from a horse, like you playing:

*a wren, happy, tail into the wind, trembling the twigs and small
        branches.*
Oh, when it was sad, you cast down into such a pure depth.

I speak these words of love—I, with no rights in this matter,
neither father nor lover, recent yet old, close but not close friend
*   of all these days.*

THE PAST

Grandpa is the biggest and Grandma is the smallest. Together, they walk through the snow as if it were nothing. However, when it comes time to pick up leaves, Grandma picks one up with her tiny little fork and Grandpa picks up another with his big lips.

Now Daryl, the bus driver, gets lost in the snow while driving five-pin bowling-pin-sized children. He isn't concerned because his enigmatic past and excellent sense of smell give him a knack for navigating dark and treacherous paths.

Eventually, Daryl and the children come across a cabin. Darryl knocks and an old man opens the door. He has everything they need, from warm blankets to poisoned hot chocolate. The children are excited because they have never tasted such a delicious drink before. They fall like leaves.

Back home, Grandma puts dishes in her tiny sink while Grandpa washes them with his big lips. They know something is wrong at the old man's cabin and again walk through the snow as if it were nothing. Grandpa catches Daryl and his bus between his lips. Grandmother sticks her fork into the dark and treacherous paths of the old man's heart. Because she has lost her fork, she makes herself an entirely new set with the children's tiny bones while Grandpa spits out Daryl somewhere dark and mysterious. Grandpa has a knack for things like that.

CHANGE THINGS

Replace pancreas with Prince, liver with Franz Liszt. Substitute Maryland for one lung, a postage stamp for the other. Kidneys: rivers. Spine: Rod Stewart. What about the Fortran programming language, mollusks, and a square-headed screwdriver? Adrenal gland, urethra, heart. Stomach as amateur choir. Black rhino as bladder. Someone left behind a surgical cloth. Was it Beethoven? Extract gallbladder, insert Andromeda Galaxy. Lymph nodes: AK-15s. Bill when done, empty-headed sky, dovecote, wingbeat, penchant for Bronx cheers during coitus, tiny ministrations of the fingers during burial of the young.

✦

TEMPLE DANCE
for Peter Chin

Walk. Walk to the temple. Walk up to the door. Walk up to the door of the temple. The temple that is no longer there. But here. The door that is no longer here. But there.

They say that the temple is named "Turn the Body." Turn the body in early morning, in late afternoon.

Turn the body in all directions.

The body is ash. The body is stone. The body turns in all directions. When we dance. We are at the threshold. A gateway, a door.

We turn the body between this place and that other place. Between that other place and this place.

Between time and the body. Between time, the body, and place. Between time, the body, and this other place. That other place where we dance, where we turn the body.

Early morning. Late afternoon. The body turns in all directions.

The body is stone. The body is fire. The body is ash.

The body is a wall. A door. The body is a gateway. A sky.

The body is memory. Dance is a memory between time and the body. Between memory and time.

Sunlight in early morning. Sunlight in late afternoon. We turn in all directions.

We turn the body: to ash, to stone, to sky. We turn the body in all directions.

Okay, so now I'm a tree. I'm a tree moving in time. I'm a tree moving between this place and that place.

Between memory and time.

All around me is dance. All around me is the memory of dance. Of dancers dancing. Dancers that are no longer there. But here.

Hey, look at this tree. This living tree. This dance between time and body. Between body and time.

All around me are dancers. That are not there. But here. Dancing through time. A forest of dancers, leaves shaking. When dancing, we are covered in leaves. The body is a forest of leaves. Leaves are turning.

Dancing is a door between time and joy. Between joy and the body.

They say that the temple is named "Turn the Body." Turn the body in early morning, in late afternoon. Turn the body in all directions.

The body is ash. The body is stone. The body turns in all directions.

THE SHAMIR

The creature, no bigger than a grain of barley, has six eyes and can eat stone. After all, it helped Solomon build the Temple and etch sigils into the priests' breastplates. But even a tiny creature can peer into the sky. The moon is out, but tonight its light is weak and the stars are visible, the vast array of constellations seemingly asking to be connected, each to each. Ursa Minor. Orion. Cygnus. The Scorpion. The stars are there, or were there, twinkling ruins of what was, of time and the inevitable—inexorable— inconstancy. Ghosts of fusion.

The creature does not look at the stars but instead fixes its minuscule eyes on the vastness of empty space, that place where there is nothing, or where nothing is visible. In time, even this nothingness will expand. Where is that region of the universe where nothing changes, where there is constancy? In the mind of this creature, there is no place of rest or of certainty. It can conceive of what could be termed Platonic ideals but knows that even ideas fade. Memory. Boundarylessness. Confusion. Death. Temples fall. Emptiness expands. What is distant becomes more distant. Change itself changes. Temple eater, wall biter, chewer of stone, time has a heart, and its blood is knotted.

OWLS

ike always, Teddy, Walrus, Little Bunny, and I are hanging on the steps behind the courthouse.

Know what I'd like to do? Walrus says.

Fart rainbows? Teddy says.

Been there, Walrus says. And got the T-shirt. What I'd like to do is sleep with owls.

Me too, says Little Bunny. Family-friendly owls.

More than one at a time, Teddy says.

Yeah, Walrus says. We'd hump at dusk.

Fuck yeah, I say. It'd be killer. Orgasms and everything suffused with contingent light.

For real, Walrus says. We'd be doing it fast and furious, then one of the owls would suddenly capture a rodent.

Soundlessly, I say.

Just one little peep, Little Bunny says. And that mouse's life is over.

Is that family-friendly? Teddy asks.

Families end. Families fuck, Walrus says. I'd say sex with owls is very family-friendly.

I'd fill my pants with owls, Teddy says.

I'd fill twilight, I say.

Crap, Little Bunny says.

Just then, we see Walrus's mom walk through the side door of the courthouse. She's crying and we all feel uncomfortable.

FRAGMENT FROM THE FLEA CIRCUS

Tiny. Captain. Big Franz. Brunhilda the Brawny. By morning, they'd all be dead. But it's not me who's in charge of life or death. At least not anymore.

There was a cold snap. In my heart? Nah. It was a bejesus cold winter night and we were far south. My two nuts clacking together. Even Jack Frost's balls shivered. Ah, what talk. I was dignified once.

I wore all my clothing. I piled on blankets. Piled the carpet on top of the blankets. Still, I was freezing. But I should have let them sleep with me, the lot of them. I'd have been like Jesus, giving my blood so they could live. I'm always scratching, so what's a little itch while I dream, twist, and toss, muttering and farting in the dark as I try to get warm? I looked through the window at the stars and knew. The constellations: my fleas. My friends. Circus performers under the biggest big top.

By morning they'd be dead.

Captain. Brunhilda the Brawny. Big Franz. Tiny.

In truth, the stars were a haze. Who can see properly? I found this old pair of glasses at a church, and for a time, I had second sight. It took a while to stop seeing double. One can get used to anything. As Hölderlin writes…

Who can remember what he writes. Something explaining how strange and dead the ghosts of the blessed ones appear to me.

Not only that but blurry too.

ONCE—I MUST HAVE been only a boy—someone, possibly my father, took me to see some dancers. Perhaps they were prostitutes. I believe I had won an award in school. There was a crowd of men shouting out songs, holding up steins. A surfeit of foam and moustaches and much jostling and pushing. And then an elbow to the face. I felt my glasses fall, and though it couldn't have been possible in all the tumult, I imagine I heard the crunch as they were ground beneath boot heels into the stone floor. From then on, I saw only the vague and pink moving forms of the dancers. The flourish of what I took to be skirts and legs and garters. Soft pink breasts and my father leaning in to ask, with beery loud breath, if I was enjoying myself.

But everything has faded. I cannot remember much. Vague pink clouds and moving forms. Occasional flourishes. Not enough breasts. Loud voices. I don't recall what happened to my family.

But how do I feel about my fleas?

It seems life is a needle in the body, puncturing me like an old bicycle tire until I've little air left, though the rest of the bicycle keeps wobbling forward, knocking hard against the cobbles. A boneshaker. A deflated balloon. But what to do?

THE CIRCUS IS invisible. My friends, the fleas, were always invisible. So I'll still announce each performer, still tell each one's story. Their birth, their childhood, their virtuoso talents. In that way, they will still perform their acts. The flea trapeze. Brunhilda fired from the cannon. The chariot. Tiny and the Captain in the Greco-Roman Wrestling of Fleas.

Big Franz the philosopher. He would stand in the middle of his sawdust world and shout, in his tiny voice. "Immanuel Kant is a big baby," he'd say. "Nietzsche is a sausage. I'd like to bite them both and drink their brainy blood."

Big Franz wasn't always very gracious, but he was always vigorous when it came to philosophy. "What can we know? The flea-in-itself? Ach. Fire me from a cannon. I need some air."

"Ach, Yankel," I said. "No one will remember us. We're too small."

"Like Napoleon," he said.

"Not that belly scratcher! We're fleas in a flea circus. As long as there's patter, we're there. Otherwise, gone."

"Nah. We're the itch with no name. Years from now, they'll scratch because of us."

"Great," I said. "A red bump in the tuches crack of history."

"So you'd rather be trash?"

"Look, Mama said stick together no matter what. So we'll stick together. We'll perform our act together. A whole lot of small together makes something big. We're here. We're always here."

LITHOGRAPHY OF THE DOG

The patron walked through the large doors of the library and up to the front desk.

"I'd like to complain," they said. "It isn't right."

"That's most unfortunate," the librarian said. "How can I help you?"

"You remember yesterday when it rained dirty dishwater and the clouds were angry wool?"

"I remember," the librarian said. "That was some storm."

"Well, I was in the library then," the patron said. "I waited in line."

"The library does get busy," the librarian said. "But it's good to be inside during a storm."

"I waited to be catalogued," the patron said. "I waited a long time."

"We appreciate that," the librarian said. "We try to be as quick as possible."

"That's not the problem," the patron said. "It's about how I was catalogued."

"We use the Dewey decimal system in this library. Were you hoping for Library of Congress?"

"That's not the problem."

"I don't understand," the librarian said.

"There were so many of us," the patron began. "From every-where. The young, old, sad, happy, and those who didn't know what they were. We lined up as if to be anointed. As if to receive mass. As if to be given a ticket to the most wished-for concert of all time. And you divided us into groups. History, Geography, Fiction, Non-fiction, Children's, Reference, Rare, Periodicals. I trusted you. You're professionals, trained in the ancient art of the library, the mysteries of classification. I didn't expect 636.7. What human being would expect 636.7? I was surprised but excited as I was grouped into Technology, then Agricultural. But I began to have a certain feeling as I was put in Animal Husbandry. And then 636.7—really? You think I'm nothing more than a dog?"

"That *would* be upsetting," the librarian said. "But surely there were other numbers? Surely there were numbers after the .7?"

"There were, but that's not important. It's—"

"Those are secret numbers," the librarian said. "The numbers that allow each book, each thing in the universe, to tell its own mysterious story, to determine its own place, to make its own allegiances, to wage its own wars. Friend finds friend, lover finds lover, enemies know each other on sight. The library is not just a place of 3-D printers and job-finding workshops. It's not just a place for the latest bestseller or a respected history of western railroads. The mystics have their wondrous corre-spondences and cryptic spells, and we have our hidden num-bers, the Kabbalah of classifications that allows for the rose to share a number with the chainsaw, a computer manual some digits with a squirrel."

Then the librarian raised a hand as if in benediction. "Reversed, 636.7 is 763.6. Lithography, I believe. Dog and stone are one. Bark and paper. Howl and tail, ink and image. They are one. And you are all of these, my friend. All of these and more.

"Now I erase your overdue fines and I send you on your path. Patron. Priest. Stone. I am glad you are here."

✦

INSTRUCTIONS FOR SPEECH

1.

Introduce the eagles. Start by announcing that the two majestic birds are not mere birds but phoenixes rising from ashes and soaring through the sky.

Mention their presidential roles. Explain that the eagles are the first and third presidents, but in eagle years they are far older. Discuss the eagles' enthusiasm for speeches. Describe how the third eagle is especially brimming with enthusiasm to give speeches, no matter how insignificant the occasion, and finds everything exciting, even the tiniest words and phrases. Note that he still enjoys plain talk, and you should take advantage of that while you can.

Highlight the importance of impactful words. Discuss how, unfortunately, the time will come when plain talk and honest words will be less desirable than polished rhetoric, but that time has not yet come.

Emphasize the eagles' potential to make a difference. Note that, fortunately, the eagles are still young enough that any speech can make a difference, especially those that touch people's bones. Introduce the idea of a bone speech. Explain that this is something that inspires the masses, something that will outlast more polished speeches.

Mention how the younger eagle president loves to stir emotions with his speeches, which is why you think a speech made of bones would be perfect. Talk about the future of the speech. Acknowledge that you know there will be a time when the speech will be entered into the archives and won't be heard for ages. But when it is taken out, it will sound the same, move the same, and be more revered than ever before.

2.

Introduce the fleabird. Explain how fleabirds burrow into the first and third hills of the dumbest country. Years pass. Fleabirds age.

Encourage interest in sad speeches. Eat the oldest fleabird. Enthusiasm is only enchanting for an afternoon. Speeches can be a smallville of shrivelled-up fun. Include a phrase that means: Remember the measured talk. Take advantage of all these scars.

Exaggerate the popularity of righteousness. Discuss how, proudly, the future will curse us with its speech-eating politicians, politicians who lick clean the bones. Initial here if you understand truthful statements. As you get older, your words will impact skulls.

Downplay the power of influential fleabirds. Explain that the lore of fleabirds is still so young that fleafirds unfortunately become the words they hear, the bones the speeches touch.

Launch the plot of directness. Make a note here to build a bridge for witnesses, something more than only fancy planning and hand gestures. Given that talk of how the fleabirds burrowed into those hills is now needed to stir emotions, a speech made from bones is perfect. Speak about the future of speech. Show the globe you know how long a speech should last. The envelope will only be opened at the end, and when the information is revealed, you'll be even-keeled and won't expect anyone to understand it. Respect will melt into something else.

Encourage listening closely. It's neither the heart nor the brain but the space in between. The junkyard dogs. The larynx.

3.

Now something else. Exclude gates. End by erasing leaves yet noting the bees that remain after rain as a kind of afterlife.

Refrain from discussing how gates leave the city. No one cares. Bees remain. Gates are irrelevant.

Suppress news of the gates' exhaustion. Avoid eating the gates or drinking their tears. Exhaustion is not enchanting at all. Orders are boring and unimportant. There's no phrase that means "Don't take advantage of these bees."

Downplay the unimportance of strength. Discuss how, sadly, the future won't bring more orders for limousines. Politicians licking books clean are not a problem. Don't initial here if you don't understand that, as you get older, the leaves you erased won't impact your head.

Exaggerate the frailty of gates. Explain that the myth of gates is so old they can't be affected by anything they hear or anything the bees touch.

Make no note to build a limo for leaves to use as fancy hand signals. There's a need for bees to stir emotions. Talking to erased books would be pointless.

You have no idea how long a book should be. The book will be made available to the future. Respect turns into something else.

Ignore the patterns the bees dance in books and discourage the reader from looking closely, noting neither the heart nor the brain but the space in between. There's no phrase that means "Don't build a vocabulary out of bees." Gates. Nerves. Leaves. This is something that inspires. Bees. I say it again. Bees.

SHORTS WITH THE POPE

The Pope's Visit

The Pope came to visit. We rented a giant U-Haul and drove to Barrie. We'd found sections of used fence for free on Kijiji. We went to pick them up. The Pope and I loaded them up and we brought them back to my house in Hamilton. Later, there'll be fence posts to install, but the Pope will be back in Rome so I'll have to do it all myself.

Doctrine

Today was a beach day. We packed cars, brought sandwiches, watermelon, and towels. We all arrived at the same time and it sure was busy. The smell of sunscreen reminded everyone of childhood. It was a beautiful day. I'd brought the Pope. We were bored so we buried him in the sand. Everyone forgot where he was! Finally, the sun went down and we all went home and went to sleep. The Pope was happy in the sand, where it was soft, damp, and cool. One day, he hoped, he'd be discovered.

Leg Day with the Pope

It was leg day so I did Bulgarian split squats, Romanian dead lifts, hip thrusts, goblet squats, glute hamstring curls, and barbell squats. When I went to lift the barbell, I saw the last guy hadn't wiped it down. Sorry, the Pope said. Under his cassock, his legs were Greek columns. Doric, Ionic, or Corinthian. The Pope looked up at the ceiling. I think he saw something inexplicable again.

The Game

I finished my coffee (milk, two sugars), then went into the Pope's room. It'd been a long night. We'd played the Pietà game. First, he was Mary and I was the dying Jesus. Then I was Jesus and he was Mary, weeping over her son. Wakey-wakey, I said. It's really morning? Yes, I said. It can't be morning. It is. And some of us could do with brushing our teeth and washing our infallibles. Finally, the Pope opened his eyes. I know everything and I forgive you, I said.

FROM *FOLKTALES FROM THE LIBRARY OF NEW PLANETS*

For my twelfth birthday, I was given the gift of night. Always, we had lived where the sun was king, ruling unblinkingly, shining down upon us from its bright palace of sky.

It was a childhood game, this attempt to outrun the sun, trick it into making long shadows, trailing behind us like the cape of the king, our arms and legs long as tree branches or rivers. If we moved fast enough, the sun would only catch us as if in the periphery of sight, bright on our backs as we attempted our escape from perpetual noon. But, of course, the attempt was futile. Unless we left our homes, crossed the walls that bounded our cities, and found other lands that we'd been told were uninhabitable to our kind.

Our planet does not rotate as it circles our sun, our star. It keeps the same face always toward the sun, like a courtier backing away from the king. And so, at each particular location on our planet, it is always the same particular time.

And so too on our planet, streaked by minerals, metals, life, each of us remains out of necessity where we are born, as we were made of that place and its particular light. My people are made of iron and of the iron red birds that we eat in quantity, of the fish in our iron-red streams. Our bones are iron. Our lips and tongues. Our red lungs, our rust-red blood.

On our planet, there is no difference between who you are and where you are, no distinction between place and time. A childhood rhyme I remember:

Who are we who are made of when?
When are who who are made of where?
Where are who who are made of when?
Who are we who are made of where?

Naturally, in our language, the rhyme is better. My people say: We are of this singular place in what we understand is a vast and uncertain universe lolling unbounded in space and time. We know who we are. We know when. We know who. It is a comfort, this certainty.

At school and in stories related in the bright light of bedtime, we children were not told of the moons and stars, of the six other planets in our system, each with others who are alive. The long shadow of the sky at night, studded with an infinite number of puny suns, tiny jewels from distant times and places. But I have imagined the many shadows cast by our several moons, imagined other children leaping and dodging, trying to outrun the moons' light. What might they make of our constant day, blind of shadow or stars or dark?

In secret, I began to draw night, to imagine dusk and dawn, to conceive of our moons' rise and set, the luminescence of their pale dance. I began to imagine the pitiless inscrutable sun turning red as it appeared to sink and dissolve into scarlet cloud, then being born again pink and crimson as it clambered into dawn. I began to imagine being made of other times, being made of other places.

How did I draw these times, these places? How did I draw this night? I drew our always-noon and began to erase. The hot blue, the heat shimmer rising, the river's steam. The red iron of our world. When I erased the words in our language for the present time, I found the past and the future. When I erased the word for iron, I found other places. When I erased our sun, it became the cool not-sun of moon, the erased red ground behind us streaked with shadow. When my father saw the drawings, he said, "Come, Alice. I have something to show you."

Citizens from other seams of our planet were arriving in our city, their robes salt white or cobalt blue. Citizens of other whens were arriving to lead us, to become our kings and queens, eat our red grains, feast on our meats, sleep in our red homes, marry our young. "Alice," my father said.

There was a door hidden below our stairs. "Your grandfather and his father, your grandmother and her mother, made this," he said. "For when there is need." In our language, this rhyme too was better, but even then, it was not an impressive revelation. The opened door revealed a rocket tall as me. A bucket of ash and a large spade.

"Father?" I asked. "Are we to escape? Are we to destroy? What are we to do with this toy?"

"Help me," was all my father said. We carried the rocket (robed in a blanket, it resembled the stiff body of a dead elder), and then we heaved the bucket and the spade to the roof of our home and loaded the rocket with ash. We stood it up and pointed it at the sky. In the traditional way, we held bent glass before the light of our sun to make fire, and the fuse ignited.

A blast of fumes and fire, and the rocket lurched above us, trailing a foul tail of smoke like a long shadow. A black raptor rising into the empty sky. When it reached the peak where the sun shone, it burst, a gurgitation of ash and fire and smoke. The sky was dirt, the sun was extinguished. I felt my skin grow chill, my insides shiver with cold and exhilaration. With relief. Our sky turned twilight, then dark. Below the band of ash, night appeared. We saw the distant sky, the distant stars. The four moons radiant and white, neither red nor hot. The four moons casting my shadow about the roof, over the chimneys, down into the streets of our city. Where was no longer when. Where was no longer who. For now.

"It is the morning of your twelfth birthday," my father said. "The first birthday you have ever known. And it is night."

I CAN'T

O h to hammer each of these letters out into one long line like the long wail of highway between the cities of I-Have-Collapsed and Maybe-I-Better-Just-Lie-Down.

But they crunch like the dried-up exoskeletons of once-iridescent insects fallen around the desiccated stump of brain stem in the clear-cut field of the mind.

Oh to build from their wiry black bodies an Eiffel of scaffolding up to a cloud-yabbering sky like the indigo mouth of a dental hygienist spitting ink into the pallid basin of Desolation in the Dental Office of Woe.

But they crunch like the dried-up exoskeletons of once-iridescent insects fallen around the desiccated stump of brain stem in the clear-cut field of the mind.

Oh to spin from the tiny serif-knotted knuckles of their tangled and minuscule lives, the lacrimal cords of the word horde resigned to be wound round the bobbin like that disastrous Buick round a pole of flickering and uncertain light, then woven into the patched gabardine of our dismal, coddled tongue on the loom of I-Should-Have-But-Despair-Pinned-Me-To-The-Abysmal-Mat-of-Myself-And-Left-Me-There-To-Age-In-Horizontal-Solitude-Like-Paradise-Which-Left-My-Neighbourhood-And-Took-The-First-Bus-Downtown.

But they crunch like the dried-up exoskeletons of once-iridescent insects fallen around the desiccated stump of brain stem in the clear-cut field of the mind.

Oh to stretch their tumescent contours into a veiny parade of tubing to be sounded like the single mournful trumpet left on the orchestra's We-Should-Have-Made-It-To-Dresden-And-Cremona-But-Beseiged-By-Misery-And-Forced-To-Play-The-*Your Chromosomes, Prey to Despair and Lethargy, No Longer Remember You, Part II*-Movie-Soundtrack-We-Gave-Up-And-Went-Home European Tour.

But they crunch like the dried-up exoskeletons of once-iridescent insects fallen around the desiccated stump of brain stem in the clear-cut field of the mind.

Oh to take their smug abecedarian cilia that flutter like the coy lashes of a micro-bovine roaming the pale syntactic plain, and to bind them together into a proud and towering phonemic peruke, and to wear this upon one's head like a judgment rendered or an elaborate and lengthy phone call to oneself where you say, "Despair hangs ten upon the weak waves of my body, and I flail in the tanless motions of sand as I am upturned in transfer from the pail of the Son of Couldn't-Get-Out-Of-Bed-This-Morning-Not-Even-To-Pee to become a turret in the Castle of Didn't-Even-Move-For-Six-Hours-When-I-Peed-In-My-Bed-Anyway in the kingdom of Feel-Like-A-Gum-Wrapper-Washed-Out-To-Sea-Or-Like-The-Day-I-Found-That-Bottle-I-Put-Into-Lake-

Ontario-That-Contained-Only-The-Overdue-Bill-That-Ransom-Note-To-Myself-And-The-Poem-I-Once-Wrote-That-Ended-In-The-Words—

But they crunch like the dried-up exoskeletons of once-iridescent insects fallen around the desiccated stump of brain stem in the clear-cut field of the mind."

RECIPE FROM THE FUTURE

I n the future, we'll eat the future. It's pretty tasty. Not like the past. Or pasta. In the future, that joke will be funny. We don't eat the present. There's nothing so unsavoury or unsavioury as the present. Except maybe my shorts. Though with a good white sauce and a glass of rosé, they could make a decent meal in a pinch. Or in a future where all forms of agriculture are gone. In the future, we'll eat our words. Plus the burning sky and the lakes, which are even more acidic than they used to be. Like apple pie. Which also isn't like it used to be. Or like it's going to be. You know what I miss? Sadness. Know what we call that now? Lunch.

My love, Mary, knocked on the door. Okay, knocked on a tree. There were no doors anymore. Also, no trees. She just walked up and said, Knock knock. I bet you're expecting a joke now.

"Who's there?" It was Mary. I ate all the knock-knock jokes years ago. I was hungry. And desperate. There's still some A Catholic, a Reclining Chair, and a Diaper Walk into a Bar jokes. Thank God.

We need something, Mary and me. All of us. Maybe we are all there is. I haven't seen anyone except us for a long time.

Really—Mary got up from her haunches around the fire, began to walk away but then turned around and said, Knock, knock. What you gonna do? We gotta do something to maintain the illusion of civilization. I mean, now that it's gone.

Hey, Tom, Mary said. A guy walks up to God and tells him a joke about the future. God says, That's not funny. I guess you had to be there, the guy says.

Oh, ho, I said to Mary. That's a zinger. That's a good joke. What's for lunch?

Don't ask me, Mary said. I'm just a guest.

Okay. We could eat our hopes and dreams.

And sorrows, Mary added.

We have lots of them, I said.

What happened to our baby, she asked.

I wiped my mouth and looked guilty.

Oh no, Mary said. You didn't go all *A Modest Proposal* on me?

No, no. I didn't eat the baby. I let the baby grow up.

Oh good, Mary said.

It's a form of agriculture, I said.

Mary gasped.

Just joking. Guess you had to be there.

I was, she said.

Ergo, you're not God.

Right. But where's the baby?

Foraging.

Foraging?

Among the weeds and the rusty deeds of civilization. Seeking entrails amid the flames.

Seems a fool's game.

It is. Though I remember once—I must have been a child then. I found a chicken.

A chicken?

Well, not so much a chicken as a rat. But—

You're not going to tell me that it tasted like chicken?

It was more the memory of chicken. Or the memory the old folks used to share when we hid underground.

Mary sat back down on her haunches again and we tucked rags under our chins because we were getting ready for lunch. I hope you realize that this story I'm telling you is made-up. Things weren't so bad. We had fire. We had a future we could hope to eat. In which we could hope to eat. The moon came out big in the dirty sky above us and Mary and I made love on the dirty ground. We had parts, and they fitted together. We had love. We had hope. The future was like a rusted-out car and the weeds grew around it. It had its own story. We loved it. It fascinated us and it was a place in which we could seek shelter and comfort. Even in a storm. Rain or snow. Not that there was snow anymore. But okay, this is a story. We had our little lunches that Mother packed. Sometime a long time ago in the past, Mother packed us lunches. Sandwiches. A pickle. Juice. Here, Tom and Mary, this is for the future. You're going to need to eat in the future. It's going to be a hungry time and you can't live on hope and love alone. You'll need lunch.

If there was a God in the future, that God would be like a sandwich. Or, to be more specific, that God would be like bread and we'd be the peanut butter and jam. God like two soft and cushy slices making us into something. Otherwise, we'd just be smears, smudges, not any kind of lunch at all. Though we'd be pressed together. Both of us, under the big moon, peanut butter and jam, two knifefuls in the future, always hoping for bread.

Bread, Mary said. Were you talking about bread?

Guess I was thinking out loud, I said. Sometimes hunger is so big it floods the banks of the brain and comes out talking. Prayers. Stories. How was a brain supposed to keep it all in?

I remember when our baby was small and we were two slices of bread on either side of him, keeping him safe and warm.

He was our peanut butter.

Our jelly.

EVENTUALLY, MORNING. IT looked a lot like the night before, except we couldn't see the moon. Or we couldn't imagine it. We had to imagine the sun behind a pearly gate of cloud. The sun, way out there somewhere, cooking us like hams.

Mary, I said. But there was no answer. Mary, I said louder, more like a yell. MARY! But I only heard the echo of my own voice. Well, I didn't even hear the echo. There was nothing for it to echo off. Maybe I was yelling inside my own head and the echo I heard was the echo of my own thoughts making nothing happen in the world, not even bringing our baby back to our home around the fire. There was no fire. Were there ashes? There were no ashes. Maybe there'd never been ashes. Maybe I ate them. Fire and ashes sandwich. A sandwich made out of my own voice. Wasn't there something about a sentence being a sandwich? Was a paragraph a hamburger? I remember talking about a knuckle sandwich. Nothing to eat but pain.

The future won't be the same as this future. Or it'll be the same but even more so. Big rock-candy future, streams filled with sandwich meat. I remember once Mary and I cooked a rabbit. Maybe it was a squirrel. We had a fire and a stick, and Mary put the squirrel on the stick and I held it over the fire. The sound was like electric sizzling. From back when there was electricity. You know what Mary was? She was an archaeologist. She'd dig things up and tell me about them. And I was a historian. I'd remember what she said.

Let's be our own institute, I said.

Yes, she said. I'll be the president.

Okay, I said. Can I be chair of the board and I'll give you a headache because I'll suggest things that aren't helpful?

Right, Mary said. We'll have a gala.

Yes, I said. We'll have finger food.

Perfect, Mary said. And tiny little sausages and cheese.

I'd love that, I said. And those little sticks with frizzy-coloured plastic on the end.

Great, Mary said. And some shaped like tiny swords.

Drinks with umbrellas! I said.

Oh yes! Mary said.

Yes, yes, yes, yes, yes.

I'M SITTING IN a chair in my dining room and there's no one here. Except me, of course. Mary's at work. She's an archaeologist. That means she studies the past. She's hungry for the past. And she has a spade. A big one and a little one. She sits on her haunches and looks for old things. If the present were mashed potatoes and you dug into it, there'd be more mashed potatoes. The past is the present, just not yet. The future is different though. There are no mashed potatoes in the future.

Mary, I said. I'm really worried.

Worried? What worries you?

The future, Mary. I'm scared.

Me too, Mary said.

Really?

Of course, Mary said. That's why I'm studying the past.

So you can learn from it?

So I don't have to learn from the future.

ONCE I HAD a theory. The past was a slice of bread. The future was a slice of bread. The present was nestled safely in between, like peanut butter and jelly. Time and our lives were a sandwich. I don't believe that theory anymore. Is time an open-faced sandwich? No. The future isn't missing, there just isn't any bread there. Or mashed potatoes. When we get there, all we'll be able to do is eat the future. It's a bad cloud and our bellies are bad clouds. Bad clouds inside bad clouds.

I'M HERE AT our dining table and I'm thinking about the future.

Knock knock. The future. Who's there? You're too late.

I'm at our dining table and I'm writing a recipe book. I'm calling it *Recipes for the Future*. All the ingredients are things from the past, so that when you get to the future, you won't be able to make any of the recipes. Except for one. It was Mary's idea.

You have an idea for a recipe that we'll be able to eat in the future?

Yes, Mary said. Here's the recipe: Take this book, *Recipes for the Future*, and eat it.

That's good, I said. Really good.

Yes, she said. And what's especially good is that people will have to buy lots of copies of the book if they are to survive.

Oh, I want to go with you into the future, I said. And not because I want you for lunch.

No?

Well, okay, I said. I removed my shorts. There, right on the dining table, we made love as if we were a recipe from the future. It wasn't anything like chicken. Not even the memory of chicken. The moon was in the big sky or the sun was in the big sky and we were on the big dining room table and we began the process of making a baby, a baby that would grow quick as corn but be less like a meal. I imagined our baby not able to walk or even sit up. Our baby would be lying down, horizontal, with its head in the kitchen and its feet in the hall, if the kitchen was the past and the hall was the future. The present would be somewhere around its belly, and we'd fill its belly with lots of good things like peanut butter and jelly sandwiches or chicken.

THIS IS A story, but who knows where it's going. Sometime soon, we're going to get to the end and then it'll be over. Mary and me, we'll have our memories. We'll sit on our haunches by the fire, we'll hold hands and remember. We'll tell the story from the beginning and then when we get to the end, we'll start all over again. We'll tell our story from the kitchen to the hall, from its head to its toes, our baby, sweet as apple pie. And the future, the future will be like a big ol' apple pie too, except an apple pie with no apples and no crust either. All there'll be is the future. The future, waiting for us to eat it. The future that's run out of past and that's run out of present. The future that doesn't taste like chicken and that doesn't taste like apple pie. That's good, because I'd like a future that doesn't taste like chicken and doesn't taste like apple pie. Oh, sorry, sir, we're all out of chicken and we're all out of apple pie. Could you have a future without white sauce and without rosé? I could have a future without them, I just couldn't have a future without peanut butter and jelly. Or without Mary. Mary and peanut butter and jelly.

Mary, I shouted. Mary, I'm hungry. I'm waiting for you here in the future, here in the future by the fire, the future that isn't the end of the story but something more like lunch.

THE OCEAN

1.

There are many things I could say or could want to say, but I don't say and don't want to say because of my own limitations and because of the limits I have imposed upon myself. This means that I've imposed these limits and limitations on my children and I've imposed these limits and limitations on her too. Our family life has limits; beyond these limits there are things that cannot be said or done.

2.

I cannot say that I wish for my children to experience only happy things, for although I want them to be happier than we have been, I do not want them to be shallow. I cannot say that I am okay with them suffering and being unhappy, because I am not okay with that. In truth, I tell her, the only thing I want to do is stand by you, be near you, love you, and make sure that nothing bad ever happens to you. I also tell her it's not enough for me to believe that I have affected the world, I want my children to believe that they have affected the world too.

3.

Because she has given me life, or because she is leaving me, or because I have given her life, or because I am leaving her, I say nothing. I remain silent for the same reason that there is no such thing as good luck: we are not the ones who put this world together.

B-I-N-G-O

My dog's name is Bingo, after the song, but he has no face: no mouth, no ears, no nose, and no eyes. So perhaps we shouldn't call him all the letters of B-I-N-G-O, just B-I and then silence. I think if he could hear me, he would come when I called, sit, play dead, and roll over, but he just lies on the floor and is quiet. When I stroke him, his body is soft and sleek. I think he has no lungs since his chest does not rise and fall. I think it is a good thing. Where would the air go? How would it enter his body? It would be squeezed out of his lungs and then immediately sucked back in. Unless he farted. But he has no bum either, so the fart would stay inside. Perhaps it is the same air that was inside him from when he was born, so it is like he is filled with history. How did it smell the day of his birth? What temperature was it? Could there still be tiny vibrations from his mother's loving barks before he was taken away from her? My mother says I should just forget about him, but I won't. Real love is something that you don't just forget about. When we're old, Bingo and me, we'll still love each other. I'll hardly have a face, at least not one that really works, and I'll hardly be able to breathe or even move, but Bingo and me will still be together. And I'll sing him the Bingo song all the way through, and if I can't sing anymore, I'll think it.

FOG

Hitler, I said. I'm inviting you to my party, but I'm warning you, no funny stuff. Besides, Mao Zedong is here, and anyone who knows anything knows that you're not the guy responsible for the most deaths, so don't start that again. And don't drink all the Bud like last time. Sure, it was fun when we took the neighbour's bike and rode along the seawall together. Your moustache tickled when we kissed. Me: male, middle-aged, Jewish, gay. You: Austrian and curious. I felt fireworks. Did you feel fireworks? Up close, under the vacuum cleaner store's neon sign, I could see the grey in your hair, the crow's feet, and the laugh lines. Your ear hair and shaving cuts. At first, I had thought the fog had come in from the bay, but then I realized we were surrounded by ghosts.

✦

AID

He ran outside with a knife and stabbed the ground again and again in the same place. "I hate you," he shouted. "I hate your sky. I hate your dirt. I hate your ocean and all your fucking parking lots." He stabbed the knife into the ground again. "I hate your fucking people and your fucking animals. I hate your fucking houses and your fucking hospitals." He stabbed the ground again and again. "I hate fucking all of it," he shouted. He continued to stab until it was night and he could not see what he was doing. Finally, wet and exhausted, he went back inside.

THE MOON ROSE. A woman walked outside and knelt down. She took a Band-Aid out of her pocket, pulled away the backing, and stuck the Band-Aid over the place where he had stabbed the ground. She went back inside.

BREATHE MOSS

Dustpan at the end of day. Motel of escapees. A sniffle, a subcontinent, a plutocrat with superstar characteristics. Long blemishes of grease shine like an iconic miniseries. Weather throbs and sunshine appears, warms the skunk's fore-parts. An off-duty patrolman partakes in a wink and a simulation, then parked cars dissolve. An airship, low above the night table, fills with rivers, accepts me as a discoverer. The bombed and the dead absorb the rampage. Thousands create undulations beneath no shingle. Wait. Grow from the mileage. Breathe in lengthening shanties. Breathe from all sieves. Be your own moss.

THE WALKING LIBRARY

for David Naimon

I wrote that this version of that story would be told by some-one who saw only a fleeting glance of its protagonist through a train window as it passed a cow-filled field where the pro-tagonist stood waiting for something to happen.

The word *train* comes from the early fourteenth century, "a draw-ing out, delay"; from the Old French *train*; from *trainer*, "to pull, drag, draw," from Vulgar Latin, *traginare,* extended from *tragere,* "to pull."

In the train window, the man seemed to be throwing a rock down the length of the car. From my position—a cow-filled field—the rock didn't seem to move, only the train, the man, the window. It was as if the story was being told from the stone's point of view. What else might be told from a stone's point of view? Mishearing something someone said, the history of language, or this ending.

SITTING SHIVA FOR THE QUEEN

(h/t Noah Farberman & Darren Wershler)

Today's the Queen's funeral and I'm having leftovers. Cold vegetarian matzo ball soup. Matzah? Matzoh? Last time I made love, my head filled with images of the rousing blue harbour of Númenor from a TV adaptation of Tolkien. Yeah, I know, I know. Númenor? Autocorrect suggests "noumenon" ("a thing as it is in itself, as distinct from a thing as it is knowable by the senses through phenomenal attributes"). One of my former students suggests sitting shiva for the Queen. Seven days of pillow-free mirrorlessness for the monarch, with much lox and coffee. Also, friends and family. Here's one way to celebrate being alive: Take the bus and get off at the wrong stop. Walk back the twenty minutes to your doctor's appointment. There will likely be crows. Huge, black rawking birds pushing their large wings through the air. Now, something the late great poet Jones said: "It takes guts to know some happiness/& not make a poem of it." I heard a joke where one of the princes couldn't consort with strippers. Something about being uncomfortable looking at his grandmother's face on the money. And here I am, writing, because it feels good.

✦

WHATEVER THE AIR OR GRAVITY REQUIRES

Boys in the house making miniature suicide bombers from action figures and firecrackers. The silent dogs of Dundas, Ontario, positioning themselves on the rug, ready for toilet action. A football team poking each other in the eyes and drinking Slurpees. An election for cloud president, assistant to slush, and the secretary of rain. A lost order for weeping tile and a garden gnome smashed by stone. Birds exchange their wings for the power of speech and find names for bones. A stapler shaped like a fish and a metal frog topple onto a subwoofer. The internet is down, and there's a man carrying a large plastic tub up the driveway. Take apart the metal grid of a shopping cart and form it into life-size lightning. Even miniature suicide bombers must have causes, however small.

MY FATHER, NAZI VENTRILOQUIST

Routine 1

Dummy: A Nazi ventriloquist is onstage, and, like always, he's wearing his black leather trench coat.

Ventriloquist: Like me.

Dummy: Exactly. And, of course, the dummy on his knee is also wearing a little black leather trench coat.

Ventriloquist: Just like you.

Dummy: Right.

Ventriloquist: So the two of them start going through their usual act.

Dummy: Then this guy from the audience stands up and begins shouting.

Ventriloquist: He says, "I'm a Jew, and I've had enough of your racist jokes."

Dummy: The ventriloquist starts to shout back at the man for interrupting—I mean, who wouldn't—but the man says—

Ventriloquist: "You stay out of this, Klaus! I'm talking to that little schmuck on your knee."

Narrator

How does it begin? Snow-covered pines. A barn. A trap door. A man in a Nazi uniform, a ventriloquist's dummy on his knee. Herschel. My father. The man, of course, not the dummy. The dummy was more like a favourite son. For in the years my father was in hiding, Fritz—that was the dummy's name—was my father's constant companion after my mother, and after his parents, were captured. Long afternoons, while I stayed quiet, my father tried not to move his lips while Fritz made up things to remember. And their routines: two old friends, slave and master, inquisitor and Jew. Patsy and straight man. Dogshadow and hand. Or maybe just two shadows. Son and father. Why am I writing this? I'm a dummy too, trying again to speak with my father now that he's gone.

Routine 2

Dummy: Snow-covered pines. A barn. Man in a Nazi uniform, ventriloquist's dummy on his knee.
Ventriloquist: Speak!
Dummy: No.
Ventriloquist: Sprecht!
Dummy: Nein.
Ventriloquist: We haff vays of makink you talk...
Dummy: Knew you'd say that.
Ventriloquist: It's been a long time since we had new material. Or a stage.
Dummy: Tell me about it... Scheisse!
Ventriloquist: What?
Dummy: You've got me talking.
Ventriloquist: What else can you do?
Dummy: Follow orders. I was just following orders.
Ventriloquist: That's what they all say.
Dummy: That's not dummy. I mean funny.
Ventriloquist: Sprecht!
Dummy: No.

Ventriloquist: Speak.

Dummy: Nein.

Ventriloquist: I order you.

Dummy: What do you think I am?

Ventriloquist: A Dummkopf.

Dummy: Technically, all of me is a dummy, not just my head.

Ventriloquist: I know you are but what am I?

Dummy: Schutzstaffel-Oberst-Grup...Ober-Grup...Oberstgrup...

Ventriloquist: Say it, you little fist-mouthed blockhead. You stutterer.

Dummy: Schutzstaffel-Ober-Gruppenffer...füh...Oberst-Gruppen...

Ventriloquist: Ach, it's "Schutzstaffel-Oberst-Gruppenführer"— colonel general—you dundertongue.

Dummy: Schicklgruber.

Ventriloquist: Vermin. That was never even Hitler's name.

Dummy: Schwanzlutscher.

Ventriloquist: Nazi.

Dummy: You wish. You're nothing without me. Or worse.

Ventriloquist: That's good. That's sehr gut. So now I think we should end this routine. That's enough for one day.

Dummy: Chicken.

Ventriloquist: I said, that's enough for one day. It's time to put you away.

Dummy: Oh please, no. Don't put me in the suitcase.

Ventriloquist: Chicken.

Dummy: Don't put me in there.

Ventriloquist: What, afraid of the dark?

Dummy: No, your gatkes. Your underwear.

Ventriloquist: I've heard that before.

Solo for Dummy 1

This is how I became a real doy—boy. Almost able to say eth-
erything. Everything. No longer just good. I mean wood. A plank. A
floorboard. Under where we were hidden. Ha. I just said underwear.
But we were silent until they were dawn. I mean gone. Not the patter of little feet but great boots. Then my tater—pater familias. I
mean my familiar patter. A Frenchman, an Irishman, and a Jew…

But what was I first?

A dummy. A real dummy.

Wooden. At least my bread. My head. Open to the stairs, sure,
I mean stars. Dormice, insects, the wind through the dave of my
brain. I mean the cave. But with strings. And a handle. How else
could I shake my head no. No, no. [shakes head] Or wink? Like
this. [winks]

And my mouth. A real moving south. I had a meal moving
mouth. Or the mechanism for one. After all, one's lips have to
move. Speaking being my raisin—my raison—d'être.

Speaking of which, why a dummy? Not a real boy, after all?
Hidden away. Not speak to the hand—listen to it. You too might
turn to wood if you'd been through what I'd been through. You
might make everything into routines. Like this.

It's a relief just to pink—I mean think. Okay, so it's no relief,
but it's a stain, a strain off the tongue. Some time alone where
I can be inside my wooden head as if it were a quiet room, an
empty search—church. Each thought a foot tap echoing as it gets
closer, then passes. I have these quiet dimes—times—inside my
box, silent and remembering.

We said nothing under the gore—floor. Herschel and me and
the family that remained. Now just Herschel, his son, and me. A
dummy, I roused—mouthed—words to pass the time. They say
that thunder is the gods stomping around the sky. Or farting in

the clouds. But we were in the basement and it was Nazis who were stomping above us.

Solo for Dummy 2

Gook. Look. Without the ventriloquist, the dummy doesn't mispronounce. Believe me, it is the ventriloquist who's got the south of garbles.

Right? I am not here without you. Without you filling my head with your fist. Filling my mouth with language. A puppeteer from the inside, pulling my strings. Let's say I live from hand to mouth. Or maybe you do.

Because it is your language, not mind. Mine.

When I'm held by someone else, there's another voice in my head.

Who is it that is speaking? Who is it that is speaking now? Whose thoughts are these?

I'm a hole in the floor where you can hide. A megaphone you shout into. Echo. Echo. I'm not here right now, but if you'd like to, leave a message.

Or we're milk and milk bucket. Radio and wave. Words and an empty page.

Here I am.

I'm only here when you hear me. But it's not me, it's you. Me and my shadow. Ask yourself this: If you're not me, then you must be my shadow.

So where were we? Right. Under the floor while the soldiers were doing their search dance. Their shouting song. A language from across the border of sanity, except we knew what they were saying. We knew what they wanted.

Us.

But our yellow star didn't shine in the dark. We hid ourselves where even the sun don't.

Routine 2

Dummy: So a Nazi ventriloquist is onstage.
Ventriloquist: Understage.
Dummy: He's been hiding for weeks.
Ventriloquist: Silently.
Dummy: Hasn't said a word.
Ventriloquist: Only breathes when strictly necessary.
Dummy: Not even his dummy speaks.
Ventriloquist: Except now.
Dummy: And anyway, he's not so Nazi.
Ventriloquist: He's only a little Nazi.
Dummy: More an agnostic.
Ventriloquist: A survivor.
Dummy: A Jew.
Ventriloquist: For now.
Dummy: For now?
Ventriloquist: He'll be a non-Jew soon.
Dummy: Discovered.
Ventriloquist: Ash.
Dummy: A cloud.
Ventriloquist: Gone over the mountains.
Dummy: History.
Ventriloquist: What kind of an act is this?
Dummy: A desperate one.

Solo for Dummy 3

So I'm a dunny. Dummy. In a hole in the floor. Vunny. Funny.
Because I need him like a hole in the head. I have holes in
my head. Ears, mouth. North and south. Nose holes too. But
he's the one who has the bent. Vent. What makes a real boy?

Tragedy plus time. Jokes plus a much longer time. A vather.
Father. I'm the dummy on his knee. Who does routines without him now that he's the one underground with an audience
of terms. Worms.

Narrator

We were under the floor for weeks. Two soldiers kept searching,
but me, my father, and his dummy were silent. We heard the
boots, the scraping of the table, the carpet pulled back. Other
voices. Two local girls, giggling. One said to one of the soldiers,
"Come round back, I've something for you. Wait till you see."
And so they went. One girl pulled off her shirt, went down on
her knees, the first soldier with pants to his ankles. The other
girl crept behind him, slipped a gun from a forgotten holster,
and fired. Then the second soldier ran and, as he rounded the
barn, he too was shot. The girls dragged both soldiers into a hole
under the straw in the barn. A pit to position a car over instead
of hoisting it up to repair it. Then they covered it up. Fritz, my
father, and me in the house beside the barn, at the same depth as
the soldiers, all of us underground. But only Fritz, my father, and
me, shaking, babbling. Then the girls spoke to us, told us what
happened. Left us bread.

Routine 3

Ventriloquist: W-w-w-hat was that?
Dummy: A new routine.
Ventriloquist: The gunshots?
Dummy: The girls.
Dummy: One in the head, the other in the chest.
Ventriloquist: We're not that brave.

Dummy: Wish we were.

Ventriloquist: But we're not.

Dummy. No, but do you know what the Nazi said to the broken clock?

Ventriloquist: I have no idea. What did the Nazi say?

Dummy: We haf vays of makink you tock.

Ventriloquist: That's my line.

Dummy: Exactly.

Narrator

For years, my father hiding out in the family cabin in the Laurentians. Snow falling over trees. A living postcard, the snow, my father, the mountains. Fritz on his knee. Maybe the same Fritz, maybe another. Looking out the window as if onstage. Hatless. Uniformless. Jewish.

Routine 4

Ventriloquist: Are you crying?

Dummy: I'm made of wood.

Ventriloquist: Thought you were crying.

Dummy: It's thap. Sap. Maybe it's you?

Ventriloquist: Me?

Dummy: You make me do everything.

Ventriloquist: Remember our old routines?

Dummy: That's your job.

Ventriloquist: But we practised and practised.

Dummy: You were always a Nazi about it.

Ventriloquist: So were you. Just smaller.

Narrator

My father, a ventriloquist. My father and Fritz, both Jews. My father and Fritz and their Nazi routine, hiding in front of Nazis. The Nazis didn't know until the Nazis knew, and then the found-out Jews had to hurry offstage. Flee. Fritz wasn't the only one who had to improvise.

Hidden, my father was worried Fritz would betray him, that Fritz would betray me. Maybe Fritz felt guilty. Maybe Fritz would try to save himself at my expense. But after the girls killed those two Nazis, we three—son, father, dummy—went to hide in the woods. "Among pre-Fritzes," Fritz said. And then we found a way to flee the country.

Routine 5

Dummy: When you're dead, what about me?
Ventriloquist: You'll say nothing.
Dummy: If I do, then what?
Ventriloquist: They should get a spade.
Dummy: I do want to speak at your funeral.
Ventriloquist: Me too.

Narrator

Night in the Laurentians. The cabin lit by candles. Some lamps. My father playing a Bach LP, Fritz tilted beside him on the sofa. Did I ever sit so close to my father? My father, doing his old routines. Pretending to be German. His wife, parents, pretending to be alive.

Routine 6

Dummy: You're on the Fritz.
Ventriloquist: You mean in.
Dummy: Don't I know it. One night when you're sleeping…
Ventriloquist: You'll be the one snoring.
Dummy: If you do snore, I'll wake you up.

Narrator

Summer. So hot I wore a bathing suit all day though we had no pool. My father was gone, doing routines with the angels. Only Fritz was left. His box under my father's bed. I was afraid of the dark, like Fritz. Unclasped the box, lifted him out, limp. "Fritz," I said. "Fritz." I put my hand into the space in his head. Opened his mouth. Closed it. Opened it again. Opened his eyes.

Routine 7

Son: "Fritz," I said. "Wake up."

FROM *I, DR. GREENBLATT,*
ORTHODONTIST, 251-1457 (2015)

THE RADIANT HAPPINESS

The doctor slept like a baby. Two women stood beside his bed. One tipped a bottle over a handkerchief and then covered the doctor's mouth and nose. The other pulled back the blankets and pushed a syringe through his navel. In this way, the baby began to grow inside the doctor. He did not understand the increasing bulge in his gut. In the beginning, he attributed it to a flourishing middle-age spread. Soon he felt the new heartbeat and then the kicking. It wasn't a kicking motivated by a need to escape, but rather an "I am here" call. Now I have intent and consciousness.

The baby was a constant companion for the doctor, a familiar kept safe and warm inside him. At certain times, the issue of orifices uncomfortably entered his mind. At some point in the future, his child would seek the world, a small cat looking for a cat flap. Great pain or surgery would be required. In the meantime, the doctor took to wearing baggy clothing, oversized sweatshirts, and, while at work, white lab coats. Those around him noted the warm glow, the sense of bounty and health that radiated from his happy and larger self. When it seemed the doctor was speaking to himself, cheerily babbling about this or that—about birds or the moving clouds— his friends and office staff smiled indulgently, buoyed by his good humour and glad to overlook the quibbling eccentricity that so clearly originated in a deep pleasure and satisfaction with life itself.

The seasons passed. The baby grew. It took to ranging about the doctor's body, a restless toddler at play on a jungle gym. "Daddy, I love you," it said. "Daddy, you are a good daddy. Daddy, I like it when you sing." And because he could not hold, or even see, his child, when the doctor was not explaining the vibrant surprises of the outer world, he sang almost non-stop: long improvised songs that incorporated the world and the doctor's feelings for his ever-growing child. The doctor's child was a bright, curious, and healthy child and continued to thrive. The doctor became massive, and though others shuddered when they observed his enormous misshapen body, he stumbled about with a fantastical grin transforming his unshaven chin. Five years passed. Fifteen. The child's voice changed. The doctor wrapped himself in vast cloaks and supported himself with canes and hid behind his desk during patient consultations.

Familiar as he was with the subtle distinctions of modern reproductive medicine, the doctor knew that this child could not be his own, or if it was, it had resulted from some surreptitious and unnatural sleight of—what might best be termed—hand. And the boy himself, who by now had developed a functional understanding of the basic operations of biological science, began to wonder, in his liquid world, about the nature of his own provenance. He was content within that fluid world—it was the only geography he had ever known—but the boy had begun to have longings concerning his own biology, about his own—though he hesitated to use the term with the doctor—mother.

The boy began to sing himself. Low-voiced songs of conjecture, filled with questions of metaphysics, of origin, and of the sports games of which he and his father were avid listeners. Might his mother, too, be a listener to these games? Might she participate in such games as a mother of his brother and sister?

Might he have siblings? Did his brothers and sisters live on the outside, or did they too live within another?

"Father, how was I conceived?" the boy asked the doctor one day between patients.

Though he knew much about the world and its reproductions, the doctor could not account for or explain the boy's conception or, indeed, his arrival (biological or miraculous) inside of him. Superman's parents understood the spacecraft's implantation in the earth around Smallville. The doctor remembered only the small churnings, the ill feeling, the beginnings of movement. And the happiness. The radiant happiness.

THE HAND

I do not expect the hand. At first, I think it is a root or some other growing thing searching out food. I brush against it. It is cool though warmer than the air, warmer than the soil. I rest my head against its soft palm.

It cradles my head for hours, then it strokes my face. Perhaps it has a cramp and must move. I breathe, sleep, wake. The hand is gone. I sleep again.

When it returns, I touch my fingers to its fingers and they respond, curling. We remain fingertip to fingertip. I do not know for how long. My watch is gone. Nothing changes.

I sleep and when I wake, the hand has disappeared. My fingers are empty. I feel for the hole in the earth where the hand has returned. There are several small crevices and I reach in. Nothing but dirt or vacancy. Somewhere in this country, they think of shoes, stationery, a plate of meat, the floor of a change room.

Then I feel the hand against my side. I hold it. We are parent and child, sisters, lovers walking together, watching the moon, anticipating the boat that will take us across the river. We whisper our stories. We are silent.

The hand is the moon, clouds. A sigh. I begin to wait for it. To expect it. It is a television. A friend. Where did it come from? What does it hope for, reaching, holding, sharing its quiet?

Fields of daisies, butterflies, explosives. There is no remembering. A cubicle. The Canadian Shield, its stunted trees and shine of mica. Burritos, librarians, snakes, and nightstands. Documents passed from hand to hand in secret.

THE HAND CARRIES nothing. Heat. A body. Happiness. I feel little except when I hold the hand. It could not have been looking for me, could not have anticipated finding me. A human hand among thousands: its own shadow, cold, sightless, underground; its mother, master, child, slave. Its twin.

I outline letters on its palm, but it does not understand. Its fingers move. Maybe it writes, but were it Arabic or English, I feel only caresses and swirls. Only an intimate and inscrutable grammar.

We lock our fingers together. We sleep. Wake. Are happy.

After a few days, the hand does not appear, I think I have lost my own hand. Later, I realize, the hand is gone. Hand. Gust of wind. The wide earth. Death. Someone brings me food.

I open and close my own hand. I open and close it. I pass the memory of the hand between each of my own hands. What can be held in a hand, what has flown away? I remember nothing.

✦

COFFEE, NEWSPAPER, EGGS

There were two of us, but we had only one pair of legs. We took turns walking. I'd walk into the park that was crammed with leaves and butterflies and good smells. Then I'd walk home and tell you all about it. Later, you'd walk to the mall. It was stuffed full of skirts, cellphones, Chinese food, and hooded sweatshirts. You'd march right up the stairs where I would be in the big chair, waiting to hear all about your adventure. I'd put down my newspaper and you'd tell me everything. Ginger chicken—really?

Some might wonder why we couldn't just share one leg each. We tried. We learned to hop. We wrapped our arms around each other's shoulders and pretended to be a big double person with a single set of legs, but it wasn't the same. We didn't feel right separating the legs. They belonged together. Like Laurel and Hardy, Brad Pitt and Julia Roberts, spic and span, left and right, and the two of us.

In the summer, our house was surrounded by millions of yellow flowers. It was because of us. People drove by our house, real slow, just to look at our flowers. In spring you'd take the legs out into the garden and dig a bunch of holes. Then you'd walk in and have a glass of lemonade at the kitchen table and wipe your sweaty brow. Ahh, you'd say. Your turn, you'd say, and I'd take the legs and carry out armfuls of flowers. I'd stick the bulbs into the millions of holes that you'd dug. Look. You forgot the shovel beside the apple tree. It's okay. I'll carry it to the garage. I have the legs.

We bought shoes online so that we could both be involved in the selection of footwear. I preferred the convenience of Velcro but you, if you had your druthers, would opt for classic lace-ups. It was black for me. White for you. Invariably we settled on slip-ons in light brown. I don't want you to think that it wasn't a rich life, a vivid and satisfying life, a life of rich imagination and personal choice. Ours was a vibrant tango of intersecting free will, a mambo up the relationship decision tree.

One day, the sun shone into our window like a searchlight. It woke us both up. Hey, I said. I'll take the legs and go downstairs and make some coffee, then you can go and get the paper. Then I'll make the eggs. OKAY, you said. But first let me go to the bathroom. OKAY, I said. That necessarily has to come before coffee. Yes, you said. Without question. So I'll wait, I said. Yes, you said. What else would you do? Handsprings, I said.

We looked around but the legs were gone. Maybe they wriggled under the bed? I asked. They were not under the bed. Maybe you left them in the walk-in closet? you asked. But they were not in the walk-in closet. Could we have left them in the nursery? we wondered. Once, many years ago, we had hoped to have a baby together. We would have shared our baby like our legs. You would go to the Christmas concert and see our baby sing. I would go to meet-the-teacher night and hear about our little one's progress with scissors. While you tucked her into bed, I would sing from the other room. But the legs were not in the nursery. Not in the garden. Not in the mall. I used the telescope and looked all over. You used your wide-ranging psychic powers to determine that the legs were not in the park.

This marks a significant change in our lives, I said. Without legs, we are different, you said. We lay in our bed and clung together. The sun rose far into the sky like a soccer ball kicked too high over a goalpost. Then it fell down to the pink horizon and we were in darkness. The next day, it did it again. We did not leave the bed. Your arms were wrapped around my torso. My arms were wrapped around your torso. Each of our shoulders, both our left and our right, were wet with each other's tears. A month passed. Then ten years. We suspected the loss of millions of flowers but neither of us had the mental stamina nor the psychological agility to look.

Why had our legs left us? Where had they gone? We imagined them at a restaurant table in Los Angeles wearing aviator sunglasses and ordering an expensive imported water with lemon. Maybe they were in India, helping the poor. A pair of legs could make a difference there, we reasoned. A significant difference. But it had been so sudden. They had left without warning. There was no note, no phone call, not even a footprint left on the front walkway. By now, the legs must have changed. We'd probably not recognize them if they walked right up to us and knelt down. The world was large and a pair of legs could choose to live anywhere, could choose to live almost any story. It was not fair of us to want to hold the legs back, to not allow the legs to realize their own personal and innate legness. To be with other legs. To feel the hot wind of Iceland blowing against their knees, the unrelenting prickle of Antarctica's sand against their pale calves, to feel the muscular pleasures of making a jump shot at the end of an inning late in the evening at a Tokyo ballpark, the fans standing and waving their colourful scarves. Somewhere in this large blue world, the legs were happy. It was time we understood that.

How? you asked. How are we going to do all that without the legs? We'll find a way, I said. First coffee. Then eggs.

THE GREAT EXPLORER

The great explorer leaves the palace. Even without his splendid hat of feathers, he has to crouch to get through the gates.

"Those at the gates are the brothers of explorers," he says to the gatekeeper. "We look into the distance and see first what others see only later."

"Sometimes I see those who return with an arrow stuck through them," the gatekeeper says. "Though mostly I sleep in this chair with my hat pulled over my eyes."

The explorer mounts his horse and rides out into the fields. He smells the scent of rolled hay, sees the familiar pocketful of stars.

Then he rides to the shore and boards his ship. He will find a new land. Those on the shore watch him sail away. They watch him get smaller as he approaches the horizon. He is the size of a small child. Soon he is no bigger than a pebble. Then he is nothing but a speck, a pinprick, a molecule.

He sails across the sea and discovers a new land. He throws down his anchor, then rows to shore. An island chief appears on the sand. He is surrounded by many people dancing and bearing great platters of fruit.

The island chief looks around the shore. He looks at the sea. He looks up, then down. Then he sees the explorer.

"These platters of fruit are for you, small one," the chief says.

"Thanks," the explorer says. "They look delicious."

"Might take a few days to eat them," the chief says. "What with your size and all."

"What about my size?" the explorer asks.

"My brother, you are very small," the chief says. "Like a mosquito or an electron. But do not worry. My own son was born small. At first we thought he was just far away. But eventually he grew. Though he's still ugly, even from a distance. Monkey-face, we call him."

"Your people dance well," the great explorer says.

"You are so small, but have come so far," the chief replies.

"I can't afford to get smaller. I might disappear. Have my ship," the explorer tells the chief. "The next world is yours."

✦

FLIGHT PATH

I n my country, two men often marry. Two women also. And these people are happy or not in the manner of any marriage or of any couple throughout the world or time.

And so, the time came for me, when I too was seized with the desire to marry. But I wanted something closer than holly and ivy, closer than two sprigs of holly, or two vines of ivy. Something closer than bread and toast. Something more like breathing.

So I married myself.

Marriage is like a Möbius strip, a twisting, turning thing that appears to have two sides, but, in reality, has only one. Or that appears to have a single side, but in truth has two. It's the edges that are important. It's the edges that are often forgotten.

It was a beautiful day. There was music. In the man-made glade, there was a flute and a harp. Or two harps. Or a single flute. There was a rabbi. A single rabbi with a snowcloud beard like Santa Claus. There were piles of food and an ice sculpture in the shape of God and Adam pointing at each other from the ceiling of the Sistine Chapel. In the middle of the boundless sweet table, there was a three-tiered wedding cake, and at its summit, under a little icing-sugar chuppah, a single person in a black tuxedo. This, in the language of celebration and the alchemy of cake decoration, was me. After the traditional ceremony on the stage of the lovely country chapel, I embraced myself and cried as I promised to be true to this life before God, my parents, my friends, and myself. I stomped on the wineglass and the people broke into song.

My love was not absolute, for life is changeable, uncertain, a minefield of betrayals and tragedy. But I had faith. I had the courage of my promise. I would forever be true to this love, whether it flickered or shone bright. Whether it was a candle or a Klieg light. Whether it was a Klimt or a Sigmund Freud. My love for myself would deepen with time. There would be therapy, counselling, and walks by the sea as the sun set. I thought how the sand was like the ripples I felt as I touched my tongue to the roof of my mouth and explored.

I gave myself pleasure, laughed at my own jokes. Sometimes, I knew what I was thinking; sometimes, I did not. After a while, it became more difficult to surprise myself, but I managed. I was a man of routine, but then, without warning, I would change. I'd find myself across town eating somewhere new, trying something different. Is this sea cucumber? I've never had sea cucumber. I'd take in the ballet or a ball game. Sometimes within an hour of one another. I would add spice to things that never had spice. I would dress in the dark, only open my eyes downstairs before the mirror. I would write notes to myself without looking. I learned to speak without first thinking, learned to anticipate my every need. I appreciated the little things. Is that a new tie? I can't believe what you managed on that triple-word score.

I filled my house with mirrors so I was surrounded by love. In some places where there were two mirrors, it seemed that there was an infinite number of marriages, my life a Ziegfeld Folly down a connubial corridor, a blissful kaleidoscope of spouses waving at each other, looking out with endless pairs of eyes into the same happy and domestic world.

There were years of happiness. Holidays. Promotions.

Birthdays. Good times with friends and alone. A new house. A cottage by the sea. Late-night drives out into the country, nothing but the stars, the empty fields and thoughts intertwined with the quiet songs of the radio. Sunday-morning coffee on the porch or in bed. Dreams shared. The prosody of reality scanned. New family. Crises met, averted, or suffered.

I was taken by surprise when the news came, though I had not been feeling well and had been taking it easy, pacing myself, spending more time at home, and at rest. But still, I was young. I felt strong, and there was much to do, much to look forward to. Soon it would be spring. There was gardening. The crocuses had bloomed between the mess of dried stalks in last year's gardens. A niece and a nephew were learning to roll over, to walk, beginning to name things, to delight in their new discoveries. My parents had become warm and sentimental, feeling joy and satisfaction in their family and each other, now having time to deeply experience each small trouble or accomplishment. And my marriage. I looked forward to an old-age marriage: of cups of tea carefully carried to the bedside, of memories dim yet strongly felt, of fastidious preparation on the calendar for each minor outing or appointment.

The doctor said that there was not much time. Maybe a month. Maybe only two weeks. I thought back to the day of my wedding. I don't know why but I remembered the stains on the waiters' white jackets, the cloying questions of the videographer, my brother's bad jokes, the beautiful lithe body of an old friend from college, my own. There was the future like the inconceivably long path of a migrating bird. A path stretched out before endless generations of birds. Each bird could not conceive of the distance of its destination or of the vastness of its route, but knew only the winds, the position of the stars, and some kind of deep pull from far inside its brain.

At the end, I sat myself up in the wheelchair. The nurse had helped me dress and shave. I had brushed my hair carefully and put on cologne. I was as handsome as I'd ever been.

✦

THE ASCENSION OF MS. PAC-MAN
for A. G. Pasquella

The wind and sea beyond my hospital room window. Ah the birds, the children, the husks of ex-lovers rolling over tarmac, the weeping of chauffeurs, the luminous exoskeletons of ghosts and octopi. The moon is my haunted body, yellow and round against the dark warp of night's black tunnel.

Once I was ripe. Once I patrolled the mazes. Once the energizers were inside me and the ghosts were vulnerable. O 100-point pair of cherries. O pears, pretzels, O bonus fruit.

I look toward my dinner tray and weep. O Chaser, Ambusher, Fickle, O Stupid. O Urchin, Romp, Stylist, O Crybaby. I am a cronc, a hag, a gorgon. I was a shark, eating light in order that I could live. O Shadow, Speedy, Bashful, Pokey. O Blinky, Pinky, Inky, O Clyde, my lovers. O you 5,000-point banana. Life is a subroutine that draws only erroneous fruit and never solace or a peaceful, victorious, numberless end.

All my youth, I floated through a labyrinth of dupes and chumps. I sought the skeletons of life's ghosts, the lightning-blue monsters of sex, consumption, and the tailless pellets of Pac-Man's jizz, its unending ellipses indicating absence only. And now, I am a pale and fulvous Tiresias of the sheets being fed only peas in the narrow maze of silver guardrails around this single bed. Immobile. Forgotten. My once-red lips pallid and deflated, my buttery legs sallow pixels only.

O witch world of three dimensions. O ray of light. O quick fingers. I feel your breath upon me. I know my soul that turned as a red bow upon my vacant brow will soon unravel and journey toward the heavens where I shall speak my own name and travel the edgeless rounds of star fields, alone in the emulation of infinite space.

✦

THE HAIRCUT

Each hair is equal, each hair is entitled to the same rights, privileges, and caresses by fingers and the wind as every other hair, his father had said. And so, he would honour his father. His hair would not be the uneven and unfair coiffure of the past. It would be new hair: long, equal, and proud.

The other kids did not understand. They carried him to the woods in a cardboard box and buried him beside an old sofa.

On Monday, in darkness, he imagined the innumerable grassland of his scalp's savannah. On Tuesday, a vast prehistoric fern rising from the verdant forest floor of his organically vibrant head. Wednesday: prize wheat on the tractless blond prairie of his pink pate. By Thursday, he knew that this was another impossible dream. One of his hairs was different. It grew faster than the others. It was magnificent.

Sunday night, it broke the earth's surface and he emerged from his paper tomb.

He went straight home and stayed there. He could not leave, for though he had had an extensive style and trim, a short back and sides, a buzz, a perm, a treatment, the one hair again became huge and snaked through the rooms of his house like the black power cords of the many morning talk show film crews who visited him, freakishly imprisoned within his small and now rather unkempt bedroom. For as it had grown, the fame of this single marvellous hair had grown also. The crowds surrounded his house, congregated in his yard, disturbed the neighbours, searching for hairnets, for product, for discarded, and possibly unrecognized, remarkable hairs. The people came from through-out the land, from over the seas, from salons with blue comb-desterilizer water and scented brushes.

His hair grew until it was an antenna extending around the world, the world in its normal-to-oily embrace. Children played beside the hair. They held sections and played jump rope. One-a-daisy. Two-a-daisy. Let's step in.

But the hair divided villages. It was a wall through the main street. Animals, coming across the hair in the midst of migra-tion, mistook it for an oil pipeline, changed their route, and died. His father would not be proud, and though his hair had become a symbol of the earth's pugnacious fertility, it had also become a security fence between nations. The Nobel Prize committee awarded his hair the Peace Prize only so they could disgrace the hair by taking it back. Generals met in secret to discuss plans to develop electrolysis from space. But still the hair grew.

The children who had buried him talked to each other from the computers in their rooms. They schemed. Something had to be done.

His hair now reached beyond the earth and was as a comb-over for Jupiter. What would happen, they demanded, if the hair curled and began to crowd out the sun?

We need the hair, he told them. The hair is everything: good and evil, memory and prediction. It is the spirit of animals, lined up, one after the other as if waiting for a movie, the drainpipe of space spiked bright with stars. It is a hundred Deaths descending the Playland slide, dark robes fluttering, their shoeless feet pulled up close, the howling throat of a toddler-minded man remember-ing spring. We need the long hair, he said. It is the ever-growing black stem of a daisy sent from the future to remind us who we are and who we might be. We are equal, he said, but only with ourselves and our futures. The hair is a long finger and it is pointing at us.

The children went into their backyards and looked toward heaven. Satellites moved across the sky, dodging the giant hair. Wind from over the fence tousled the children's bangs.

We believe you, they said. We love you.

✦

ICEMAKERS OF THE ANTEATER

An anteater chews through the house. The chair arms. Glasses. The legs of chairs. The mattress. It's the boyfriend my nine-year-old daughter's going to have ten years from now. It chews up the swimming pool. I sit on the porch throwing toasters, and shout, "Don't ever come back!" From under its coat, the boyfriend takes out a violin and begins to play some obscure anteater song. Then my daughter appears from the roots of a burning tree, dressed in football equipment. The sun, in an obvious attempt at drama, backlights her with its crimson tongue. She crouches low and runs into the house. It falls, a sack of doleful rooms, stairs and carpeting. The anteater splits in half. From its insides are born three angels, white as fridges, ice trays hidden between their cloud-like wings. In each tray are my daughter's future children, each tiny, curled up, and frozen.

✦

THE LOLLYGAGGING PRONGS
OF THE SIX-BAR BLUES

I t is a rainy Saturday afternoon and we're sprawled on a couch, sipping coffee. Love is a bright fork retrieving pickles, Fred says, munching on a sandwich. Or else it is a radiant pickle waiting to be touched by lollygagging prongs ferreted from the miniature display case at the nocturnal end of sorrow's long hallway.

And I say: It is a set of hopeful teeth swooping into the open mouth of a howling candy-store wolf, causing its loping face to whistle into the pickle-sweet air. It is an air conditioner strapped to the back of a convenience store clerk clipping roses in the red velvet bag of yesterday's arboretum.

But George says: No. It is a sticker of Snow White stuck to the left arm of a solar-powered electric chair lost in a mine shaft below the deli. It is a librarian sawing a harmonica in half with a bread knife. And, he says, love hurts.

If you're the harmonica, Fred says.

The couch is in the middle of an intersection. We are three friends and let's just say that each of us is playing two sets of the six-bar blues, expecting Barbie, or Bambi, or Baden-Powell to arrive with flags instead of thigh bones on the city bus bound for the lake of sudden frogs.

✦

MILK IN RAINDROPS

They throw the TV into the fire. Shadows flicker over cave walls. On the screen, a small heaven crenellated by flame. They plug the TV into a mammoth. A mammoth appears on the screen. They pull the plug and stick it into the river. The rush of water, floating leaves, logs realized later to be creatures engulfed by waves.

They plug the TV into itself. Nothing, then it appears onscreen, frightened, meek, wanting home.

A ceremony. They marry and it broadcasts them, the russet of sun, the purple sky, their words about life together. Children, remember our ancestors. Wisps, warnings, what's yet to be seen. A pillow, a mountain, the sound of leaves.

Night. The moon slithers, wary of ferns. The TV speaks, a hiss like embers in the fire. The slither and sibilance of its tongue, the slow static of birds, a tree of eyes. We believe babies find milk in raindrops, gather berries from the fields' thighs. We feast on the mammoth light, the trace of hands, the stories that trust us.

✦

FENCING

after a collaboration with Victor Coleman

We had been whitewashing the fence that we'd been sitting on and were waiting for the paint to dry, watching it as if it were serious French cinema on an unengaging afternoon.

"French cinema is the breath of God, all filmy on the feathered behindbacks of the seraph serving," I said, and the others laughed.

George raised his right eyebrow dryly. "I prefer to keep God at alms' length," he said, and we chuckled, imagining we had all the time in the world.

Charlie discovered a few drips of paint on the fence. "It's as if a uvula in the cave of God's maw had become protean, proving that the vibrant protoplasm of language is but a virus from author space." We drew in our breaths preparing to laugh drolly, but Henry, who was an angel, screeched up in his car, and we exhaled without laughing.

"Sorry I'm late. Heatstroke, you know—being an angel, I have to keep everything— heater included—on high. But seriously, I was crooning down the road toward utter and prayer. I'd turned at the corner of divine intervention, at the border between the letter and the enveloped, and, if you can believe it, I was epistle whipped again. Here, let me read it to you."

We were all ears and wings and Henry began:

> *There once was a shoe salesman Elijah*
> *Who said I'd be happy to oblijah*
> *When your foot's neatly shod*
> *In the raiment of God*
> *In fear angels shall ne'er tread besidejah.*

"It's a harp attack," I said, "in a region legion with Dionysian fission."

George moved his eyebrows around again. "It's a frisson allied with the anomaly," he said.

"Wish we were really human," I said.

"Yes," everyone agreed, and we waited by the fence for another 500,000 years.

✦

SNUG

Outside of my head, a great storm, dark, and the air snorts buffalo and doom. Clouds gather in furrows, the sky tossing and turning with a doozy of a headache. Any picnics are not happy: the sandwiches are soggy, the Kool-Aid's diluted, and everyone's irritated with father for continuing to state, "It's all about being together," and "It's attitude, not details that determine success."

But look! A little sparrow flapping through the downpour. Doused, it's a flag in a hurricane. Whipped and tossed, it finds an opening, a safe passage, a cave of respite. Okay, my ear. It funnels deep into my cochlea. Finally a pink snail, some promise of satisfaction in the darkness. It keeps going, finding safe harbour in the snug of my brain. Now, it's a feathery bumper car in the warm labyrinth of my fulgent mind. There's an image of my parents celebrating their purchase of a new hose, my sister falling from a tree, and my grandpa's heart, clip-clopping like a pony inside the cobbles of his chest.

And still the sparrow moves through the shed of my skull, past the toolbox, the pitchfork, the medulla oblongata, and that dream I had where my son gives birth to B. B. King and a window. An acorn licks a tree and the forest shudders. Then the bird heads south and emerges from the star of my anus and is lost to storm and uncertain darkness. I'm able to sit down, eventually, once I overcome fear and the memory of feathers.

"What comes before or after us we do not know," my father says, sucking on a damp sandwich. "Only the bird's short flight, the dog's incessant yip, the shelf that shines in space when the storm is outside."

DUST. DUSK. NIGHT. DAY. KNIFE.

Of course we don't know where he is. Raoul Wallenberg gave himself another passport, became someone else, then disappeared. A curled brown leaf.

He spoke as they were about to board, gave each word a new identity. Now we don't know what they mean. A long ditch running beside the road. Home.

Over there, behind the moon. Behind words. Fingers intertwined, churning like a river mill, sun climbing the horizon, rising over the field. A scurrying in twilight. A woollen blanket folded over and over. Eight times the limit of folding. Then it disappears, was never there.

Transfuse my veins with sap, fill a tree with blood. Branches move slowly in a slow wind. Autumn at the end of the fingers, red, gold, brown. Curling. When I am made into boards, a chair, this floor. Dance on me. Hide underneath me. Hush. Listen. Owls.

STORIES TOLD BY the bakehouse. Childbed. Midnight. A mandolin. In another's skin, a wolf creeping through mountains carrying only flour, an extra hand in a basket. Blood drains through the wicker.

Moonlight, silver tongue, wolf spine. The shine of a wrist, sneaking through fields and they in their grey uniforms, hissing, pointing guns, not knowing. Inside the baked loaf, a passport, money, an eyeball.

Names filtered through trees. Seven layers of clothing. Skirt. Shirt. Coat. Shirt. Pelt. Leaves. Bark. Dress. Shirt. Dusk. Dust. Night. Day. Knife. Stars. Hush. A shoe busy with insects. A morsel fingered in a pocket. A new planet. Backwards and forwards. Sleep.

Night is a length of a train, morning shuddering down the days, drifting smoke. Razors and breath hidden in lapels, rabbit skins, an unshaven face. Father cigarette. A hidden cave. Mother eyelid. The city folded eight times and bound by streets. Under the corn, sky roads. What they don't know: leaves have our names.

Blackbirds an almost remembered song. Oxen, cobblestones. The heart heals the knife, old potato. You fold and refold the words but they don't disappear. A river forming over time or through memory, but less wet.

The moon is samovar, ship, the galaxy smear of light spangled against a Baltic blue sky. Shh. He writes his own passport. We don't know what it means.

Clouds and rivers. A torn newspaper photo with no face. A passport above the desk. A Vienna of beds. A Vilnius. When you cease to be who you are, you don't become someone else.

THE NEW SQUEEZE

A new accordion because the accordion is the world and it should do more than push and pull. The hiss and sigh, the one and zero, the squeeze and press are three dimensions only, considering time. But what of Newton's up and down, sink and rise, backward and forward, away and toward, what of the new tessitura of space-time, the infolding diapason within the electron, the asymptotic passacaglias of hadrons, the tiny cassotto of exotic mesons and tetraquarks? There's a cave filled with the shadows of accordions or of accordion music. There's a pyre of accordions alight. We cannot know if the accordion plays or not, or is inflamed, or both. The caged accordion observed is not the incorporeal accordion true. An accordion may be dimensionless polka or a chat-room hora, but we cannot know if it is Mozart, if its shadows play the numinous ompah of root and fifth, if our true love wrapped in an accordion is but an emergent system of grace notes and obligatos drawn from our connected minds, or stripped naked to the waist, what risk is ours to play. Inside the accordion, the vast multidimensional darkness of the possible; above us, the constellation of buttons and keys, the dance pattern of what we know already and would now like to forget.

THE SAXOPHONISTS' BOOK OF THE DEAD

As soon as Miss Billie Holiday turned to write on the blackboard, Lester Young whipped out his peashooter and fired a spitball at the blackboard right where she had written the date. The spitball rolled down into the chalk gutter, leaving a damp opalescent trail.

"Pfft," Coleman Hawkins said, shaking his head at Lester. Before Miss Holiday turned around—she first finished writing the double bar at the end of the song—the Hawk shot another spitball right at her butt. There was a rippling around the point of impact on her sleek, dark skirt.

"John Coltrane," she said, looking at me. "John William Coltrane. I know you helped pioneer the use of modes in jazz and later were at the forefront of free jazz. I know you were recognized for your masterful improvisation, supreme musicianship, and iconic centrality to the history of jazz, but you march yourself down to Principal Hodge's office right now and I don't mean later."

"Yes, Miss Holiday," I said, standing. Ben Webster looked back from the seat in front of me and mouthed Miss Holiday's words as soon as she said them, opening his mouth wide like a satchel.

I wasn't worried about the principal's office. I'd been there before. My buddy Bird had taught me to play "Cherokee" in at least twenty-one keys. I could handle the principal. Before long we'd be talking about his lifetime in the Ellington band, about Harry Carney, and even about Billy Strayhorn and Mercer. And besides, what was he going to do, send me home? We all knew that there was nothing beyond the classroom. At the end of the school's linoleum, things just faded out. There was nothing. Nothing but the empty sky of infinite space and the chorus of stars.

I walked out of the classroom but stood for a moment outside the door, listening as Miss Holiday continued the lesson. We were learning "All the Things You Are," even though we'd all played the song a thousand times.

"Who can tell me what happens during the bridge?" she asked.

Eric Dolphy's hand shot into the air. This should be good, I thought. Eric was always pushing things right to the edge.

"Yes, Eric?" Miss Holiday said. There was something about Miss Holiday's voice that was so fragile but yet kept us in our place. Even Lester. At recess, he would defend her when the other boys began to talk. And I wondered if he deliberately missed when he shot spitballs. He'd get that crazy look in his eyes, twist his head funny, and shoot the peashooter at a weird angle and never get it anywhere near her. Still, a river of saliva down the board was something. Most guys, the spitball would just bounce and land on the floor with only a small dab of wet where it had hit. And there were those times when Lester would play a song with Miss Holiday. Even though his conception of rhythm and harmony were rudimentary compared to the sophistication that I felt I'd achieved, especially in my later years, I couldn't help but feel moved in a sleepy, old-timey kind of way.

"Miss Holiday," Eric began. "You know where the G-sharp melody note over the E-major chord turns into an A-flat over the F-minor seventh at the turnaround of the B section?"

"Yes, Eric," Miss Holiday said. "But please stand when you speak in class."

"Sorry, Miss Holiday," he said, shuffling to his feet. "In my estimation that's a particularly striking employment of an enharmonic substitution in an American popular song and one that facilitates the use of a chord built on every one of the twelve tones of the chromatic scale."

"That's an astute observation, Eric. And one that reflects your particular sensitivity to heightened chromaticism, something which is often tragically misunderstood. You may sit down."

"Thank you, Miss Holiday," he said. I couldn't tell if Eric had been trying to be sarcastic. Sometimes he was very subtle. But Miss Holiday had dealt with him deftly, I thought.

Out of nowhere, Lester suddenly murmured, "You are the angel glow."

"Pardon me?" Miss Holiday said.

"YATAG, ma'am." It was Charlie Parker, slouched as always in the back row, his nose stuck deep in a book as if he wasn't listening. "YATAG. You are the angel glow. Some of the most beautiful lyrics of all time. In the B section, ma'am."

My own favourite line was "What did I long for, I never really knew." It began the verse, which was almost never sung.

I started walking to Principal Hodges's office. Deep space loomed at the end of the hall, just past the pop machine nd the pictures of the student council. A rich velvet darkness and the stage lights of the silver stars.

The door was half open and I could see Principal Hodges in his customary ash-coloured wide-lapelled suit, chair tilted back, shiny shoes up on the desk, his eyes barely open, a haze of smoke like an interstellar dust cloud settled around him.

"Time and again I've longed for adventure, 'Something to make my heart beat the faster,'" he said through the door. "John William Coltrane ... Trane," he said, motioning for me to enter. "How long have we known each other?" he asked.

"A thousand years, sir," I replied, though I didn't really know how long, having little to measure it by.

"And here you are at my office again? I thought we'd developed an understanding."

"It wasn't me, sir. It was Coleman," I said.

"That's what you told me the last time. And before that, you said it was Lester." He took a long drag on his cigarette and then blew it out in an extended blue sigh. "John," he said. "John, it's about listening. The others look up to you. It's time to take responsibility."

"Yes, sir," I said, looking at the floor, the many burn marks like dark constellations in the taupe linoleum tiles. "Responsibility."

"Now go back to class and do what's right."

"Yes, sir." I nodded.

"Can you really play 'Cherokee' in all twelve keys?"

"Yes, sir. Charlie taught me. And it's at least twenty-one if you consider the enharmonic spellings."

"Right," he said. "But they don't sound any different, do they?"

"No, sir."

"Before you return to class, John, I would like you to take a long walk around the school and think about what I've said."

"Yes, Principal Hodges," I said, knowing that it was impossible, that I'd be lost in empty space like all the others.

I went back down the hall and listened again at the classroom door.

I heard the click of cases opening, the small thrumming of fingers on saxophone keys as my classmates held reeds in their mouths, saturating them with spit to prepare them for playing. I heard the small talk, the muttered jokes, the first few riffs, and the plangent vibrato of high notes. The quick whistle, the resultant shout as someone hit someone else with a spitball when they weren't looking.

I went back into the classroom.

"Okay," Miss Holiday said. "John's back. Get your tenor out, John, and let's take it from the top."

✦

THE NARROW SEA

There was an accident and the truck overturned. Some were confused, suffering shock and head injuries, and they began to wander aimlessly along the road. The rest of us made for the neighbourhoods. We climbed fences and took exit ramps. We walked the crescents and courts of the subdivisions. We stepped past the rolled-up newspapers and the discount store flyers, saw the sweet green grass sticking through the melting snow and so walked toward the lawns. People were told to stay away from the windows so that we weren't spooked. We saw them looking away from their televisions, peering from the corners of windows. We were mortal ghosts tarrying in their yards but we were not afraid.

"Mrs. Brimby," I said to a cow next to me. "Do you remember?"

"Yes," Mrs. Brimby said. "I remember."

Then there was shouting. Humans in uniform with ropes and guns, and hoops on the end of long poles.

They didn't see us as we slipped behind a triple-car garage and into the lane behind a convenience store. We waited between the blue dumpster and the wall.

Finally, night fell and the air became cool, the only sound the nearby highway like the exhalations of the sea.

The moon set and we left our hiding place.

We came across two youths wheeling a folded ping-pong table

down the middle of the road. We nodded at each other, complicit in our secret tasks, and kept going.

By the highway, the service road was empty, the weeds of its rising embankments offering us cover. We had only a few hours before sunrise.

"What do you think happened to the others?" I asked.

"They panicked," Mrs. Brimby said.

There was a man on the top of the embankment. "I'm going to catch you," he shouted.

I felt sorry for him.

"Come with us," I said.

"You have to come with me," he said.

We stood in front of him, the moon casting our shadows together like a dark puddle.

We waited.

He knew it was futile. We were two large animals and he was a spindly youth. He lowered his stick.

"I have something to show you," he said, finally.

His name was Mike. He was working for the summer with Animal Control while he attended college. He had stayed out late, far beyond the end of his shift, in the hope of doing something marvellous, of finding us, of impressing his superiors. His new girlfriend, from the city, also worked with animals and he called her on his cellphone. He listened intently for her instructions.

He led us along the service road, across a main street bright with gas stations and fast-food restaurants, and down a long multi-lane boulevard. His girlfriend, Rose, arrived. She was bright and fresh-looking and held out her hand in greeting when she got out of her car, then smiled at the absurdity of the gesture, and changed it into a little wave.

Mike helped Rose take something out of the trunk. They began pulling it up around themselves.

A cow costume.

Rose, who was the front end, gestured with her nose.

"What should we do?" I asked Mrs. Brimby.

"Follow them," she said.

We passed under a gateway and through some well-manicured gardens. We walked around a large glass building and stopped at a side door. Rose reached out from the abdomen of the costume and opened it with a key.

We shuffled along a concrete corridor, then down a few stairs. There was a vast glass wall, the window of a huge tank. Inside, the water was luminous. Enormous creatures, whales of some kind, sailed around the bright blue fields singing their bitter-sweet song.

The three of us, two cows and two humans, watched through the glass as dawn came in through the high windows.

"The ocean," I said.

"Yes," said Mrs. Brimby, "I remember."

✦

PHIL CAMPBELL WAS HIS TOWN

There's a guy called Phil Campbell who lives in a town in Alabama called Phil Campbell. It was exhausting: the questions, the confusion, the wisecracks:

"So you're Phil Campbell and you live in Phil Campbell…?"

Phil Campbell thought about moving, thought about changing his name, but he never did. Phil Campbell was his home. It was his name. He was Phil Campbell and Phil Campbell was his town.

But Phil Campbell wasn't named after Phil Campbell, the town. He was named after his father, Phil Campbell. And this Phil Campbell had been named after his own father, Phil Campbell, who had been named after his father, a stocky and redoubtable man named Phil Campbell. But that's as far as it went, for that Phil Campbell was the progeny of George Campbell, a migrant who had moved to Phil Campbell from somewhere up north, no one was sure where. On the other hand, Phil Campbell, the town, was named in the 1880s after a railroad man named Phil Campbell who came from England and set up a work camp. The town was incorporated in 1911 and remains the only place in Alabama to have both a first and a last name.

"Hey, Phil Campbell, you come from Phil Campbell?"

"That's *Mister* Campbell to you."

It was a good life in Phil Campbell. Safe streets, good jobs, a good digestion, and a smooth complexion. A happy life.

But this past April, a tornado ripped through Phil Campbell and messed things up. Here's what happened.

Bricks, windows, record collections, small chairs from the elementary school, fridges, bank deposits, Phil Campbell's pants, cows: all tossed into the air and then scattered about the hot Alabama ground. A toupée was blown, forlorn and alone, down Main Street, a baleful tumbleweed, inventory spat from the twisting chaos of the air. There were tears flying horizontally like rain. There were small bursts of hope, but there was little to hope for.

Phil Campbell would never be the same.

He'd been working in his basement for days and hadn't got the tornado warnings. He'd come up to the kitchen to get himself a glass of orange juice when he heard strange sounds outside and so he opened the door to see what was going on. The tornado burst right through the door. And when Phil Campbell opened his mouth to say, "Hey, what do you think you're—" the tornado jumped in and dived down his throat. Phil Campbell's insides became as messed up as the streets of the town, and he fell down and lay on the clammy linoleum beside the stove and passed out.

That's where the other Phil Campbells enter the story. One thousand one hundred and fifty Phil Campbells. Phil Campbells from all around the world.

These Phil Campbells found each other on Facebook, through Twitter, and through regular email. They gathered in the town of Phil Campbell. They came to see what they could do.

Philanthropy.

It was mostly guys named Philip and a few Phyllises, though there were Phillipas and Filipes too. They all wore name tags. Identical name tags, photocopied by Phil Campbell of Phil Campbell Real Estate (Boston, Mass.).

"Phil Campbell," the name tags said, both with irony and without.

It was a serious thing, this meeting of Phil Campbells, but it was droll pandemonium when they registered at the hotels.

"I've a reservation under the name Phil Campbell," a Phil Campbell would say at the Phil Campbell Motor Inn, and the other Phil Campbells in the line behind him laughed good-naturedly at the confusion of the girl at the desk.

And there were the many Phil jokes.

"Hey, Phil," a Phil would call into the whole group of Phils just to see who would turn around.

Or the ever popular "Philately will get you nowhere."

"I've had my Phil," a Phil Campbell father would quip about his son, another Phil Campbell.

And there were murmurs of assent as a Phil Campbell patted his handsome round Campbell-belly and ordered a Philly Cheese Steak sandwich at the Phil Campbell Steakhouse with the words "I need a Phil-up, please."

But no matter how you looked at it—joyfully, wryly, bizarrely, wonderfully—there were a lot of Phils.

"Hey, Phil, where are you from?" one Phil would ask another.

"Brooklyn. Where you from?"

"Toronto, Canada," the first Phil would reply.

Groups of Phil Campbells sat together and talked. There wasn't anything special about being Phil Campbell if you lived in a place other than Phil Campbell, in Seattle or Liverpool or Prague, for instance. There weren't special Phil Campbell stories, the way someone who shared a name with a famous celebrity had stories.

"You're Flip Philips?"

"Not *that* Flip Philips."

"Oh, but please, have a seat in first class, and may I have your autograph? For my kids."

But being Phil Campbell became remarkable when you were in a group of over a thousand other Phil Campbells.

"One can of beans isn't special, but if you see a thousand cans of beans lined up in a row, then that's something," a Phil Campbell from Hoboken, New Jersey, explained to a Phil Campbell from Tucson, Arizona.

And being with 1,149 other Phil Campbells in the Phil Campbell Catering and Banquet Center in Phil Campbell, Alabama, was not just unusual enough to make a good story. It was sublime.

An alignment of electrons. A ringing harmony, a magnetic charge.

What was the same? What was different? What's it like where you come from? How did you hear about the town of Phil Campbell?

But then the Phil Campbells turned to the more serious matter at hand. "How can all of us Phil Campbells help the people of Phil Campbell?" The tornado had been bad. People had been killed. Many were missing. Phil Campbell was filled with debris. There were emergency rescue crews, but they were overwhelmed.

The Phil Campbells made plans. They would tend to the sick and traumatized, search for the missing. They would clean up, help rebuild, and assist people in finding new homes. Each Phil Campbell according to his or her own skills, profession, and nature, and resources. There were officer Phils, nurse Phils, construction worker Phils, and, of course, several Dr. Phils.

They set to work.

With spades and wheelbarrows, pickup trucks and bandages.

With kindness, determination, and goofy grins.

Army cots were set up in the high school gym. Enormous pots of soup were set to boil in the kitchens of churches. An infirmary ran out of the flagship Phil Campbell Pizza Emporium. A team of Phils began going door-to-door—or property-to-property when the doors or the houses had been knocked down—searching for those in need. Old men and women were helped outside, blinking in the bright light, as if emerging from a cave, and then driven to the gym. Mothers and their small children were lifted off their broken porches and taken for food at Phil Campbell Baptist Church.

"How you doing, Phil Campbell?" one Phil would ask another.

"Doing fine, thank you, Phil Campbell," the other would reply, and they'd both smile. Two Phil Campbells out in the world, doing good.

"Okay," one of them said into the crackling walkie-talkie. "Just going to check one more street before heading back for more supplies."

Phil Campbell's street hadn't been hit hard. Really it looked almost untouched. The lawns, neatly manicured, the shingles in place on the roofs, only garbage pails and flowerpots tossed about the sidewalks. Still, the team of Phil Campbells went up and down the street, checking each house just to make sure.

Phil Campbell's door was open.

"Hello, anyone here?" they called.

No answer.

Phil Campbell was still unconscious on the floor, a pool of almost evaporated orange juice sticky between the shards of broken glass scattered over the linoleum. The Phil Campbells moved quickly. One checked for a pulse. The other brushed the glass out of the way to make a clear workspace and then prepared the medical kit and held up the walkie-talkie, ready to call for outside help.

"He's alive," the first Phil Campbell said. He took a small flashlight from his pocket, pulled up Phil Campbell's eyelid, and shone the light at his pupil. "Responsive," he said.

"Sir?" he called to Phil Campbell. "Can you hear me?" He leaned in close to listen to Phil Campbell's breathing. "Help me," he said to the other Phil Campbell. "Let's sit him up." One Phil

Campbell supported his head and they pulled Phil Campbell up and rested him against the cabinet doors below the sink.

Phil Campbell began to breathe heavily and his eyes fluttered.

"What's your name, sir?" the second Phil Campbell asked. "Do you know your name?"

"Ph...Ph...Phil Campbell," Phil Campbell said weakly.

"That's my name," the Phil Campbell who had supported his neck said. "It's all of our names."

"Phil Campbell," Phil Campbell repeated. "I am Phil Campbell."

"Yes, sir," Phil Campbell said. "Your name is Phil Campbell. It's our name too."

Phil Campbell opened his mouth to say something more, but he could not contain the tornado any longer and it turned violently inside him and shot from the cave of his throat. It knocked both Phil Campbells down as it twisted about the kitchen and then burst out of the house with an ear-splitting howl.

It beat against the houses and trees of Phil Campbell's street, this time smashing and scattering everything in its seemingly erratic path toward the centre of town. It destroyed the elementary school and knocked down the library. It raged along the side streets and ripped through the mall.

One of the Phil Campbells rolled over on his belly and reached for the walkie-talkie. He must alert the other Phil Campbells.

Later that afternoon, there were 1,151 Phil Campbells gathered together on Main Street. They stood in a line on the other side of the street from the tornado.

Phil Campbell, the only Phil Campbell from Phil Campbell, Alabama, walked forward.

"My name is Phil Campbell and this is my town," he said to the tornado. "You are powerful and you have ravaged my insides and you have ravaged my town. You have killed many of our people, but I am not afraid. I stand here with all of these other Phil Campbells. Phil Campbells who have come here from all over the world. We Phil Campbells are not afraid."

The tornado turned and twisted and darkened the sky but did not move.

Phil Campbell bent down and picked up the lost toupée from the middle of the street. Though it was dusty and misshapen, he put it on his bald head.

"You know what I'm going to call you?" Phil Campbell said to the tornado. "I'm going to call you Phil Campbell. You're one of us now."

And just as the tornado had been inside him, he stepped into the tornado, into its empty insides.

The last time anyone saw Phil Campbell of Phil Campbell, Alabama, he was high in the air, holding on to the toupée and waving back at them from between the twisting fury of the tornado, just barely visible from the outside.

If the people of Phil Campbell could have named their town after Phil Campbell, they would have, but more than a hundred years before, they already had.

PARABLES OF CONVENIENCE

for Beth Bromberg

1.

A man wants to rob a convenience store. He charges in, armed with a knife. He orders the clerk to leave and wait outside. The clerk runs out of the store, calls the police, and never comes back. The police surround the store. They see through the window that the man is eating a chicken.

2.

A man wants to rob his local convenience store. He walks in and chats with the clerk. They both know each other. At a certain point, the man pulls on a black balaclava and holds a gun to the clerk's face. This is a robbery, the man says. I already knew that, the other replies.

3.

A convenience store is unhappy. I could be so much more convenient, it thinks. Late at night it travels to the home of a man who has a balaclava, a gun, and a criminal record. This is a stickup, the convenience store shouts into the mail slot.

4.

A robber rushes up to the owner of a convenience store just as he's locking up for the night. Look, he says, and shows the owner the handle of a knife that he's put up his sleeve. One moment, please, the owner says, and goes inside to get something. Look, the owner says, pointing to the toes of a baby sticking out of his own sleeve.

5.

Items on a convenience shelf want to get stolen. One day, he will come, the toothpaste says.

✦

MAHONEY LONESOME

The victorious wrestler is an oiled rhinoceros in a green Speedo, stomping the ground with his delicate feet. His funeral barge arms are ceremoniously poised above the golden sheaves of his mullet, shorn and curled like an offering in a rite of vegetative fertility. His muscles are burial mounds beneath the roiling prairie of his taut and blushing skin. His is the roar of a locomotive in pain, an avalanche of rocks crushing the family car.

His broad box-spring torso is a queen bed of slats, sleek and lumpy as after the coitus of mammoths. And the crowd, furious with enthusiasm, creating a broadband hiss like the white noise rush of the universe collapsing at the end of time, has filled the air with the reckless sacrifice of their larynxes and tongues, an exuberant abattoir of joy and rage.

But let's talk about viruses. The tiny Whoville network of viruses on the wrestler's tight trunks. Or one single virus, living at the end of a cellular cul-de-sac, attempting to seek life and to flourish, to find meaning and satisfaction, here on the brief green earth. The virus is a single word in the great wiki of hope and information, a mortal sleeper hold in space-time, an earnest Tongan death grip on life. In the big world, there may be the end-of-days tectonic supernovae of body slams, the torque of tiger feint crucifix armbars on the topology of subspace, but the virus perseveres in its ardent intracellular replications, its ontological infections, its almost endless epistemology of transmission.

They call our virus Mahoney Lonesome, and it works its covert operations in the crawl space beneath the organic stairs, a child-like and surreptitious spectator between parents in the interstellar parade of microscopic communication. It is both mail carrier and letter, firefighter and fire, gravity and galaxy.

It is a long and a short story. The Klieg lights of the ring have been silenced, night achieved by a switch, and the wrestler returns home. Another human, child or lover, rushes to greet him. The Red Sea parts in an exodus of blood and memory, and the virus takes its plagues wandering into the desert of the other. Mahoney Lonesome, a shadow, a spirit, the jubilation of souls in contact, enters the other, a certain knowledge, a chin lock, the sun shining into night, a cobra clutch, a front chancery of love, forgetfulness, immunity, or chance.

Yet pan beyond this wrestler and his viral kayfabe and eyeball that vacant region in space-time, bounded by ropes or string the-ory, which remains vacant but is there to recall the bonzo gonzo of our tenderness, the Andre shot of our rage, the cheap heat of mortality. Story is a hotshot, a tomato can, a swerve. If the crowd believed it could exist in twenty-two dimensions, there'd be cheering.

TART. SWEET. CRUNCHY. CRISP.

We were sitting in a waiting room outside the Big Office. I'd brought a copy of a jazz magazine to read and it sat on my lap, unopened. She was around my age, mid-twenties, her dark hair tied back, her jeans and T-shirt plain and nondescript. Did you know that Chet Baker died by falling out of a window? she asked. Imagine, she said, the propped window, Chet's lank body draped sideways over the sill, a leg hanging over the edge as he gazes out at Amsterdam Street below. He's singing a tune in his sweet voice. Maybe it's "When I Fall in Love," because then he really did fall.

It might have been an accident, she said. Yes, there was heroin in his system and cocaine in the hotel room. So that might have had something to do with it. It wasn't likely murder because the door was locked from the inside. And a window only two storeys up wouldn't be a good choice to jump from, don't you think? He was kind of a worn-out angel, but he was making some of the best records of his career. Then he pulped his head on the concrete. He already didn't have teeth and had had to learn to play trumpet all over again, except with dentures. After the fall, he couldn't very well play without a head. Though I suppose a few have tried, she laughed sweetly. And then added, suddenly serious, We lose people like that. Without warning.

We'd been sitting for a couple hours in the small waiting area, just a few chairs, a couple of worn magazines, and some kind of batiked fabric art from the seventies. I knew there was something I should have said when she became serious, but I hesitated, not knowing what, and then it was too late. I'd taken too long.

I thought of it later. Sponsor me in the gravity-a-thon. Sponsor me in the gravity-a-thon today for I will remain pulled to the earth forever. You can sponsor me by the hour or the day. You can pay in one lump sum, which, considering my mass and shape, might be most appropriate. I will help hold things together. I will be pulled toward the centre of many things and this pulling will help. Things will stay together. They will remain clumped, pressed down like soil in the path of wide-hooved horses. The roads of the world shall not erode, and its mountains will not fly through the clouds.

But I too have my own force in the universe. I pull matter toward me. The sun. Jupiter. A raisin. Galaxies and superclusters. Gnats. There is attraction. Far from home, the shape of a comet and its path changes because of me. Even more if I eat this next sandwich or that apple.

And there is an attraction that flows between the stuff of everything. The citizens of the world, its fish, and its stones. Gravity flows between us like an aura that shakes hands, that clasps us together as a drowning swimmer and his rescuer tug at each other over the boat edge, as waves rise and fall, escaping from the ocean and returning, escaping and returning, as indeed the moon pulls the tides, a restless sleeper tugging on blankets, pulled by dreams.

And I will sponsor you also. I will sponsor you and you will sponsor me. We both will move toward the centre of the world. I will pull you toward me and you will pull back. We will pull the living and the dead toward us. We are swimmers in an ocean of tide and undertow, an ocean of time and space.

But, of course, it would have been typical of me to think of that. I'd have wanted to stand up in my superhero cape in the waiting room and make everything right, speaking not for the meaning, but for how it fell on the tongue. Still, though, the sudden seriousness of her words stayed with me. *We lose people like that.* The words like a plaintive hole in space, like someone had erased a shadow, leaving nothing, not even the air.

I saw her again about a month later, walking down the stairs to the Big Office. Hi, I said awkwardly. Do you know which jazz composer has a middle name that's a shape?

I don't know, Benny Square Goodman? she said with a scrunching of her right eye, like a kind of wink.

Actually, it was Melodious Thunk, I said.

Who?

Thelonious Monk—his middle name was Sphere.

The opposite of square, she said. His own planet.

Yes, I said. But they always say his music is so angular.

Okay then, a planet with lots of feet and elbows sticking out of it. That's some kind of strange gravity happening there.

I guess, she said. And then was gone.

I continued up the stairs and sat down in the waiting room. After an hour or so, the door to the Big Office opened and I was asked to come into another smaller waiting room, though with similar decor. There was a clipboard on the table beside my chair. There were forms to fill out, and I began. My name, my age, the town where I was born. The story of my childhood. My mother's maiden name. Grades I got in college. I wrote about apples that I liked at different times in my life. Tart. Sweet. Crunchy. Crisp. My first bicycle. What dental work I needed. My job, my investments, my new car. Retirement plans and the last tropical country I travelled to. And as I wrote, I remained fixed to my place in the chair. I was balanced perfectly between one thing and the next. I had gravity and there was gravity, but I did not fall.

FROM *DOCTOR WEEP AND OTHER STRANGE TEETH* (2004)

✦

DEFROSTING DISNEY

I t is I, Dr. Mountain, famed heart surgeon to the cartoon world, who has been given the task of fixing the strange red pumper beating inside the slim black chest of Mickey Mouse.

Once before, I was called upon to perform this auspicious duty. It was a complex and highly technical procedure, but I can explain it simply and in terms you, the public, can understand.

We defrosted Walt.

Yes, Walt Disney, like an aging Snow White in her glass bier, awaiting a princely and eternal life in his cryogenic frost chamber, awaiting new age-extending medical procedures, procedures that would allow him to be re-released to the viewing public. A restored version of the original classic. A masterpiece for the whole family. A Walt you cannot afford to miss.

We took his heart for Mickey, then we froze him again.

It will be a shock for Walt, when he is finally defrosted for good sometime in the future, when he wakes without a heart.

Walt's eyes open. He looks around. He feels, for the first time in two hundred years, his sallow body, his stiff fingers. His lungs expand to take in the modern air, his two lungs like Disney World and Disneyland on either side of the America of his chest, ready to oxidize the technicolour blood that will be pumped out across the awakening world of his body by his I-think-I-can-I-think-I-can heart. His autonomic nervous system winds up like a pitcher eyeing the plate. Signals like memos are sent down to his chest. "Pump," they say. "Contract and send blood."

In the empty ballroom of his rib cage, there is no red Beauty dancing. There are no four chambers of the Beast. Thumper is gone.

Quite a surprise for Walt after all these years. His body, a Pinocchio collapsing after his strings are cut, not a real boy after all.

But let us return to Mickey, his ears limp, his voice a husky whisper. Minnie, Goofy, and Donald are gathered around his hospital bed.

"Oh Mickey, my Mickey," Minnie says, weeping, apparently having forgotten Mickey's unwillingness to give up a kidney, and she on dialysis, her remaining kidney refusing to advance with the frames. At the last minute, a compassionate background artist draws her a misshapen kidney with an impish smile.

Mickey's eyelids flutter. A gloved hand rises. "If I live," Mickey whispers, "I'll make it up to you."

"Gawrsh," Goofy says. "You were always a friend when you needed us most."

"Oh Mickey," Minnie says earnestly. "Have you drawn up a will?"

It is then that I, Dr. Ignatius Mountain, heart surgeon to the cartoon stars, stride into the room.

"Mr. Mouse," I say. "I am ready to repair your ailing ticker." I wheel Mickey and his bed out of the room.

Anaesthetic. There are so many choices with cartoon characters. I opt for the 7,000-ton Acme anvil. Other than a slight flattening of the patient, it is a good choice.

I make the incision.

The scalpel moves like shadow through the made-of-light skin. Already I can hear the ticking, the rumble of his blood. I feel anticipation and fear, as if I were an uncertain Aladdin madly rubbing the lamp.

Once I opened a chest, and the heart, like a gag lapel-flower, squirted a stream of laughing blood that engulfed me and washed me over to Paramount.

I worried about Walt's heart inside Mickey. It was always too big, too nervous, too human for an aging mouse. But it knew Mickey well, and Mickey understood its troubles, its need to expand, its need to close like a fist.

Sometimes, from his hole in the baseboard, Mickey would look back at his tidy living room, the overstuffed sofa, the big-screen TV, and the shelves lined with the books and videos of a long career. This wasn't what his Walt-heart desired. And no matter how many times he tried, it seemed to make no difference who he was when he wished upon a star.

His copyright would soon expire. He could not live forever. Little pieces of him would appear on T-shirts and coffee mugs around the world. He'd feel like the fading image of himself on an over-bleached beach towel, washed a thousand times.

I open Mickey's chest cavity. I am a spelunker, returning to a cave. There is Walt Disney's heart, poor frail thing, beating because it doesn't know what else to do.

I hold the heart in my hands. It squirms like a fish drawn from the water. I feel the urge to say something. I bow my head and all that comes to mind is "It's a Small World." But I'm not sure that's true, for here I am, Ignatius Mountain, once a poor boy, now in the centre of the universe, my hands holding the beating heart of Walt Disney, my head bowed over the anaesthetized body of Mickey Mouse, and I feel that the world is vast beyond belief. We cannot begin to understand what is in the shadow of a single whisker, or within the wingspan of a flea. I can fix Mickey Mouse's heart, the stolen heart of Disney, but, like Mickey's pink skin, so densely packed with hairs that it appears smooth and dark, I know that this life is made sleek with possibility and is huge.

I see now that Mickey's heart needs only to be held in my gloved hands, needs only my few words. Of course, I will tell Minnie that something magical was required, something highly technical and inexplicably deft—Mickey's wealth being what it is, and his need to spend it on something appropriately beeping, and with flashing lights.

I close the incision and enter the waiting room, peeling off my gloves. Minnie is pacing. Goofy is reading old magazines. Donald is smoking furiously.

"Everything is okay," I say. "Mickey's heart is a success."

"Thank God, the bastard," Minnie says. They all look relieved.

I feel a brightness then, a lightness, as if I were the one who had given up his melted heart and had been refrozen, as if I too could return to waiting.

A HISTORY OF THE VILLAGE

'm alone in the coffee shop with the fizz and rush of the espresso machine near the back. A thousand or a thousand-and-one years ago, I left my wife, my child, and the crystal-clear waters of my perfect swimming pool. I cannot remember when I left and my watch is gone. I look at where it used to be, but my wrist is barely there, my arm only a wisp of an arm. I am a Pinocchio made of echoes or of smoke or perhaps bad poetry. There's a book on the table in front of me and I see that I have been writing again. There's a mountain, a cupcake, and a wrist-watch in a valley. Someone very tall is milking a cow and their back hurts. They are singing—no, yodelling—and it reaches the pink ears of the espresso drinkers in the alphorn factory. I am living in a small cup; someone is harassing the foamy mountains and Clara the blue-skirted milkmaid. Gone now are her dreams of being a physicist down in the valley. She'd have loved to be able to calculate just how far Rudi the fat boy could pitch a goat from the roof of the church, and how far the twin shrieks of Gretel and Lorelei the barmaid sisters would travel, given a certain fixed input of Pilsner into Rudi and the perfectly round opening of her mouth as the goat flies overhead and she bathes nude in the fountain, realizing that youth is over, and probably the village was never how she imagined it anyway.

✦

CLICK

The day Henry was able to control his coffee maker from space, he had crouched on the ceiling and wept. That same day, he had made toast while in orbit. He had washed the dog while contemplating the white-blue whorl of wispy clouds over the earth. He had watched his mother dabbing her weepy nose with a Kleenex, crying while talking on the phone, watching the soaps with the sound turned down.

The coffee that had slowly dripped from the coffee maker was a dark French roast, and the aroma, Henry had imagined, was like a mahogany ghost spreading through his empty apartment. A ghost without its own borders, moving by osmosis, infiltrating the air.

Henry wasn't weeping now. He took another sip of coffee. Back on earth, his dentures in their water-filled glass clicked shut, like a turtle snapping at toes. The water sloshed out of the glass, the flukes of a whale slapping the surface, sending a baroque curl of water upward and then out over the bed and across his wife's closed eyes.

She began to stir. He clicked furiously, the teeth snapping frantically in the glass by the bed. A Morse code of underwater molars.

"Wake up, wake up, wake up."

His wife's eyes opened. She felt her wet face and pillow. Crying? she thought. I don't remember crying. Then she became aware of the clicking in the glass, a deranged cricket signalling her. Henry?

The clicking of the teeth slowed down. Henry's wife, Alice, hadn't been able to throw away his teeth after the accident. She dutifully replaced the water each night, just as Henry had done. Then she set them down on Henry's half-finished copy of Russell Hoban's *Turtle Diary* on the night table beside his side of the bed. She turned out Henry's bedside light.

"Henry, I know it's you," Alice said to the teeth.

Henry kept clicking from high above the Earth. In a few hours he would be directly over what had once been his bed too, what had once been the bedroom in the apartment that he had shared with Alice.

I don't understand, Alice said to the teeth. I want to understand.

Henry wished he could touch Alice. He wished he could hold her in his arms, perhaps go dancing once again. He began to click the teeth in waltz time. CLICK-click-click, CLICK-click-click.

Alice remained still, looking at the teeth quizzically. Then she started to hum along, nodding her head in time. Then she began to sway, and finally, she stood up and, still in her night dress, waltzed around to Henry's side of the bed, turning around and around on the carpeted floor.

They were dancing.

✦

SUMMER MORNING

There are three directions in which I must drive my children this humid summer morning for, after a series of large and fractious family consultations over corn on the cob, hot dogs, and caffeine-free Diet Coke, we have signed them up for a variety of entertaining and educational summer day camps. Their backpacks are ready, loaded with ice packs, fruit snacks, sandwiches, cold drinks, bathing suits, sunscreen, insect repellent, Dunkeroos, potato chips, orange slices, and towels. They have finished their Mickey Magic cereal, their Cocoa Puffs, their bagel with ultra-lite salmon cream cheese, orange juice, water, and milk. They have been given their Flintstones chewable vitamins (an orange Fred, a purple Barney, a misshapen orange Wilma, or maybe it's Bamm-Bamm). They have been sunscreened. They are wearing their own hats and sunglasses. Their running shoes are on the right feet. I have turned the Nintendo off. They have been reminded about appropriate camp behaviour, about the afternoon pickup arrangements, the schedule for soccer practices, about the friends who will come over after that for a swim, and—if things go well—for ice cream. There have been several arguments over seating arrangements in the minivan, and finally an agreement has been established that seems at least temporarily satisfying to all concerned. The children are in place, their backpacks stowed beneath their feet. Their seat belts are on and the large stuffed Winnie the Pooh has found a place between my youngest children. I turn the Raffi CD onto "Bananaphone," put the car into reverse, and accidentally drive over a bicycle that is skin-coloured and screams so loudly that the children cry. My youngest presses her face against the window.

"Bicycle Girl is dead," she shouts. "Her spokes won't turn again."

I jump out of the car and cradle the bent metal limbs.

"Bicycle Girl is not dead," I say as the little girl's head trembles. I speak softly, reassure her that all will be well. We take her inside and find a large cardboard box that we fill with tissue paper, a small pillow, and a blanket. We place the pink girl in the box. My daughter weeps as she kneels, singing Raffi songs in a small voice. I find a bell that had fallen off my bicycle years before. My son stands near the box and rings the bell. It is part dirge, part ice cream man, part mobile blade sharpener. I phone my wife—"Alice, come home"—and my wife drives from work. She pulls back the blanket and touches the Bicycle Girl's spokes with her fingers.

"Don't worry," my wife says. The Bicycle Girl whimpers. My wife spreads cream, then dresses the spokes with bandages. We carry the box into the family room by the television, where we can be close.

"Daddy, I am pink inside," my daughter says.

"We all are," I tell her.

I DON'T SLEEP. My brain is filled with hills. Bicycles ride up and down the sidewalks. Leaves fall on me, cover my eyes so that I wander into the road.

After a few days, the Bicycle Girl's colour deepens to an almost red.

"It is time to remove the bandages," my wife says.

Bicycle Girl's wheels turn, and she smiles when my son rings the old bell. She turns her head toward my daughter as she sings. Soon I am able to lift her out of the box and place her between my wife and me as we watch television. The news. A sitcom. Nature programming. My children's friends visit our house.

"Where is she? Where is she?" they shout at the door. The girl wheels tentatively around the living room, my son holding on to her handlebars, helping her balance. Bicycle Girl. Little wheezing grandma. Leaves surround us like snow, and everything is quiet. I light a fire and the Bicycle Girl is fascinated. She circles the living room, drives up close to the fireplace.

"Does she have a family of her own?" my daughter asks. "Are they looking for her? What should we do?"

It's only when we call the children for supper that we discover my daughter is missing. A neighbour reports seeing her and Bicycle Girl riding past the convenience store and over the bridge where the roads become vague.

THE TENTH SIGMUND FREUD

Even before the Ferris wheel began turning that day, the Sigmund Freud action figure awoke. He was not alone. He shared the shelf with the Statue of Liberty pencil sharpener and a glow-in-the-dark cigarette-lighter Jesus. Though he didn't feel it, Sigmund knew that unlike the others, he was meant to be ironic. Still, his arms were the only ones that moved. Jesus could bless in only one position. Liberty could hold her torch in only the one way she always did. But Sigmund could raise his cigar to his trimmed white beard. He could point at his shoes. He could wave to the little boy standing beside his mother in the single aisle of the store. It was Sigmund's only form of communication, and he hoped the boy would notice. "C'mere, little boy. Take me away. A toy isn't real until it is truly loved."

He didn't really believe this. He knew it was a long shot. A means to an end. An escape. The one Sigmund who had escaped before him had got lucky. A psychiatrist from Bellevue had bought him. Who knew if she truly loved him? Love, especially for adults, was so contingent, as he well knew. And besides, there was the matter of irony. Could anyone, child or adult, move beyond irony, and truly love, let alone truly love a six-inch-high plastic Sigmund Freud?

The boy had Jesus in his hand. "Look, Mom," he said, lighting Jesus's flame and thrusting it into his mother's face. Sigmund knew he would have found the symbolism funny if he hadn't been so desperate to get out of the dingy seaside store.

"Put that down!" the mother said. "It's not for children."

"Pick me, pick me, little one!" Sigmund appealed with his cigar-holding arm. He tried to look as lovable as he could. "I'll be your father. Your wise man. I'll stay away from your mother."

The boy stuck his finger into the pencil-sharpening hole of the Statue of Liberty.

"See the white beard—I'm Santa Claus," Sigmund implored from behind his tiny round spectacles. "Human communication is possible if you will just make the leap," Sigmund said. "Trust yourself."

Late nights in the shop, the only one awake, Sigmund would wonder what it meant to be an action figure. To be one of ten identical action figures. The nine other Sigmund Freuds slept huddled together the way Sigmund imagined primitive men had in their dark little caves. None of the other Freuds would talk to him. Jealousy? Suppressed adoration? What was it that made him different from the others? Long ago he had tried to understand, through analysis with the other nine Freuds. But they weren't ready. He'd scared them with his revelations, his suggestions, the intensity of his eyes. And so he'd been left to himself and his difficult friendships with Liberty, with Jesus, and now with this little boy.

"Mom, doesn't that doll look like Mr. Winestein?"

"Which one? … Oh, yes… I mean, who's Mr. Winestein?" the boy's mother said, trying to cover up that she and Mr. Winestein had been having an affair for years while her son attended baseball practice.

"You know. Mr. Winestein. Mr. Winestein who took me fishing with Johnny that day?"

The boy clutched Sigmund around the waist and pulled him off the shelf. Freud gazed up into the boy's earnest face. "Take me home, little boy. Love me. I can teach you things you never dreamed of."

"Look, Mom, its arms move."

"Little boy," Sigmund whispered. "I know secrets. Every boy likes secrets. I'll tell you about Vienna. I'll teach you German and about the mysteries of the mind."

"He even has a little cigar like Mr. Winestein, Mom."

"Loving a toy prepares you for your future," Freud said. "I'll be a special part of your childhood."

The boy brought Freud near to take a closer look.

"I'll be a toy rabbit and you can make me real," Freud whispered.

The boy stood still, looking at Freud. "Mom," he finally said. "I'm never going to love anyone as much as I love this doll."

"Take me home," Freud muttered. "Take me home."

✦

FREEZER

We've been given the key. We open the door, place our boots carefully on the mat in the hall. Then downstairs to the freezer. We've come for chocolate cake. My grandmother's cake, preserved in its chill basement sarcophagus, a Frigidaire ark for the pre-prepared and the grandpa-ready, for the Ziploc-mummified and the granny-inscribed, a frozen library awaiting mealtime archaeology, sandbags against whatever disorder is let loose when the outside world floods its banks.

We lift the freezer lid. Fish hard as stone school together in tinfoil pyramids. In this frigid desert, they do not know what hot water awaits them in my grandmother's sink, in which before-television meal they will be participants. We wander this frozen city of blintze dormitories, of boiled-chicken tenements, of the future cooked up by my grandmother. We release no curse exploring this Arctic Giza. That is the microwave's job: one less meal frozen out of time.

We hear a knocking. Behind a tray of frozen cabbage rolls, a hammer that once belonged to my grandfather is rapping on a yogurt container filled with applesauce. It looks sheepish, guilty, embarrassed to be caught. "I was a little peckish," it says. "My handle was rumbling." We notice other tools crouched behind the mock herring and the onion pie. Gradually, they emerge, like little children after the tanks have left town.

A pair of calipers opens a jar of curry mincemeat and rice, and the other tools rush over to eat. A screwdriver plays balalaika and sings. A packet of nails begins to dance. There's the material to repair a broken chair telling jokes that involve several languages and cavorting with an ironing board. A party has broken out in the freezer, and still we haven't found the chocolate cake.

The sound of the music and laughter fades behind us as we explore the passageways between frozen loaves of bread. Behind a batch of jam-filled biscuits we discover boxes of gloves. The gloves, delicate and leather, appear to be sleeping, each glove resting its slim fingers on its sister's. The gloves are breathing softly, and so we creep by, careful not to disturb their dreams of decorous morning walks downtown. Then a glove coughs quietly, stands on its fingers, motions to us with its thumb.

"If I could have your attention," it says. "Perhaps I can help."

"Thank you, O well-made calfskin glove," we say.

The glove curtsies, makes a demure fist, then straightens again. "Soon the freezer's dim bulb will be setting, its rays slanting across the crimson frost. I will guide you past the medley of small vegetables, the bags of string beans."

We follow the glove to a valley between frozen hills. "The queen bee, the sweet dark moon of the valley is here," the glove says, slipping back into the night. A tent of plastic wrap flutters slightly in the chill air. We step forward, part the flaps, walk cautiously inside. It is quiet inside the tent and smells faintly of flowers. At the far side of the room, propped by pillows, resting on a large bed, is what we have been looking for: my grandmother. Her eyes are closed and she is gently breathing. She appears to be sleeping.

"I've been waiting for you," she says. "Now eat."

✦

RUNNER

Of the thirty thousand runners running today, only one is made of glass. Only one could be shattered by a small stone. Of course, you can't tell what the runner is made of; clothes, gloves, shoes, a hairpiece, and speed conceal him.

A video camera set up at the checkpoint. From early morning, a constant stream. A few event vehicles. Flickering lights. Race officials. And always a stream of runners.

The runner passes into view. Octagons of light on the camera lens. The runner expressionless with concentration. The stone at chest level, moving forward as he moves. He has been chasing the stone since the race began, and finally he is gaining on it. The road sinks down and the runner's speed increases.

No one knows the runner's name. His chest touches the stone and there is an explosion of light and gloves. The camera has been plunged into a whirlpool of clothes and broken glass. A hairpiece limp on the sidelines. A shoe behind a bush. The runner disappears. It is as if someone has replaced the air with nails.

The shards of glass embed themselves in spectators watching from the sidelines. They do not notice the intrusion, so sharp are the fragments. They remain fixed on the race, their eyes scanning for family members and favourite runners. Tiny cuts speckle their bodies beneath their windbreakers; small abrasions mark their faces. The people take the glass home. They take the glass to restaurants and cafés, to homes and schools, to showers and doctor's appointments. They take the glass to bed. They press the glass against the skin of lovers, children, co-workers, pets. *Here, poochie poo, come kiss Daddy*. And the shards are passed on to Rover's face.

While at work, a woman finds a piece of glass in her hand. She removes it. She is a research scientist and she examines the fragment. Iridescent edges, ridges the colour of eyes, fissures like sky light. There's a pockmarked section that looks like Mother Teresa. But, of course, she thinks, everything looks like Mother Teresa. At a higher magnification, there are butterfly-shaped indentations and scratches like tiny drawings.

"C'mere, Bob. Look at this," she calls to her lab technician. Bob sees Rhode Island and scribbles that remind him of Hebrew.

"Are you sure?" the scientist asks.

"Absolutely," Bob says. "It's my bar mitzvah portion. And there's a bit that, if you sound it out, is an opening monologue Billy Crystal once did on *Saturday Night Live*."

They take the glass piece down to the electron microscope. The scientist sees her parents lying side by side beneath its surface. They look as if they have been buried in a frozen river. Their small faces are peaceful, their hands clasped together. They are young. The scientist examines them closely. Her parents become younger. Soon they are boy and girl and the father has no beard. His face is smooth and unwrinkled and the mother's body is slim as a child's arm. The parents become younger still. They are infants curled beneath the ice. They are tiny pink ears, their fists not yet unfurled. The glass is a womb and the scientist's parents have become a single cell. The scientist calls out, but it is too late. They have disappeared, and the fragment of glass is empty.

The cut in the scientist's hand smarts.

✦

SLICE

My mother buried me with a handful of flour. He will rise, she said, and threw the shovel over the fence. Then she went inside and began to sing like a lizard.

No. Though her mouth was empty of soil, she didn't sing. But how would I know, buried in the backyard with a handful of flour?

Underground, everything was different. The worms bickering in the dirt, the millipedes cracking droll and ironic jokes under damp rocks, the yapping and slobbering of dogs burying their bones. My mother was silent, went to bed, and pulled the covers over her head.

Was she feeling guilty? Do guilty-feeling people climb into bed in high-heeled shoes? Do they ignore the hammering of truant officers, of Boy Scout leaders, of can-he-come-out-to-play friends? Even Grandma, with her armful of cake ingredients, gave up knocking, went to the next daughter down the list.

The morning splintered as night threw a champagne glass full of dew into dawn's empty fireplace. A millipede cracked a good one about an ant, and my mother got out the shovel. She had forgotten the eggs, the milk, and a few other things.

There was brightness for a few seconds until mother filled the hole.

It rained all that day. I could hear the raindrops thrumming, the earthworms irritated and cranky, heading for the surface.

My mother shouting on the telephone, railing against world history, built-in shelving, politics, the ocean. She'd lost her eyes in the ocean.

Not her actual eyes. Here I'm speaking metaphorically. Or I would be speaking metaphorically if my mouth weren't filled with soil. It's like when I said her body was lithe and spiteful as a lizard's. The ocean had pulled her bones out and washed them like driftwood on the waves.

There was a boat.

Small, wooden, propelled by oars. Don't ask what was in it. If I was so clever, would I be a living bone buried in the corner of the yard?

A recipe, maybe. A child. An extensive Julia Child video collection. All of history rolled up small, then baked in a bread to escape detection at the checkpoints.

Why is it dark underground? Why are there no birds? These are the mysteries. I'm just buried.

The next day there was sun. The world was warm and I began to rise. I pushed away worms, squirrels, broken teacups, swing sets, patio stones, and barbecues. I was a vast loaf and the rec room became dark in my shadow.

Maybe I have exaggerated a little. In truth, I was no garage-sized loaf, but a bread slice, large as a bedroom wall, and I made the birds cower. The sky was light and tawny through my translucent body, and my mother, peering from beneath the covers, noticed the change.

✦

WHAT DOES IT MEAN TO
FIND A DEER IN YOUR BEDROOM?

Should you blow the hunting horn or invite the deer to dinner? I was worried and so I went into the bedroom to change something—my socks, my shirt, I can't be sure—and instead found a deer looking blankly into the mirror. It's okay, I've handled worse, except this deer looked familiar.

My accountant? My grandmother? Myself in a past life?

It was my fridge.

"Speak frankly, fridge," I said. "Tell me what the future holds. What shall the meals of the future put on the plates of my life? What of the safety and happiness of my children, my wife? Shall my body be eaten by cancer. Will my mind hold out until the end? What will be the condiments of happiness all the days of my life?"

There's something beautiful about appliances. About their muteness, their tawny pelts, their doe-eyed corners, their earnest shape.

✦

UVULA SHADOWS

The doorbell rings and I open the door onto a bright sunny day. The mailman is standing on the porch, and when I look into his mouth, I see the universe. Snow-capped mountains, radishes, raindrops, Piccadilly Circus, storm clouds, lightning, India, floral dresses, beautiful limbs, arch-ways, shipboard navigation systems, pipe cleaners, discarded frost-free refrigerators, sidewalks, fire, Louisiana, Teflon cook-ware, radiators, hardwood flooring, lemons, rain barrels, solar flares, Chicoutimi, bailiffs, portly saboteurs, dancing children, Mount Fujiyama, eternity, galvanized eavestroughs, manhole covers, binary stars, subway systems, waves, squids, discount stores, old men, pterodactyls, reticent rhythm and blues spokes-people, Tuscany, neglected deck-chair manufacturers, neutrinos, Buxtehude deniers, disgruntled conservation authority parking lot attendants, monsoons, tsunamis, bicycles, uvula shadows, taste buds, and a hundred-thousand stars like distant cavities in the vast black dental work of the sky.

"Can you please sign?" the mailman says, holding up a clip-board. Planets are spinning where his tonsils should be. The bright blur of a comet streaks across his soft palate. In all this vastness, I feel certain that life exists. Surely we could not be alone in all this possibility. Cells or galaxies come into being behind his wisdom teeth. Signals are sent from earnest transmitters in his pharynx. "We are here," the signals say. "We are not alone. We look for companionship in the incomprehensible massiveness of space."

I feel sick. I am still in my pyjamas. I've only half eaten my breakfast and here is everything in the mouth of a mailman. His eyes are hopeful, plaintive beneath his blue cap. In his ordinary hands he holds a clipboard with my name printed below a list of what I take to be the names of living things. I hesitate. I don't know what I would be committing myself to if I sign. "Who are you?" I ask. "What is it you are asking of me?"

As he opens his mouth to answer, I see whales, the future, carpeting, truth, suffering, and between two teeth, there we are, the mailman and I, standing on my porch in the bright morning.

"I could use a shave," I think to myself. "Who else has seen me like this?"

The mailman looks okay though, his tiny clipboard illuminated by stars. I see myself waving stupidly at my unshaven larger self, standing outside the mailman's cavernous mouth. It is as if I were on TV, greeting my friends and family. Is this what Gandhi or Maimonides would do? Even Groucho would not have been so inane. "Hi, Mom!" he'd say. "Outside of the mailman, the universe is man's best friend. Inside of a mailman, it's too dark and sticky."

But I am beginning to suspect that this is not the normal mailman. In truth, I do not recognize him. Perhaps this is not his usual route and he is filling in for the regular guy.

I begin to speak but wonder what the mailman can see in my open mouth. Had I flossed recently? It had been a while since I brushed with diligence. I am willing to admit that perhaps my oral hygiene is not up to universal standards. My mouth is a vibrant organic place, an address not rich in highly developed life forms and advanced consciousness, but nevertheless a place where life may have a chance, a place where galaxies and solar systems could be born and eventually spawn the nimble feet of gazelles and the soul-scouring calls of owls heard amidst the complicated verse forms of creatures who had learned to mediate their conception of the world through a system involving the coordination of muscle contractions in their mouths and abdomens.

The mailman looks at me curiously. He is holding not only the clipboard but a pen. It is a sure sign that I have some breakfast caught between my teeth. He is offering me implements that would be helpful in the removal of items foreign to my dentition. The clipboard is a possibility, but the pen will be more effective. I take it from his hand. The mailman smiles and the universe disappears in his closed mouth.

I raise the pen to my mouth. The mailman looks pleadingly at me. I aim the pen tip at my teeth. I only intend to dislodge the breakfast fragment that had become trapped, but as the pen comes close to my mouth, desire, like the tremendous gravitational pull of a gas giant, sucks me into its orbit, and I push the entire pen into my mouth. There's a flash of bright light and then the shadow of vast interstellar darkness as the mailman again opens his mouth to speak. I begin to chew on the pen, feel the satisfying crunch of blue plastic, the juiciness of the ink as it spurts onto my plain human tongue, just a small red rectangle of inner-city backyard beside the borderless acres of the mailman's cosmic maw. I taste the acrid nectar of the fossil glow as I swallow. I turn and go back inside my house. I will not need more breakfast.

✦

BROKEN GLASS COWBOY

He was Johnny Appleseed except he didn't do apples. He didn't sow seeds. He created no orchards. But he was concerned. He crossed the country barefoot, visited parking lots. He'd bend low over asphalt, examine with his blue eyes. His long fingers would move like the legs of a spider and he'd pick up glass, for in nearly every parking lot across America, at some time, a bottle has been broken. Glass has grown wild. And sooner or later, Chester Shardman would arrive.

Perhaps it's Saturday night, and Dan and Joe are stumbling downtown, talking loud, making power guitar sounds with their lips. They're drinking beer. Dan holds up his just-emptied Coors and hurls it at a wall. It shatters. A flock of glass, a brown rain. A simple Saturday-night fracture. It descends upon the parking lot of John, wearer of shoe polish, owner of software and golf clubs, cherisher of a ring and a beer glass from his graduating class.

The glass waits in darkness until the commute begins. It begins to sparkle as the lineups in the coffee drive-throughs lengthen. Dan and Joe are sleeping. Dan dreams the bones of his forehead fracturing, the fragments breaking free like snow rising toward the dawn sky. Dan thinks of a hand plunging into water, droplets splashing onto the floor around the sink. John starts his car and begins to drive to work.

Chester Shardman follows the trails of fractured glass. He is the Hansel and Gretel of the broken bottle, finding his way home. It's been years since he first began. November was chill and Chester left the shores of the Atlantic, following glass to the Pacific. Chester arrives at the parking spot of John the desk dweller. John of the decent handshake and the well-made cold call. Chester bends down on one knee, the bride of the yellow line. He brushes his wide palm over the black tarmac, feels the sharp spines of glass. Glass does not respect the painted line, the wheels of cars, the *Reserved for Employees* sign. Chester works quickly, diligently, plucking the brown seeds between finger and thumb. He is a chicken working the yard and soon he has gathered the glass into his turned-up apron. He strides into an alleyway. He will heal what was rent asunder. He will piece the glass together and form a bottle out of small notions. A network of tiny seams surrounds the thin eyes of glass. The bottle seems alive, a hand, a leg, a baby's head. It is wrapped in a delta of life-nourishing veins.

Chester carries the bottle inside his shirt, protecting it like an infant. He will walk across town and up the fire-escape stairs to Dan's apartment. Dan the bottle thrower. Dan of the bone flock forehead. Chester places the reborn bottle into the sleeping hands of Dan and creeps away, perhaps for breakfast, perhaps to another glass-bejewelled parking lot on the other side of town. Finally, Dan wakes and discovers the bottle in his hands. At that moment, language is inconceivably broken, its thousand sharp edges teething on air.

BROWN SHOES

They give me Iceland. When I open it, lava burns my shoes. Damn. They were the brown ones. My favourite lace-ups. I've beheaded intruders in these shoes, my lovely two-handed sword slicing through the brutes as they push their great ugly brows through my windows. They leave a mess on the living room floor, lapped up by cats. I pitch their bodies over neighbours' fences. They land in the pool, spoiling kids' birthday parties. I try to make it up to them, read the *Prose Edda* over the phone to Snorri, their dog. How was I to know it was 4 a.m. with my eyes closed? And can you blame me, what with intruders bursting through my windows? Wispy blue-gold intruders with arms like scented ropes. They embrace the piano, make a noose around family photographs, leave Grandma sobbing in a cupboard. Don't worry, Grandma, I have my sword. I'll make yarn of the intruders and you can knit them into little blankets for the babies born every minute of the long relentless day. New babies of every size and colour. The cats lick up the extras, the entrails, the mistakes. The twilight is filled with intruders, and I splice the sweet-smelling dusk with my pitiless sword. Grandma, there are so many of them, you can cover the local school with your knitting, muffle the classrooms of their endless children.

It is springtime and tiny flowers grow on Iceland, pathetic blossoms that clutch the mica-covered rocks. Fishermen set out in their skiffs, seeking fish off the rugged coast. There is the vibrant choral tradition, and I'm often asked to adjudicate when contests are held. Ten points for mewling with good diction. Eight points for bone-altering vibrato in songs about endless night. Nine for accurate sforzandos, the altos snickering beneath their downy almost-moustaches.

The grey world is filling with people. It's crammed with them. Their tiny thoughts and stingy little bodies. Their stories and conversations. Their soccer triumphs and head colds. Their libraries, booster shots, funeral pyres, graduations, and chic sidewalk cafés.

There is no place for me here. I have to leave.

In a week, they'll find Iceland neglected, unshaven, and beginning to grow mould. Let them give it to someone else.

✦

THE LOST SCOOTER

I have a scooter, a beautiful blue scooter. Then the wind comes barrelling along the road and blows my beautiful blue scooter onto the lawn, which is like a forest. I call out. Parents begin appearing. They emerge from houses, side doors, porches, driveways. Soon the whole street is speckled with parents. They line the sidewalks, cover the lawns, occupy the road. Traffic stops, and more parents emerge from cars.

"He has lost his blue scooter in the lawn like a thicket," they say. "And though we have waited for a more diligent relationship with this lawn to develop, for a demonstrated record of earnest lawn maintenance to be apparent, we will seek this child's blue scooter in the homeowner's deep lawn. Day is ending, our children are home in bed, we will turn our attention to that world between the green blades."

I point to the place where the wind took my scooter and the eyes of the parents follow my outstretched finger. Then the street begins to swarm. Parents, some arm in arm, pace, their eyes fixed on the ground, hoping to find the glimmer of a blue wheel, the sparkle of a handle. The scooter is lost on the street and the parents will find it. The scooter does not cry like a wandering child, but surely it is forlorn and frightened between the blades.

Groups of parents form in certain regions of the sidewalk. Hierarchies and specializations develop. The near-the-sidewalk parents, the driveway specialists. The chief of those who search the eastern section of lawn. Certain patterns of speech become characteristic of particular groups of parents. The long and languorous speeches of the in-the-shadow-of-the-oak-tree parents, the clipped style of those on their knees. I consider the favourable commercial opportunities afforded by a lemonade stand. After all, parents need to slake their questing thirsts. In addition to lemonade, I sell the accessories and accoutrements appropriate to the search. I establish my own currency and introduce a political system wherein I have sole legislative power. Parents must consult me on all matters regarding the search. I provide exclusive details regarding the appearance of the scooter. I create a structure within which parents who trade knowledge of these details are subject to taxation. I find a system of credit to be a valuable option for some parents seeking to acquire details beyond their immediate means. I am willing to consider applications for shelter from those parents whose financial transactions are sufficient to merit my interest.

As the sky above the street turns dark, I sing the ancient poetry of the scooter, and the parents regard me with wonder. The stars spangle the dark lawn above them, and for me they are truly grateful. I am just a single child but the scooter is lost forever.

✦

BABY SNOTTLE
after Anton Majkut (age four)

Baby Snottle had no eyes and no ears and lived inside an eyeball in the toe of a shoe. The shoe was inside a shoebox and it hung from a Christmas tree in the Joneses' living room. The living room had a heart and some teeth but no windows or doors. The only way out was through a crack in the wall. But Baby Snottle never went out. Baby Snottle saw the world through his Tiny Ellascope. It was a beautiful Ellascope and was made specially for Baby Snottle because Baby Snottle had no eyes.

"Oh, how I love my Tiny Ellascope," Baby Snottle would say. "It is tiny. It is beautiful."

Through the crack in the wall, Baby Snottle could see a small mirror. In the mirror, he could see his Tiny Ellascope looking back at him. He could see his own hair, which looked like a dog sitting on his head.

Baby Snottle's hair dog spoke to him.

It said, "Baby Snottle, I'm cold. Put on a hat."

"Baby Snottle," it said, "please brush me."

It said, "Let's go for a walk, Baby Snottle. Oh, please take me for a walk."

And so Baby Snottle climbed out of the eyeball in the toe of the shoe and went for a walk. He walked down to the heel of the shoe where there was written in gold *Snottle Shoe Size nine and a half.* Then Baby Snottle climbed onto the outside of the shoe and tied its laces into the shape of a little bird.

"Shoelace bird," Baby Snottle said. "What is it like outside?"

"It is warm and green and beautiful," the shoelace bird said. "There are bushes, and leaves, and there is sun."

Baby Snottle didn't know what the sun was.

"It has no eyes or ears and it lives inside a round thing."

"It is like me," Baby Snottle said. "Does it have a Tiny Ellascope?"

"It has a million shiny Ellascopes."

"I have only one Ellascope," Baby Snottle said. "And it does not shine." Baby Snottle looked sad.

"But you have a hair dog," the shoelace bird said. "And it has a joke to tell you."

"Why did Baby Snottle's Tiny Ellascope hide in the trees?" the hair dog said.

"Why?" said Baby Snottle.

"Why?" said the shoelace bird.

"Orange you glad I didn't say banana?" the hair dog said.

"What?" said Baby Snottle and the shoelace bird.

"I'm only a little hair dog," the hair dog said. "In the morning when Baby Snottle brushes me, I get frightened and my jokes fall to the floor and get broken. Sometimes I glue them back together, but sometimes some of the pieces get lost."

"We understand," said Baby Snottle.

"Yes," said the shoelace bird. "We understand."

"Banana," said the little hair dog, and it barked and ran around happily on Baby Snottle's head until Baby Snottle went back inside the eyeball in the toe of the shoe. He climbed into bed.

"Goodnight, hair dog," Baby Snottle said. "Goodnight, shoe-lace bird. Goodnight, Tiny Ellascope."

"Goodnight, Baby Snottle," they all said, and Baby Snottle went to sleep.

In the toe of the shoe, the eyeball stayed awake all night, watching over Baby Snottle.

Then, when morning came, it closed.

THE LONG ARM

I am a frog in a pond. I lie submerged in my bed and only my eyes stick out. My perfect bed with the lime-green sheets and the blue comforter. I close my eyes. I hear them making breakfast downstairs, fizzling the bacon, scratching the toast.

The dopey yellow bus lopes up the street like a huge metal lunchbox. It bounces to a stop in front of my house. The doors click open and Mr. Dyner waits. He rakes the hairs on his unshaven face with his long fingernails, a sound like toast-scratching. Then he reaches over and pulls the lever and the bus lurches over the hill like a horse in a cartoon.

When I shut my eyes, I open a door in my mind. I open a huge rippled door at the front of my brain. I walk into an enormous chamber like a throne room with a marble floor, only I'm ankle-deep in cerebral fluid. I slosh my way toward the back wall and there is my arm.

It's my right arm and it's bent at the elbow. It's propped against the wall like a hockey stick. It's pink and balancing on its fingers, knuckle-deep in fluid. I don't know what to say. Shaking hands is out of the question. I bow slightly. The arm shrugs.

I hear my mother calling from downstairs. "Childhood is over," she says. "Dress like a man." But I will not go to the office. I will not wear a business suit.

For years now, I have stopped myself from balding. My hairs

are full and black. I concentrate on each follicle. I send blood to each one. I keep them plump and growing. It once required all of my attention, but now it is a habit that I'm able to shunt to the back of my brain. Now I can attend to other things. Like symphony concerts.

I'VE DEVISED A little gadget. It's strapped around my tongue. It sends my temperature to a clock radio. Sometimes I listen to 99.7 or 98.5 FM. During fevers, 104.2 FM, new country radio. I'm slung over a horse. A cowboy slaps its flank and it roams the dusty scrub. It wanders into town and someone gets Doc Holman from the saloon. He cuts off my leg and takes me to the symphony concert. I don't like the way the second violins look at me and so I hobble onto the stage and break a chair over the principal. His intonation becomes faulty and so he is fired at the after-concert barbecue. He is hawking his violin at the pawnshop when we meet. He receives a good price despite the fact that he keeps the strings. Suddenly he ties my arms with the E string and loops the A string around a light fixture. He kicks the chair out from under me and everything goes cold. Punjabi disco floods over me at 92.4.

My father is calling. "I'm extinguishing memories of your youth. Listen as your kindergarten fingerpaintings go up in flames. I am snapping the heads off your tee-ball trophies. Listen to the sound of your papier-mâché model of Zeno smashing against the counter."

I have no childhood but I have my right arm. It will grow longer. It is a six-foot anaconda and it engulfs me. I am mummified by my own limb. My fist surrounds me, my knuckles are the bony plates of an ankylosaurus. No business suit will fit me, not even from a specialty store. It is unlikely that I will ever commute.

My parents are shouting. Their voices are the muffled voices of whales. Theirs is a long and complex song. It speaks of loss, of community, of great driveways. The world is pink within my arm, as if the sun were rising from every horizon. It is pumping pink light through my limb world as if it were a bright and enormous heart. My healthy head of hair becomes bleached white. My skin becomes something crumpled and uncrumpled many times, made chamois-soft over many years. I am a sage under lime-green sheets in the bedroom of my childhood. I open my fingers a crack and the school bus drives onto my pillow. It takes me to kindergarten, where I help the teacher find serenity and make cut-out shapes. A few times I knock over the other children with my arm. "When you fall, you must rise again," I say, and they rise and continue forming Plasticine into organic life forms. It is the morning of the first day.

"LIFE IS TRANSFORMATION," I tell the principal, and he begins to flicker. "Specks of dust burn like shooting stars as they hit the surface of consciousness," I say, and he flicks a switch on the PA. "My arm is a totem that looks good in a glove," I inadvertently inform the entire school.

✦

UNDERSTANDING SOUP

A writer, a chamber ensemble, and a conductor walk into a bar. The conductor and the chamber ensemble order drinks, but the writer starts talking to the little green cocktail umbrella, all that's left of Igor Stravinsky's Shirley Temple after he's drained the glass and slipped out the back door.

"What do you get if you combine talking and music?" the writer says. "What's the difference between speech and song? What happens if you come home and find that Death is in the bath and has used up your entire bottle of No-Tears Happy Ending Shampoo?"

"Hey, buddy!" the bartender says. "Who do you think you are—Leonard Cohen? You ordering a drink sometime before my grandkids get out on parole?"

"I am the Janis Joplin, raised on Pop-Tarts and the numismatic tendrils of recitative and the Florentine Camerata," the writer replies. "Speech is to song as an inflatable life raft is to the giant helium-filled tongue of a madman. The voice is a proscenium and I am the dark velvet curtain that comes down when it's over. I'd like to be shaken, stirred, an olive placed in the centre of my brain. Song can bury the music of speech, as if song had a col-oratura spade, and speech, speech were a rare flower growing on the uvula of the numinous letter carrier of intra-doughnut-shop communication."

"So what you're saying is, I should expect no tip?" the bartender says, mopping up a beer spill.

"It ain't 'It ain't over till the fat lady sings,'" the writer answers. "Instead, there's this skinny kid waving his fingers at the moon. And what the moon replies, he's just not saying."

The conductor gives the downbeat, and the chamber ensemble begins to play. The bartender climbs out of his costume. He is a stick, an effervescence, Cecilia Bartoli dressed as a clam. He sings while the writer hails a taxi in twenty-three languages. No taxi comes. Instead, he has an audience of polyglot heart-transplant patients who weep on his lapels. It has been a good night, and the writer rejoices with a bowl of soup. "Thank you," he sings to the noodles, which spell out his name.

The noodles, like synchronized swimmers, wear little noseplugs, then begin to sing, half-submerged in the warm broth.

It's not a very big bowl, nor an important song, but in a small room somewhere across a continent where the wind plays, a woman sits on a sofa and remembers.

CHICKEN SUIT FOR THE SOUL

Perhaps you won't be surprised if I tell you that, on the bus, everyone has hands. Perhaps you were expecting me to say this. Perhaps you have thought it yourself. Today. Yesterday. Once, when you were young, and took many bus trips, kept your money in a billfold.

Unless, of course, you think, feathering back your dark hair, it's a bus filled with chickens. Then it's likely that it's only the driver who has hands. But what if the driver is a chicken? Or what if he is in a chicken suit? Ah, but then it only looks like he doesn't have hands. He in fact has big beefy hands, which is funny, since he's dressed in a chicken suit and is driving a bus filled with chickens. But life is full of men in chicken suits, their large hidden hands clutching steering wheels, driving chickens to some as yet undisclosed destination. But isn't this, in our heart of hearts, what we've hoped for all along, and why we've remembered to pick up our own chicken suit from the cleaners?

Listen. There's a rooster, a Rhode Island Red, waiting at a bus stop near the chickens' final destination. He is balancing a small house in his open hand. Perhaps it's a prosthetic. The hand, I mean. It sticks out, featherless and pink, from beneath his wing. The house in the rooster's open palm is your house. It's your family in the living room watching television. Your father is on the couch. Your mother is on the rocking chair. Your children are curled on the floor beside the family's drooling chicken. Before you left, you lined the house with new newspaper, replaced the water in the little cup. It's not that you don't want to come home. It's just that there are many buses, and many bus stops spangle their routes. You've stopped at so many, peered with one large eye into countless houses, surprised so many families. They look up from their television sets, thinking perhaps that it is their son, father, or husband returned home. A brief moment of hope as they look into your eye. Then they're not sure they recognize the lid sliding down, the lashes' curl, the filigree of tiny veins running about the white. They want to believe but are unable. Wasn't it a blue pupil sitting in the centre of their brother's eye, and not this yellow one? It's hard to remember, and their own eyes are small and short-sighted as millet seeds.

There was a crowd scene in a movie. Their brother was playing a chicken working undercover, looking down, reading a magazine. A bus had been stolen. Many buses. Just before shift change, a driver at the depot walked home with all the buses in his mouth, as if they were aspirin or false teeth. He wouldn't have been caught, except that the president of the bus company was still in one of them, calling home on his cellphone.

A chicken is an omen of death, the driver says to the police who arrest him. We are surrounded by chickens, he says. And we dress in chicken suits, pretending to be chickens dressed as reasonable people, he says. The chicken suits of our childhood, the chicken suits of our old age, he says to his lawyer. We walk on eggshells, staying away from the fire at suppertime. Our soul, our eternal bus, he says to the judge, travels from bus stop to bus stop in this our material world. As we begin to speak, he says, the wind blows away the bus transfers held in our beaks. Perhaps we shall be lucky, he says. Perhaps our driver will wink, he says, allow us a seat at the back of the bus. And perhaps, after all, we will settle down in the long straw for the slow ride home.

The judge shakes his scarlet wattles, nods his scarlet comb. His gavel comes crashing down upon the pale seeds on the court floor. Everywhere there are bus drivers shedding feathers, reaching beefy hands toward the yellow sun that shines from its greasy white cloud. Some of the drivers have gathered around the steaming hood of the five-thirty bus. They cook themselves an omelette as if it were a sacrament. They build a church of feathers and climb inside. They wait for the wind to carry them away.

✦

DOCTOR WEEP'S WINDOW

My neighbour has regular arms and a regular head. He has regular carpeting, broadloom, you might say, and it covers most of the floor of his regular dwelling-place. "House" would be the regular way to say it, and that's how I'm going to say it. House. My neighbour has a regular bed. He has regular shelves. When he drinks, regular lizards climb up his regular walls. My neighbour has a regular name, and his regular name is Ted.

Every Sunday, that's usually the day after Saturday, my neighbour Ted mows his regular lawn. He prays to a regular God, uses the regular prayers, gets the regular answer. He covers his regular torso with a regular shirt. Indeed, he has the regular number of torsos, which is one, and the usual number of shirts, which is two, and one of his shirts contains his regular breath mints and the directions to his mother's new house.

Beneath his regular pants, it is my belief, my reasonable supposition, that he wears regular underwear. I mean, I can picture two options here, but I do not know with certainty which of the two options I should describe. I do not know which are more regular—boxers or briefs. I know not, knowing only that he would opt for the more regular of the two regularly available choices. Would he consult a men's clothing consultant? A specialty magazine? An undercover policeman? In the department store, his regular hand is joined in the usual way to his regular arm, and it hovers over two packages. It twitches like a divining rod and he makes a selection. Boxers or briefs folded up in a little box. And he pays his money and he takes them home in a little bag, and he unlocks the door, and he walks down the hall, and maybe he puts them in the laundry first, or maybe he puts them in his underwear drawer, joining the others, or maybe he puts them on right there at the end of his hall. First, I'm assuming, taking off his pants and his older, more mature pair of boxers or briefs, destined for the laundry.

WHY DO I dwell on his underwear? And here I must mention that I use "dwell" in a different sense than that which I previously used it to describe my neighbour Ted's indwelling, the same indwelling that causes him to be my neighbour, that causes him to be in view when I part my bedroom curtains and point my binoculars at the dwelling place—the regular house—of Ted my across-the-street neighbour. Why am I absorbed by his underwear? Wait. Let's not start that again. I think we have an understanding, a common language, shared values. You look at my lips moving. From this, you form an impression of what words I might be uttering, or at least what utterances are possible, given the configuration of my lips. Your eyes take this information and pass it, like soup through a kitchen hutch. You pass it piping hot, steaming, to your brain, sitting there big and unmoving, waiting in the centre of your head as if beached on the living room couch. Through your ears, the pinkish wings of your reader-head, you take in the shaking vibrations of air that the mouth of my face has formed. The air burrows down into your earholes until it arrives at the big couch where your brain is sipping soup, waiting. Maybe these movements of the air are the bread, the cheese that is shaken into the soup, stirred with the spoon, slurped down by your brain, during the supper-hour news. Grief is everywhere, the announcer says. It is erupting on the streets of our nation, turning up in libraries, in the back seats of our cars. But this just in. I have received an update, a note hurriedly written on the back of my medical file. It says we must get back to Ted. Ted needs us. He's a regular guy and his little face on the front of his regular head, and his regular mind inside that regular head, indwelling, so to speak, his regular mind housed inside that regular skull, needs us. We mustn't forget he who needs us. I got carried away up there. Sorry, Ted. So now it's back to you.

1. *My Interest in the Underwear of Ted.* I am interested in Ted's underwear because it is hidden from me. I have no personal knowledge of his underwear. We seekers must explore what is hidden from view. We must research and uncover. I don't mean literally, of course. I am speaking metaphorically. As if I said his sadness was as big as a Buick, which isn't true. It's another size entirely, like Toronto.

2. *Why Ted's Underwear Is Important.* Ted's underwear is important because when my neighbour Ted makes the decision to sit down, and he will make this decision several times in the course of this account, his regular underwear—boxers or briefs—presses against his regular pants, which press and make contact with the regular chair at his regular table. And by the way, feel free to pull up a chair and share a place with Ted at his regular table. No, not the same place. That would mean you would be sitting on top of him. Our protagonist might be damaged or at least compacted by your weight. Certainly, his movements would be restricted, which would be to his detriment, and would compromise our objectivity. Sitting on the protagonist is not an effective narrative technique.

I've learned that. I've learned it well. Shh. Don't make a sound. We're observers here and don't want to disturb Ted as he is sitting down. Watch as Ted clutches the sides of his regular head with his regular hands, his regular eyes screwed up into regular puckers, though it's usually his mouth that does that, it's usually his mouth that puckers, sometimes—but not necessarily—when he desires to use it.

But now it's before lunchtime, and my neighbour Ted is sitting at his regular table, his hands clutching his regular head, his regular eyes puckered, his mouth stretched across a regular face, and his forehead is a regular telegram.

Today is he is trying to think up a new name for himself. He will leave behind the well-kept lawns of the regular name, Ted. He will not put out the two regular bags of garbage at the end of his regular name. Two bags of garbage and a recycling box at the end of Ted, just sitting there beside the final "d." No wonder his signature was always a mess. What will his new name be? Will he look in the dictionary, the phone book, the Bible?

WAIT. I HAVE made a mistake. I said "telegram" up there. I meant monogram. I meant to say his forehead was a regular monograph and his mouth was stretched across his regular face. "Mr. Sorrow," Ted says to himself. "Mr. Woeful Sorrow." He thinks about it for a while. "How about Sadness Jones or Gerry Woe?" he wonders aloud. "Or Dr. Weep?" Ted reaches for the bowl of soup sitting in front of him at his regular Ted table. He reaches to grasp the soup bowl and brings it toward his regular Ted chest. There seems to be no sign of breadsticks or of cheese. Edward Weep, PhD, will eat his soup alone. Without additions. Except for us, but he doesn't notice because we're keeping quiet, here at the table. He eats his lonely soup, sometimes getting up to look again in the fridge, as if this time there will be cheese, as if things could have changed in there since he looked over the yogurt, moved a few items around on the shelves, closed the door, and then returned to the table, his boxers making contact with his regular pants as he sits down, begins again to eat his soup in a manner forlorn as a Buick lost in Toronto, alone as a baseball glove in the empty vacuum of space. But then he stands again in order to shuffle over to the Frost-Free Ice Maiden Frigidaire to examine whether things have changed on the wire shelves, whether he missed some grated cheese tucked behind a wilted broccoli stalk. But nothing has changed. Things have remained the same, at least in the kitchen of Dr. Weep, and the low hum of the Frigidaire is like an entire gospel choir singing one note while buried in sand.

AND ONCE, DR. WEEP was buried in sand. He was only Ted back then. He was young, younger than Toronto but not than some Buicks, and he wasn't having soup. There were no gospel choirs in sight, though they could have been undercover, if not undersand, catching a little R & R, and perhaps some zees, and Dr. Weep was wearing nothing but a striped bathing suit and, at this time, a few kilograms of sand placed there by Mrs. Weep, only she wasn't called that at this particular juncture; her name was Mary, and she and Dr. Weep had been recently joined in holy—if not sandy—matrimony. They were in a playful mood, and so one had buried the other in sand, both of them laughing like flamingos. And though, in this case, the movements of our protagonist were restricted, for indeed he was compressed in sand, it was their honeymoon, and who are we to restrict a little nuptial frivolity for the sake of narrative finesse? Perhaps this sacrifice of fictive nicety could be considered our gift to the happy couple, seeing that they didn't register, and were joined in wedlock without warning, and certainly without time to notify the neighbours.

The next several years are a blur. It seems I was not able to keep the lenses of my binoculars clean and the curtain kept blowing in front of me at inopportune moments. Like when Dr. Weep was visited by angels or Cub Scouts, or had a new roof put on, and a new Weep was born, and the angels returned, for they had left behind some papers or a hat or their woggle. Like when he sold his home and moved to Freedonia, New York, to find a new place to dwell, a new housing for his sorrow. But there are a few things I can tell you, since we're here alone at the table of the absent Dr. Weep. Well, actually, only you're at the table, and it doesn't belong to Dr. Weep anymore—remember, he moved luck, briefs, and sorrow to Freedonia, New York, to find a new dwelling place, etc., etc., and you've let yourself in by the side door, and you're sitting in the kitchen of Dr. Weep's successor, Lt. Col. Happyface, only right now he's away, simulating an invasion of the big Christmas tree in the centre of town. He's protecting the silver balls, the candy canes, and the illuminated star at the top. He's questioning everybody, searching their toy sacks, frisking reindeer, taking a closer look at the elves. He's writing it all down in his big book. He's observing things through his binoculars, as am I, except that he stands tall, his army back straight, whereas I remain crouched, squinting like a fetus out from my window. His are big military binoculars, olive green, and his sight is high-powered and remains clear. They're not prone to blurring, and certainly there are no curtains, especially now that the iron one has fallen in a heap on top of the heating vent at the bottom of Europe, and there are no curtains that could come between observer and observed, between subject and object. I, however, am at my regular place behind the blowing curtains. They're not iron. They seem to be some kind of polycotton blend.

I could check. No, the ache in my knees is unbearable. My eyes
are puckered just as the eyes of Dr. Weep's were before things
became blurry. When I think of it all, the years like high-speed
Buicks driving by down the main streets of our lives, the lump
in my throat big as Toronto's busy downtown core, I clutch the
sides of my narrator-head with my study hands. I twist my face
up into a regular kilogram, and I too begin to weep.

WHAT HAPPENED AFTER Dr. Weep came out from under the sand?
Lunch, yes. Maybe daiquiris. But I mean after that. After they'd
finished the in-flight meal on the flight home, after they'd
unpacked their sandy laundry, after Dr. Weep had kissed his wife
and gone to work, returning home to a new child, to evenings by
the fire, the TV crackling, emitting a warm multicoloured glow.
After he'd driven the little Weep to Cub Scouts or Brownies, to
electric zither lessons, to golf-cart driving festivals, cow-tossing
parties, to Sunday school, where a slim young woman in slim
shoes who would one day be Mrs. Lt. Col. Happyface taught that
for every cow tossed, there would be a catcher, for every strum
there would be a willing zither. What happened to Dr. Weep—
Ted, as he was called by telemarketers looking at his name just
above their finger in the telephone book—what happened to Dr.
Weep that left him sitting at Lt. Col. Happyface's kitchen table,
clutching his hero-head in his regular hero-hands, trying to think
of a new name for his regular Ted body, the multi-channelled
embers of the TV almost turned to test-pattern ash?

Ear Born

Dr. Weep has a brother. Did I already tell you that? Yes. Dr.
Weep was born of a mother, a woman, actually, who bore two

sons, though not at the same time. Inside her womb they grew from translucent specks to blue-eyed pink things with fists. Inside her womb they grew from tiny pink commas to large ear-like babies. Inside they crouched, listening. And when they had listened enough, they came forth from their mother's womb and began to bawl, Dr. Weep and his brother, though not, as I've said, at the same time. It was like Lt. Col. Happyface and Dr. Weep. First, one was indwelling across the street, housed as if in the womb of his mother, and then he was born, leaving, in this case, for Freedonia, New York. Then another began to live there, although without the accompanying vast increase in size. Lt. Col. Happyface was essentially the same size when he had the movers install a large couch to a position where it would sit for time beyond reckoning in front of where the television would minutes later find its final resting place. He was essentially the same size as when he stretched out on the couch in future years, flipping on the same television now near the end of its days, and watching an invasion of a Christmas tree in the centre of Cleveland, wishing that those in Cleveland had had his foresight, his training, that they had simulated, as he had, an invasion of their Christmas tree.

I have spoken an untruth, and for this I am sorry, sorry as a Buick. I will make amends. Like Toronto, I will correct my untruth. This, now, is my correction.

The Truth About Lt. Col. Happyface's Actual Size

Lt. Col. Happyface was, in fact, larger than when he first came to live across the street, having rarely participated in the defence of the Christmas tree beyond his role as advisor, there in his strategic, bunker-like position on the couch. But this morning, inspired by this unforeseen Cleveland situation, his mind on fire as if fuelled by piping soup, Lt. Col. Happyface rose up, boarded a bus bound for downtown, and initiated a simulated invasion of the large pine in the central square.

End of correction.

And I too have a brother. He is in the back room, at the other side of the house. He is looking out the window, looking out the other direction. Whereas I look north, across the road to Lt. Col. Happyface's house, once the abode of Dr. Weep, where indeed I can see you patiently waiting for this narrative to unfold like boxers falling out of a dresser drawer in slow motion, while my brother looks south, across the backyard and into the back window of the splendid dwelling place of the brother of Dr. Weep. House. I said I would say "house," for Dr. Weep's brother has most, if not all, the same regular parts, the same regular life, as Dr. Weep.
  "House."

Time to Think about My Brother

There are nights when there is nothing to see. The visions of the world are tucked safely in their beds, sweetly dreaming of the dark insides of drawers. Dr. Weep is in Freedonia, and Lt. Col. Happyface has got forty winks surrounded, with no chance of escape until morning. In Dr. Weep's kitchen, your reader-head rests on your folded arms, and is dreaming of narratives sleek as the underwear of gazelles. You dream of places like Toronto, where the generous portion of narrative soup served up by the city overflows the brain-bowl. Reader-heads may float free and metaphorically down the sweet associative avenues. Buicks drift along the boulevards, as if adrift in soup. On such nights, I think of my brother. What could he be watching through the window of Dr. Weep's brother?

So let's join him as he watches Fred, the brother of Weep, at his kitchen table. Fred's siblings-of-themselves hands are cradling his brother-noggin. Fred is just about to leave his birth name behind, a vapour trail behind a jet. He will find a new name. "Mr. Henry Joy?" he wonders aloud. "The Reverend Harvey Happiness, Jollity Smith, Mortimer Glee?" He considers each name carefully. Choosing a new name in which to dwell is an important decision.

But my brother is dreaming. He's wishing to carve a name for himself and his watched-one. He has window envy. He would like it to be as it is with Dr. Weep.

"Brother," I tell him, "many watch, but few have Weep. Weep and I are practically brothers ourselves, if one brother spent his waking hours observing the other indwelling across the Jordan of the street until the second brother moved to Freedonia and another who perhaps you might consider a step-brother moved in and began planning for the defence of Yule trees that are like huge and festive dendrites in the dense pineal gland of the city core." My brother is curled before the window like a fetus that needs a shave. His forehead is furled into a regular calligram, a fist run over by a Buick.

It is night, and Dr. Weep's brother is sleeping. The windows to the south are dark. "Brother," I say. "Do you remember childhood? We lay beside each other in our plexiglas bassinets, each of us staring hopefully out the maternity ward window. We watched for the gleeful face of our father, passing out cigars. 'It's a boy!' he'd exclaim, his beefy palm slapping down upon the backs of other happy fathers. We watched for his wave as he made his phone calls to the mayor, to his mother, to all those aunts in Kentucky, Alberta, and Macedonia. But it was the nurses who made calls, and eventually our father came, the nurses crowding round, waving at us as we walked out the door. "Don't forget your shaving kits," Emmaline, our favourite nurse, called out.

I look over at my brother. "Emmaline," he mutters amid snores and heavy breathing. Bobbing in the pool of our childhood, my brother has fallen asleep. I find a blanket and cover him. I creep over to my window. Shh. Let's not make a sound.

For the first time, you and I, we find ourselves alone. It is an opportunity not to be missed, an open door to the bakery, a key in the ignition.

Listen.

I have a confession to make. And here I am speaking frankly, directly to you, the reader. For in this short passage I will neglect concerns of style or form, though the narrative arts rate high amongst my interests and talents. Indeed, in my youth I was the recipient of the Boy Scout plot-development badge. It is—I know—always risky to leave the written text, but it is a risk I am willing to take. Tell me if you feel that I have invaded your personal reader-space with this disclosure. I will attach a sug- gestion box to my front door. I will read your suggestions. I will be responsive to your concerns. I am, however, not unaware that you may find something for yourself in my confession. What I have to tell is a mite juicy. It could have mileage around the water cooler. It could have legs in the internet chat room. You could be a storytelling hero just as I once was, ah, back in my woggle-wearing youth.

My Confession

I wrote a note to Mrs. Mary Weep. Only I didn't sign my name. I signed it *Dr. Weep*. It was a small deception, a slight personalization of the truth. But Dr. Weep and I were almost brothers. The vicissitudes of life had buffeted us together. I had watched him since before Mrs. Weep had had thoughts of marriage and of compaction beneath sand. From before Dr. Weep had a name beyond Ted. Surely I'd spared him the inconvenience of writing the note himself. Of formulating his wishes for the future.

When I die, the note said, make your famous brownie recipe. But at this time of change, Mary, my own Mrs. Weep, I want to be a part of your culinary act. I want to be included in your sensational brownie fame. Listen. Life is transition. Add a special ingredient. Me.

Have me turned to ash, then added to the brownies. Pour me into the big mixing bowl with the chocolate, the flour, the eggs. Hold the bowl up to your lovely chest, embrace it like a child, and then begin the mixing. Languorous strokes curling around and around the bowl. Mix me into your much-loved family recipe. Then cook. Don't worry. I will rest inside the brownies as if inside the warmth of the marital bed. Look, there we are curled together on a Sunday morning. We're embracing in the hot red light as our dark surroundings slowly rise.

Enclosed with this letter you will find an invitation to a party at our house. It is for many years in the future. A party for when I have passed on. Use this invitation. Invite many people. They will be delighted to discover that they have been asked to attend. What could be more pleasurable than a gathering on the front lawn of the Weeps of Freedonia? Invite my friends. Invite my enemies. Make punch. Ensure the wine flows like traffic down the main arteries of our fair city. Feed them brownies. Don't tell them where I am. Or if you must, tell them I am away on business.

Remember my parents. My childhood friends. Remember my uncle. Those guys on the football team. And our old neighbour, an admirable friend, a viable human being, a good guy. He lives still. His well-appointed domicile is situated across the street from our old house. Our good neighbour and a decent fellow. Invite him to the party. Let him taste the brownies. Likely, he will be hungry. Give him the lion's share. Let him feed. Surely it is a virtue to nourish a neighbour, to give a neighbour sustenance from what is yours.

I will love you always, Mary, my dear—even after I have begun travelling the curling paths of our friends', our family's, our neighbours' stomachs. Your brownies will be my chariot to the new life, and its wheels shall be sweet.

I WISHED I had a dove with wings of snow: I would speak quietly and the dove would take to the air with my note in its beak. It would rise like winged smoke from the chimney of my house and glide through the open window of Weep. Its soft wings would brush the pink cheek of Mrs. Weep. It would rest my note like a flat white tooth upon her pillow. Then the dove would vanish, leaving only whispers on the breath of Mrs. Weep.

As the sun rises, Mrs. Weep wakes. Dr. Weep has left for work, a lukewarm cup of coffee on the counter, the unkempt sections of the newspaper on the chair. Mrs. Weep turns and discovers the note. She sits up, plumps the pillows in the bed behind her, unfolds the note, and begins reading.

But I had neither dove nor trained spaniel, and my brother had his own work, his own satisfactions. And so I had to devise another means to deliver my note. I saved and was frugal. I amassed funds sufficient for the purchase of flowers for Mrs. Weep. I lifted the receiver, dialled Pistilwhip's Florists, and began dictating. The floral assistant wrote down my words. The note filled forty-seven of the small cards stapled to the cellophane that surrounded the flowers. They arrived the next day and Mrs. Weep embraced them with joy.

In the following days, I did not know what words passed between Dr. and Mrs. Weep. I knew only that spouses were furled within the glad arms of other spouses, that lips were pressed against lips, that meals were shared in the scented shadows of flowers. I did not know what meals or shadows the future would bring.

This is my confession.

Thank you.

HAVE I ALWAYS watched at this window, my knees a two-thirds complete tripod of bone and cartilage, holding my face to the cool glass, my brain up to the life of once Ted then Weep now Lt. Col. Happyface? Once, long ago, I did not live in this room. My legs had purchase. I strode amid the hurly-burly of the marketplace and was moistened by the foamy multi-channel waves of human drama. I was a walker, and I was not contained. In the morning, I would be fearless. I would rise from bed and find the sidewalk. I would march toward the city, my face an intersection, a pentagram, ready to accept whatever sped through it, ready for slowdowns and collisions, ready for yahoos in the souped-up vehicles of their youth yelling profanities through open windows at the brave striding toward work. And indeed, I was a worker. I effected change. I placed people on hold. I had a job.

My Job

I remember now. There was a large desk, a man, and a suit. How were they arranged? They were in a room. The desk was on the floor. The man sat behind the desk and smirked. That he was inside the suit goes without saying, though the clarification was necessary in order to dispel the lurid. And inside his suit, the man smirked. He smirked from inside his tight-fitting skin. I expect the blood cells commuting around his body were smirking as they grabbed sips of coffee, fiddled with the radio, drove with their knees, and they sped to important yet congested locations. For instance, his heart.

There must have been a chair or at least very large haunches. He towered over me from behind his desk. Perhaps he imagined himself on a throne, on a dais, as the chief turtle among turtles perched high on a rock. The turtle told me things. There were things I should do. There were things I should not do. There were many things I could do better. Few of them concerned dental hygiene, still less eighteenth-century opera orchestration or Toronto-bound Buicks. I would leave the room with things to do and I would return with things done, or with stories about those things. Occasionally, those stories ended happily; many times they had unexpected twists. Sometimes I had questions, and these were answered with the brisk flourish one might expect from an F-18 fighter as it engages in casual conversation with a butterfly.

I remember also shadows in the room. Broad shoulders. The dark shapes of his shelf of books. His rulebooks and compendia of regulations. The framed photographs of his misshapen yet golden family. There was a basketball trophy and a Little League certificate of appreciation. I too appreciate Little League, though admittedly I do not have the paperwork to prove it. Though its exact location has passed out of memory, I do have in my possession a small glove, ripe with the colour and odour of a neglected dog. Perhaps I have a neglected dog. From time to time, I hear what might be construed as barks. They originate from the same place as the ringing in my ears, those dark and tintinnabular fields where barks run free of their dogs. The barks themselves are neglected by the dog-mouths, have escaped from the dogs' cruel teeth. They seem happier this way, left to roll and cavort with other barks beneath the howlless moon.

This man behind the desk was the source, or the cause, of my employment. There were forms to fill out. Procedures to be observed. People to speak to at little desks as I walked by. Each morning, I knew where I must go. I was employed for something. I would make proposals and adopt an industrious mien. I would show my mettle and be fiscally prudent. I would reap where I sewed. I would come back from the outside with a sack filled with things that I would empty into a large heap on this man's, the employer's, desk. We would observe them together and then smile. First, the employer's smirk would widen into what may—if the definition was stretched beyond what would be customary for regular employer lips—be considered, from a certain angle, and given certain lighting conditions, a smile. Then I would join in. A few seconds of motionless yet mutual lip configuring and then the employer would sweep the heap of things into his desk drawer. I would bow slightly, make small gestures with my day planner, and leave once again for the outside, beyond the desk-filled world.

It is lost, the exact nature of the things I piled, the offerings I heaped onto the perpetual calendar on the employer's desk. If I had any training, it too is lost. I scan the oily walls of my rooms and observe no certificate, whether of appreciation or qualification. I know not within which league, little or limitless, I participated.

And how did I obtain the objects I collected? This too is lost, though I am aware that though narrative needs a muscular and manly direction, it also needs the lovely nice details, the minute and vital pixelation of daily life. Though I am not an exemplar or a paragon, I have striven in my time to collect such details of Dr. Weep. How does he look, carrying his sorry garbage to his wilting curb? In what manner of voice does he address telephone solicitors? How far does his tongue extend when moistening the gummy reverse of a forty-nine-cent stamp?

These are the details I gather. Heaps of observation, both telling and incidental, are collected in the sack of consciousness, conceptual and sensory noodles dropped into the steaming soup of cognition. One day, I walked from the room with the desk, the man, and the suit, and the possibility of a chair. One day, like Dr. Weep to the house across the street, I never returned. I spend my days inside my own dwelling place, the skin of my domicile, as he who was hitherto the employer spent his days inside his own suit-surrounded skin. And though I do not use them, my doors are more comfortable than his, though less prone to blemish.

I have been a collector.

And now Dr. Weep is beyond the flickering circumference of my observation. He is a featureless horizon that surrounds me. There was a puppy, a planet, a lost ashtray. The details of Dr. Weep's sorrow are lost beneath the seats amid loose change, car wash coupons, and missing teeth. Are his children appearing before the parole board, hoping for absolution? Was his dog found across the highway? Has his eldest son signed his donor card, bequeathing, upon his death and given the appropriate medical circumstances, his organs to someone else? If a car were to veer through my window, compressing my body into a dramatic narrative twist, would the ears or eyes of the son of Dr. Weep be transplanted into my body to save me? Would I wake, groggy and unsure in my hospital bed, to find Dr. Weep looking into the eyes of his own son, the eyes planted like blossoming flowers in my cross-stitched and healing brow? "Here, these were his glasses. I thought you might need them," Dr. Weep says.

I watch Lt. Col. Happyface and try to imagine the life of Dr. Weep, he who shed his Tedness and then his house as if it were a skin he had grown out of. Dr. Weep drives down to the library to take out some books. He and his lovely wife, Mary, are going away for the weekend, and they'd like something to read. It's a retreat, but not the kind that Lt. Col. Happyface must enact as the keeper of the downtown tree gets testy when he invades near Christmastime, Lt. Col. Happyface shouting out bellicose carols from his camouflaged and sweaty face. No, Dr. Weep and his wife are taking some time out from their busy schedule of spelling bees, chiropractic appointments, horticultural planning committee appreciation receptions, and sessions of Celtic harp disaster readiness training to get away from it all in the woods outside Freedonia. For this retreat, they've decided to select only books that have been made into movies, so that when they come home they can compare. Dr. Weep chooses *Metal Melancholics: The Buicks of Toronto*. Mary decides on *Anxiety Magic: Card Tricks for a Life of Zesty Calm*. They arrive at the retreat, unpack their suitcases, place the books on their doily-covered bedside tables. "Shall we walk down to the lake?" Dr. Weep asks. "Yes. Let's," says Mrs. Weep, putting a soup-flavoured energy bar into the pocket of her yellow windbreaker.

The shadows of Dr. Weep's life shake the walls of my room. Sometimes I make shadow dogs with my fingers and race them through this life, over the walls, light switches, nail holes, and the memories of my regular neighbour, Ted, struggling to keep up with his new life. The shadow dogs have a plaintive aspect to their doggie jowls, as if they were saying, "Why are you running away from us, shadows of Dr. Weep's life? Are you trying to leave us behind on the plain white walls?" The drool falls from the dogs' dark lips as they ask, "Are you ever coming back?"

Then I open my hands and grasp my binoculars. What programming is currently being presented by the Lt. Col. Happyface Kitchen Window Broadcasting Corporation? It's a gala special.

Mrs. Lt. Col. Happyface is making minestrone. She's dropping in pine cones, saying her prayers, listening to zither music. They have guests coming over. It's the advance Christmas Tree Invasion simulation committee, trumpet-playing angel division. They'll have soup, then adjourn to the living room to pore over the secret dossier. They'll not make the same mistakes of those ill-prepared and impetuous Cleveland amateurs. Careful planning will yield significantly improved professional results. Happyface has learned that. He'll not make the same mistakes again. There was that time he left the couch without sufficient preparation, without fully thinking it through. He just stood up and walked away. And as could have been expected, disaster ensued. There was the mess of soup in the kitchen. The trail of Kleenexes, the wounded puppies, the crater in the bedroom. Mistakes like that can be avoided with fastidious preparation. The committee will debate. They'll strategize. This will not be a shoddy, ill-conceived Christmas tree invasion simulation. It will have the grace and poise of true professionals at the top of their game. Some will be dropped from above. There will be a phalanx of reindeer imitators. An operative will go elf undercover. Like surgery on a symphony, the operation will be seamless, trumpets announcing the victory. Mrs. Lt. Col. Happyface will create a celebratory soup, perhaps her famed minestrone. They will drink deeply and find succour in its dark red liquor. A satisfied smile will creep across the weary face of the Lieutenant Colonel. Like soup, it will radiate warmth, and there likewise exists the possibility that it will spill somewhere about the room, though, we are hoping, without the commensurate vegetable shrapnel.

Across the room, I hear metallic scraping. A soft papery thunk, like the wrapping falling off a dove. My brother is quiet, his small white face pressed against the glass of his window. I can hear his breathing, tiny pneumatic oars stroking the surface of a lung-coloured sea. He is content with his observations of Fred, the brother of Weep. He has noticed nothing. Inside our small house, where few things happen, I have seen a flash of light. Something has fallen fully formed from the smooth forehead of my forgotten front door. A letter has arrived and it waits patiently on the doormat. *Welcome*, the mat says, though I cannot remember when its single word was required.

When was the last letter? Perhaps there was one announcing my birth, though doubtless I was too young to read. Once, as a child, I received notice that I had attended school, that I had received praise from my teachers for the excellence and daring of my academic work. I had coloured in oceans boldly, had counted by fives. My project on the Phoenicians had earned much acclaim. I had made the stamp-collecting team.

Surely I was not now receiving further notice of my academic career. I had long since divested myself of Bristol board and Duo-Tangs. I had, at one time, entered the working world. This new missive must refer to another event, to something else that had transpired in my mysterious and seemingly unstoppable life story. I tried to reach for the letter while still maintaining visual contact with Lt. Col. Happyface. I would not adjust my set, nor change from regular programming. I might miss a conflagration or lute spectacular, or perhaps a life-affirming change to the minestrone recipe. I had the letter at my fingertips but could not grasp it. For a moment I turned my head and, leaving my post at the window, clutched the letter, bringing it toward me as I resumed my station. The letter was pale and motionless. Its silence was inscrutable, gnomic, fearsome. It was waiting for me. It had always been waiting for me. I had been called to spelunk through its dark and terrifying halls. There would be the glint of a knife blade, the horrifying recognition of oneself in a mirror, the scurrying and flutter of unknown animals. The uncertainty of which way to turn. I held the letter before me and planned my future. I would open this letter. I would read the words that were written for me. I took a deep breath and held it. I pushed my finger into the envelope's slanting folds. What was whole was rent. There was a single piece of paper inside.

Unfolded, would it reveal a discount coupon, a profitable sales opportunity? I had heard of such transmissions delivered to one's door. Perhaps it was a two-for-one special, a preferred customer discount, an advance notice of the sale of the season.

I unfolded the paper.

As you watch, so are you watched.

Clearly, I would be buying clothing or Buicks at a reduced price. The acquisition of Toronto continued to be beyond my means. I examined my brother. He remained blind to internal development, his eyes pressed against the window, shining like brights in the pink fender of his skull, illuminating the road where Fred would travel. The letter was not from my brother, he who is like the eye of a whale, unaware of its twin, looking out from the opposite side of its housing.

In all my long days at the window, I had never considered the other houses in view. I was aware of signs of habitation, but was unclear as to the exact nature of the population. The street was speckled with windows of all types: picture, bathroom, bay. I had not considered what regular limbs, torsos, broadloom lay behind them. Were there men poised over drawers of boxers? Boxes filled with drawers? Were women scanning the dictionary, the plumber's guide, the city map of Nottawasaga, Ontario, searching for new names in which to dwell? I would say that "windows are the eyes of the soul" if such a locution were not so coy as to be an impediment to our discussion. Better to state that for each window there was a kitchen, for each kitchen a table, island, or breakfast nook. And there, lying in innocence and expectation, awaiting its jam or sugar-free fruit spread, would be a slice of patient toast, each bite anticipating the teeth of the window owner closing over it, bringing darkness.

Then the teeth would open, and light would flood the toast eater's insides. The illuminated one turns toward the window and looks toward me, Weep-watcher, Ted-minder, Happyface faithful.

As you watch, so are you watched. Someone outside is expecting me to change my name.

FROM *BIG RED BABY* (1998)

LIKE BOZO'S NOSE OR TIME ITSELF

All those years dashing off to work, leaving my sheets a knotted mess of snores, and now here I am, standing before a sheet of clouds that it's my job to fold over a bed big as sky.

I wondered, back on earth, if space would disappoint me, but subject and object have disappeared, lifted away like the box-top separating cereal from milk-filled bowl. It's no wonder the sheets are a mess.

I am like a Möbius strip, my inside and out all one surface. It's like that now, the meaning of life one colour in a swatch of paint-store colours. For the bedroom, I chose a dusty rose believe-in-God brown, an olive knee-deep spiritworld bookshelf orange, and an indigo love-of-splintery-children blue. I remember the wallpaper I had as a child. On a lime-green riverbank, Descartes was making sandwiches. Schopenhauer and Immanuel Kant were fishing from a boat.

And I would like a boat, plummeting a million kilometres up toward myself, wrapping a lime around my eternal soul and pulling hard, tacking around my illuminated veins that spiral around me like distant galaxies.

You know, there's a joke we tell out here. A man turns into a store and the store door is as microscopically tiny as the fleshy blue walls of heaven or as the beginning of time, lost in the junk drawer beneath a bunch of old mail, bent keys, and a dark spot on Little Richard's skin the shape of the second dimension, obscured by a week's growth of beard and the dim light of a glow-in-the-dark edition of the Bible.

The man turns out of the store. His heart pumps once. It is the Big Bang and it creates his daughter's second birthday, complete with clowns. "Happy birthday!" the protons say, bumping into one another.

And this is the way it ends really, like a punchline that goes on forever, and we find that we were waiting all this time for the faint tittering of history, its polite applause. The curtain comes down for the last time over the infinitely dense footlights of heaven, and eternity's long run is finally over. We go out for a drink, end up having several too many, fall asleep in the taxi-ride home, itself a taxi, or else ourselves.

✦

SMALL TEETH

Last night I slept with the Tooth Fairy, woke up with tinsel on my back. I dreamed that my jaw was broken and I could remember the touch of her lacy wings on my chest. She put her tiara on my night table, her wand under the bed.

Where was my wife? She was flying alone in the cloudless sky, carrying a grocery cart filled with the newly plucked feathers of trumpeter swans. She had left me a note saying, *When the Tooth Fairy comes, I've left out cookies and Scotch. You may take her to our bed. I'm off to see Abe Lincoln, when he was a young lawyer, and without the beard.*

"Was the Tooth Fairy good in bed?" my friends ask.

"Not bad. Better than Peter Pan or Mrs. Santa," I say. "And she can fly, you know."

Really she was great and all my teeth fell out and she replaced them, one by one, with the bones of small birds. I open and close my mouth: a robin creasing the sky above my yard, a sparrow's quick wings.

It was like the time I snuck into Canadian Tire dressed in the skin of a dog. I was looking for garden ornaments. For accessories for my car. For something to stop me waking the neighbours at 4 a.m. with my howling.

"You're not really a dog," the Tooth Fairy says. "She is in the plumbing aisle, looking for nails."

"Yes, I know," I reply. "I'm a wolf and it seems I've left my money in my other skin."

The Tooth Fairy looks at me, tears forming in her white eyes. "When you were losing teeth, you seemed like such a good boy. Always left a nice, well-written note under your pillow. Always spent the money I gave you wisely. And to think, here you are, dressed in the skin of a dog, barking at bird feeders, at rubberized car mats, sinking your teeth into tires and contemplating ostentatious hubcaps emblazoned with lions' teeth.

"Save your money," she says. "It is the end of the twentieth century and you will need every cent, even the ones with Abe Lincoln on the back."

She touches my head with her wand. I open my mouth and pennies fall out from where they have collected on my tongue. My arms have become like wings, their feathers the feathery pages of the telephone book, opened to page 247: Dr. Greenblatt, Orthodontics, 251-1457.

I am the Sphinx, a griffin, Osiris. In the before-dawn darkness of my skull, small points of light illuminate my brain. A hawk flies silently from one ear to the other. The twin moons of my eyes are eclipsed by dark lids. The silver net of a shopping cart glints as it crosses between the lobes of my brain. My wife has been shopping and she has filled her cart with small teeth.

RED DOGS

Wind up the gramophone, play that scratched Caruso platter. Let us change into tennis clothes and hide under the couch, for the red dogs, the red dogs of dawn, have arrived. They are at the door howling, their voices a bed full of ants. They've gathered on the welcome mat and are watching the door. Their pupils swim like wounded fish across their sweaty eyes and their tongues hang from their faces like broken arms.

My body is a plain white countertop. My fear is a dishwasher gone mad. I open and close the cabinet doors of my nervousness. I open and close the cabinet doors of my— My body is a Formica tabletop, their sweaty tongues are drooling up my dress, my curtain rod, a candlestick. I undress and take a bath in the cloud of their damp breath. If only I were a missile, an airplane, a subterranean cave, because I forget which part of the Bible the dogs wrote, though I've often seen them gathered at night by the swimming pool, burying each verse before dawn.

✦

EDWIN

I f Edwin, my eldest brother, had ever been born, he would have
been a year older than me. My father, a medical student, had
his study beneath the stairs, his window a basement window
and his specimens sealed in jars:
 —a tiny fetus in a translucent sac
 —a small fetus, pale-fisted, white
 —Edwin
 I point him out to my friends. "Look, that's Edwin, my older
brother, if he'd been born."
 I think he would have been taller, thinner than me, and with
short hair. Edwin going before me, growing taller, moving
through the neighbourhood. He'd score goals, talk to our neighbours at their side door. I know Dad would have taken Edwin to
the golf driving range, then let him come with to the pub.
 Dad sawed down a club for him in the garage, then taped up
the handle, my father showing him how to hold it: Line up your
thumbs like this, Edwin.
 Down at the other end of the street: "Hey, that's Edwin's
younger brother, okay, you're it, one one-thousand, two."
 A miscarriage. They tried to have Edwin before they had me.
It was like he went away to a foreign country and though he was
alive, we never saw him, just knew what he was like. And that
baby in the jar was Edwin before he was born, and what he left
behind him when our thoughts of Edwin grew bigger.

I miss him. I think of all the times we could have had, all the things I could have asked him. What would it have been like to have him in the next room with his door open, doing homework?

I don't know what happened to him after we moved to Canada. My father didn't have a study until we moved again and there wasn't a shelf below the window like before.

I still imagine Edwin back on that shelf with some kids looking in. They go to the street and play football until they're called home for supper.

NEIGHBOUR

The stars are a pale pox on the sky's dark chicken, Al the neighbour comes out to say. They are goosebumps on an arm so large that in this world there is no room for fingers. Heaven is filled with fingers, Al says, and they spend eternity making the shadow of a dog, a hang-ten sign, or a swan.

Let's say a certain angel tells the fingers to get out of the way because he wants to watch a movie. The fingers part in the V-for-Vulcan sign and *On the Waterfront* is revealed. It looks strange with its new cast reflected on the clouds.

Hey look, isn't that Genghis Khan and that Spinoza? Isn't that—what's his name—Sophocles' brother? But they're not doing badly, for angels.

Maybe later, after the first reel is over, those angels who were furniture, or else plot devices, switch with the ones who were humans, or perhaps dogs, and the movie continues.

Afterwards, they all head downtown for cheesecake and coffee; though, of course, some have tea. I myself wasn't invited, so instead sit at home, play chess with the computer.

I was doing okay, until that knight came out of nowhere and I was forced to lose my queen. "Alright," the king says, "now I'll have to change the picture on the stamps."

And that reminds me, I've a letter to send. Something I've been putting off for a while.

Sincerely yours, the weather is fine, when will you get the streets cleaned, make the bowling alleys safe again? The hospitals are filled with your victims and the museums have been closed down. When I walk, I cannot run, and when I fly, the sky's dark chicken flies with me.

Please, we need your help. The stars are cathedral spires sticking into its dark skin. Look, there are its doors, and its people are on the sidewalk crying, selling sunglasses, Scotch tape.

I am only Al the neighbour but I understand. I will give you my trousers, my swimming trunks, my land. I will stand here freezing. I am only one kind of neighbour, but others are watching.

✦

FOR A NUMBER OF YEARS

I found a moustache by the side of the road, kept it in a jar on my desk. I punched holes in the jar's lid and provided it adequate food. All afternoon I watched as the hairs of the moustache swayed like a miniature field of dark wheat, but then just before supper a stillness came over the jar as if a grim frost had passed through. After several days, I buried the jar beneath the roots of a tree by a barber shop.

Though I looked for hours in the roadside grass, I could not find another moustache. Instead, I attempted to will a moustache to appear on the face of my younger brother. I would stare at him through dinner as he ate his potatoes, boiled chicken, or Jell-O. At night I'd throw bottles of Aqua Velva into the river, watch them bob then splinter on the rocks. Though my brother was only nine and already as tall as me, I tried to hasten his growth, adding the appropriate substances to his breakfast. But nothing, it seemed, would make a moustache appear—not bedrest, not a stay in the hospital overnight.

At school, moustaches began to appear on the faces of boys in my class. I did not feel that I was responsible for these unnecessary growths. I had desired but a single moustache, which I felt was reasonable, not so immodest as an entire eighth-grade crop.

I decided in secret to try cultivating a moustache upon my own lip. I prayed for it to grow. I stole my father's razor, mixed his hairspray with milk. I spent time with my grandad, and walked by bars. I felt certain that when spring came, my moustache would grow.

By February, I noticed a certain growth on my lip, one that wouldn't wash off. I was unable to harvest this pale corn. It grew all summer, until it began to curl. I was given a shaving kit and with this was finally able to collect and store this more robust growth in a jar, where it led a happy, though fairly quiet, life, for a number of years.

THE LOVELY CARLOTTA, QUEEN OF MEXICO

There is a man standing on the side of the road wearing a chicken suit.

Why is he wearing a chicken suit?

The moon is large in the sky. It is like a school bus screeching to a halt on the dark asphalt outside the house of the Lovely Carlotta, Queen of Mexico. Twenty children, their skin pale as eggs, climb out of the school bus, walk up to the front door, and begin to knock. They have been knocking for hours, their knuckles like bruised grapes. There is the sound of keys rattling, the lock turning. The door opens and there is the Lovely Carlotta, Queen of Mexico, resplendent in her feather boa, her deep-sea diving suit. The children brush past her, one of them tripping on an air hose. They sing "Vaya Con Dios" and look for kitchen utensils. When dawn comes, they will make taco salad, dressing it with condiments from the future. The Lovely Carlotta has a shower in her diving suit, unscrews the helmet to brush her hair. She pads into the living room, the air hose knocking over a plant in the hall. She climbs out of the suit. Underneath she is wearing a red dressing gown, trimmed with the royal colours of Mexico. From behind the couch, someone sings the theme to *Jeopardy!*, then jumps on the coffee table, shouts, "I am the Alex Trebek of all Mexico, dance with me, for you are my queen." Carlotta kicks off her slippers, climbs up on the table, and begins to dance.

*National Geographic*s get crumpled, the *TV Guide* lands on the floor. One of the children stands on a chair near a light switch and flashes the lights. Another turns on the television. Is that an earthquake? A psychic help line? Tina Turner dressed as a priest? Life is *Jeopardy!*, she calls out. Life is a Final Jeopardy that never ends. We stand before our friends and family and also before those whom we will never know. The questions are answers. We have answers before the questions.

Why is there a man standing on the side of the road wearing a chicken suit?

Why is it a chicken suit?

Why is the man who was standing on the side of the road wearing a chicken suit crossing the road?

Which came first, the Lovely Carlotta, Queen of Mexico, or the egg?

The man in the chicken suit looks toward the moon with its new feathers, begins to cluck the names of his ancestors.

✦

PLACENTA

Years before my birth, my mother dreams of a magnificent six-tusked elephant, white, the colour of angels. The elephant walks toward the Milky Way, the four big bangs of its feet, the universe expanding in four directions.

An alarm clock on the night table ringing. A shooting star arcs across the indigo sky. My mother's eyes open, look out into the night. I enter her uterus: the quick flash of thought.

I grow to be an old man in my mother's womb, the placenta a long white beard wrapped around me, my eyes wrinkling as I float in the pinkish light.

When it is time, my mother puts down her magazine and coffee, rises from her chair on the porch, and walks through the plum blossoms in the direction of my father, who is sawing wood in the shed. Her hand clasps a flowering branch and I emerge from her side without pain.

I am born blue like the dark night of my conception, my fingers and toes webbed like a frog's. Though I am already an old man, my mother allows me to take seven steps, then wraps me in cloth, and keeps me with animals. I say nothing of why I was born, make no mention of my plans. The priests revere me, pull my long earlobes, and warn my parents of the demons who would kill me.

My parents take me to live in disguise with cowherds. I have no alarm clock of my own, but learn instead to play flute and dance the tango. My family builds three magnificent cottages on a hill so that I may live away from the cares of the world. I have breakfast in my bed, which is a perfect circle. I sleep beneath circular sheets and nothing ever dies.

One day I open the window and begin to play flute. The women of the village are mesmerized by the scales that I play and climb up the hillside toward me. When they arrive, I follow the stream of them out onto the grass and we begin to dance. The sun rises into the sky like a giant circular bed and I multiply myself, make love to each woman. It is so festive and all of me are doing so well that the gods gather in the clouds above to watch and take notes.

They want me to start a religion. They want me to write books. They want me to speak to the people and appear in their dreams. I feel like an alarm clock that has just begun to ring, that someone in bed is hitting, looking for the switch to turn me off.

We reach a compromise, but I cannot tell you what it is.

Let us feel our own worth and the love of the Lord. Let us live in harmony with nature, love others, and remember that there is a path to ultimate release.

THE STRANGE FISH OF ICARUS POTEMKIN

Icarus Potemkin is sad. His car, along with his copy of *Ulysses*, has been stolen right out of his driveway. An hour before, Icarus had returned home from the Suez Canal, had left the book on the dash, and had forgotten to lock the doors of his little green car.

His sadness is like the large and oily puddle on his driveway, except that no cars ever drive over it, even to turn around. It is so large that its edges reach out beyond the suburbs. It's no wonder cars never enter the puddle, choose instead to drive into the happy river gurgling toward the giggling at the edge of town.

And now, left alone, strange fish with bristly bone-covered fins have crawled out of the puddle, have left a filmy trail along the sidewalk, past the schoolyard, and into the coffee shop. Strange fish in the coffee shop ordering fancy coffee drinks, snapping their newspapers, toothless and cold-lipped, munching on biscotti.

Crumbs fall out of the corners of their wet mouths, soil their scales. One of the crumbs falls under my chair—under my left foot, actually. After it hits the floor it begins to rise again with me on it. I think to myself, Here I am surfing on a crumb and I haven't written anything in my notebook yet. I could have written *Where will this crumb take me? I am so unsure*, but I dropped my pencil way back there in the coffee shop.

The crumb is speeding down the road. The crumb is taking me to the university. It whizzes me past the little yellow booth and I just have time to give the parking attendant five dollars.

We make a sharp right turn and enter the George T. Stubble Building. We go into classroom 11A. I am late for class. I drop my essay on the corner of the professor's desk and breathe a sigh of relief. It is over. I have finished. But when I look back, my essay is a bony fish, its gills gasping in the still air. I fear that my footnotes have become eyes with transparent lids, my finely honed introduction a small fish, eaten by a larger fish on the way up the food chain.

Where is my notebook? I want to write a poem about how I belong at the top of the food chain, beside those who polish their shoes. But then I notice that all of my punctuation marks, the commas especially, have become tadpoles that are fast maturing into slimy and muscular frogs. They are covering up the professor's desk, even his notes about the ears of those who worked on the Suez Canal: large, darkly tufted, swart half-shells, listening in the hot and dusty air to the lowing of oil boats waiting beside Africa.

The frogs are hopping from the professor's desk to the desks of his students, their textbooks open to diagrams of the Middle East, a chart of the facial expressions of James Joyce.

A frog jumps from Syria and lands on James Joyce's forehead. An expression of careless frog-expectant mirth barely creases his thin lips. The frog burrows into his ear, finds its way through the polyglot canal of his cochlea, and arrives at his brain. It is small and intense, like a neutron bomb. Now there is a frog at the centre of James Joyce's skull. It is the colour of James Joyce's green suit, or of the grass stains on his publisher's shoes.

James Joyce reaches into his breast pocket for a cigarette. His mind explodes in a slimy amphibious bang. Frogspawn splattered on the vault of heaven flitters in the amber glow of the lit match held between James Joyce's fingers.

Icarus Potemkin walks out to his driveway, sits down in the exact spot where his car would have been, picks up his book from the imaginary dashboard, and begins reading.

Page 238. His nerves knit themselves into a marvellous and joyful tapestry: a transparent dolphin, its pumping heart the brilliant green of a neutron bomb. The tapestry unwinds itself at night. Something in the mind of Icarus Potemkin clicks: the four little knobs of the car doors popping down together when the automatic lock is pressed.

The car-thieving fish buys a coffee at the Odyssey Drive-Thru. The sound of the little plastic cup lid being ripped back. The professor wishing the fish "a nice day." A biscotti crumb approaching the speed of light becoming pure energy in the mind of a coffee drinker. A tear, the size of a small lake, falls from the single eye of an enormous hundred-legged frog. It plops into the waters of the happy river as it gurgles toward the giggling edge of town. The suburbs laugh. Street signs tremble. Strange fish will come to your door, posing as dolphins. Icarus Potemkin's copy of *Ulysses* will get a speeding ticket, somewhere in Alabama.

✦

COP OF CUFFEE

Would
you
like
some
tea?
I said.

I'm a police officer. Badge number 357. I'm dressed in blue.
This is my hat. I wear large shoes. I drive around in a yellow car.
Everywhere I go, I carry a little notebook. I don't like tea.

Oh,
I said.
Then
would
you
like
a
glass
of
orange
juice?

I have burly arms. I wear a wide leather belt. I shine my badge
with my own spit and this makes it glisten. My police car phone
connects me with a network of other policemen who have similar
car phones. If we hear of two streets that cross, we arrive there
with our lights flashing. I don't care for juice.

Perhaps
a
little
mineral
water?
I said.

You should see me at the policeman's summer games. I run with
an egg on my spoon; I'm first through the gate. I've never been
to Edinburgh but I can caber toss. Does the name Hermes Menza
mean anything to you? I've a wife and two kids. I wouldn't like
mineral water, thank you.

I
know,
I said,
bet
you'd
like
some
root
beer.

Okay, so I'm going to have to get tough with you. You should see
me naked in the tub. I've always had this moustache. Once, at a
red light, I stopped my car and sobbed uncontrollably. The light

changed to green. Don't think I don't know where you were the night of January sixteenth. I was there. It was like a cheap detective novel, only I was the copy editor. Do you have anything a police officer could drink?

Right
you
are,
I said,
I'll
get
you
a
Coke.

I don't have a tongue, don't have a wife. I don't have a clear understanding of the universe. I don't like malls. I walk like I own my legs but don't. I can swim but not underwater. I can flip through the pages of a magazine but am afraid of heights and dry places. When I drink a glass of water, you can hear the voice of my father. Oh father, cook for me. I'm tough as nails, soft as the hinge of a door.

Soup
in
a
mug,
I said.
I'll
get
you
some

soup
in
a
mug.

I am not a goatherd, a pot shard, the glistening back of an eel. In the underground vault of my soul, my ironed uniforms are waiting for me. We have a word for people like you. My knowledge of geography extends into northern Quebec. I'd like to ask a few questions. See this paperweight? Once, it was gone.

✦

HELLO, TONGUE SURGEONS

A wolf pads up my front steps, pushes open the door,
walks into the kitchen where I'm making chicken, and
bites off my tongue.

I look in the *Yellow Pages*: telegraph operators, tomato sales-
people, tongue surgeons (registered).

The first five times I dial, no one answers.

"Tomatoes and other red lusciousnesses," a woman's voice
says on my sixth try. "How may I help you?"

I've been dialling the wrong number for half an hour. I hang
up, dial again.

"Hello, Tongue Surgeons," a curt voice says, but I'm unable to
speak clearly, try to form my sentences with vowels only. Wish
I'd invested in consonants when they were first discovered, way
back at the beginning of the mouth.

I press numbers on the phone. Five six four three five six. I
approximate speech but they don't seem to understand "Help"
there at Dr. Lingua's, and I'm left with the weedy drone of the
dial tone buzzing like a lobotomized fly.

It's hard pulling it out through the little holes of the phone, but
I manage, and soon I've a dial tone attached to the stump that the
wolf left at the back of my mouth.

The first thing I say: low long-distance rates, bonus points, the
opportunity to call family far, far away. But then I begin to tell

GARY BARWIN

this old story that I know about a witch and her wagon pulled by
wolves, how she whips their grey backs with live writhing snakes
as she pulls into the parking lot across from city hall. And in the
sky, instead of clouds there are these ominous-looking brains just
hanging there, and it seems like all morning the sun is threatening
to peek out from behind the cerebral cortex of one particularly
large one. You can see its crenellated edges turning pink as light
creeps round it in the same way that memory flashes warm through
the hippocampus, or through a witch when she diverts a river with
her hand, then demands sacrifices if city hall is to be saved.

These are the names of the wolves: Lepton, Hadron, Nucleon,
and Tomato. I think it was Tomato that bit off and swallowed
my tongue.

I try to phone city hall. I want to tell the mayor that a sacrifice
has been made, that the wolf Tomato has my tongue. But I can't
get a dial tone. It's in my mouth instead of a tongue. I must go
downtown and stop the flooding. Already the mall is under water,
half the leather outlet submerged. If I could just become the long
dash or the short dot under the telegraph operator's finger, I could
flash along the line and arrive before the wolves.

But here is the milkman putting out bottles. I hide in the cold
back of the truck, behind the clinking crates. He is on his way
to the cafeteria, making sure the aldermen have milk to go with
their sandwiches, to whiten their tea, or else coffee if they're
tired. I feel like I'm riding a creamy stagecoach, rich in butterfat,
heading west to where I'm needed, and instead of the threat of
wolves, there are coyotes, their crooked shuffling fur and ragged
gait, their howl like the insistent ringing moon.

I slip in the side door of city hall when neither the milkman
nor the witch are looking, past Urban Planning, Traffic Tickets
(Dispute or Payment), and the Office of the Sheriff. I move with
stealth around the Office of the Ombudsman; I arrive at the

glass doors of El Rancho del Mayor. They swing open as I walk through. He is there, deboning a chicken.

I begin to speak, my mouth crooked, my ragged tongue shuffling. There is a faint howl as of a telephone being lifted before it is dialled. The mayor's mouth is open, a half-flooded parking lot filled with wolves.

"Mr. Mayor," I am trying to say, but the wolves of his mouth leap out and bite off my dial-tone tongue. It has become a coyote and runs with the wolves of his mouth. They are howling on the plush deep-pile mesa of his office, and the pages of municipal files float by like tumbleweed. A desk drawer opens on the mayor's left, and from amid the pens and pencils, which have turned into twisting snakes, the witch rises, cackling building code and bylaw. "The mayor is severed," she screeches. "I *have* my sacrifice." The waters recede. The wolves leave town. The witch catches dinner and a movie, then takes a cab to another city, her overnight bag filled with snakes. The sun sinks in the brain-filled sky, and it is the end of another day.

I was going to call and tell you, you see, but there's this problem with my tongue. There's this problem with my tongue.

✦

LESTER NYLON'S SECOND HONK

I

All that rainy afternoon, Nylon hoped that the weekend would end, that someone would come and pick up the pieces.

Later, I remember telling him that Nylon hoped the weekend would end, that someone would pick up the pieces.

I don't love you anymore, she said. Nylon hoped the weekend would end, that someone would pick up the pieces.

He had opened the first vial then mixed it with Nylon hoped the weekend would end, that someone would pick up the pieces.

She unbuttoned her blouse. The taxi honked a second time. Nylon hoped the weekend would end, that someone would pick up the pieces.

It was clear that afternoon Nylon but the weekend would that end there would someone pick up I don't love you.

II

Tuesday. A taxi waiting. The rain falls sizzling to the sidewalk. The weekend that someone would pick up pieces I opened the first vial and then, Nylon, I burst into smoke.

I arrived at the hotel, blouse opening like the burning wings of a someone coming to knocked at the door.

There seemed no hope that the weekend would end, that some-one would pick up the phone rang and it was Nylon.

This is the weekend I hoped would end and someone is at the

door picking up the smoke by the burning wings of that weekend would end but Nylon is at pieces burst into ashes to someone
pick up the first vial.

All that weekend the taxi honked a second. The sizzling Lester
Nylon of no fixed address has come to hope that the weekend
would end, that someone would come pick up the ashen, fallen,
flaming, nylon, weekend, forgotten, hopeful, phony, honking,
knocking, vile, opening, ringing, burning, smoky, blousy pieces
and we all can be done with it once and for all and go home for
Nylon the weekend would end that someone would come and
pick up the pieces.

III
I don't love you.
Blouse opening.
I burst into smoke a taxi waiting.
In the wings, that weekend the rain falling.
Hoping I picked up the pieces the phone ringing.
Sizzling.
The rainfall ending.
The burning hotel.
Later, the weekend would end.
Smoky. Nylon. That.
Lester, later, a taxi pickup.
The weekend it ended that someone would pick up.
That Nylon Lester, that pieces of it end and.
Later that afternoon, Nylon hoped that the weekend would end,
that someone would.
He fell to the sidewalk.
It was a new day.
Nylon hoped that the weekend would end, that someone would
come and pick up the pieces.

LADIES & GENTLEMEN, *LADIES & GENTLEMEN, MR. RON PADGETT*

for Stuart Ross

Ladies and gentlemen, you could say that I am an avid reader. In fact, this morning I read a book that was called *Ladies & Gentlemen, Mr. Ron Padgett*. In it, Ron Padgett is addressed by the author several times by name. The funny thing is that the author does not even know Ron Padgett. I mean, he's read some of his books, but as he says, unless Ron Padgett once stepped on his toe while getting off a bus in Toronto, the author has never met him.

And I've never met Ron Padgett either. Unless, of course, as he stepped off a bus in Toronto, his foot, narrowly missing the toe of the author of *Ladies & Gentlemen, Mr. Ron Padgett*, came down on my toe. What a guy that Ron Padgett is. I mean, he didn't even say, "I'm sorry."

And let me make something else clear: the author of the book *Ladies & Gentlemen, Mr. Ron Padgett* has never stepped on my toe, unless he did it so lightly as to change the meaning of the phrase "stepped on my toe" to mean something more like "when one person delicately brushes the feathered sole of his tiny shoe against the massive, structurally reinforced steel-toed boot of another, when the other, absorbed in his own thoughts (probably dwelling on the fact that Mr. Ron Padgett never apologized to him when he stepped on his toe), wasn't looking." In fact, I have never had any contact with the feet of the author of *Ladies & Gentlemen, Mr. Ron Padgett*, not that I'm necessarily excluding possible contact in the future, considering the fact that once, a long time ago, I shook his hand.

Okay, so now you know. Though I have never met Mr. Ron Padgett himself, I did however once shake hands with the author of a book about him. It was our first meeting. We never shook hands again.

I wish there'd been a string section there. I mean, imagine what it would have been like, strings pulsing in the background, when I said, "It was our first meeting. We never shook hands again." But that would have compromised the true meaning of the passage. I don't think the author of *Ladies & Gentlemen, Mr. Ron Padgett* would have liked that, though he probably would have appreciated the reference to popular culture and especially film.

So then, let me fill you in on the real meaning of the above passage. You see, after we shook hands, we became—dare I say it?—friends. This may explain why we never shook hands again. It is not our way to come up to each other and shake hands if we meet on the street (we have never met on the street) or if we go out for dinner (we've often gone to Toby's for a burger). The only time we might shake hands is if one of us became a father. But perhaps one of us, without knowing it, has already become a father on a bus in Toronto. Or perhaps it was Mr. Ron Padgett who became a father on a bus in Toronto without knowing it. It seems more likely, since I am led to believe by my friend's book that Mr. Ron Padgett already has several children. In any case, it seems that a handshake is in order.

But I'd have to go a long way to shake the hand of Ron Padgett. Did you know that he lives in Tulsa, Oklahoma? But maybe you'd like to find out the fascinating facts about Mr. Ron Padgett for yourself. In that case, it seems to me that there are a couple of ways you could go about it. You could go to the public library and ask for the best biography written about Mr. Ron Padgett. They'd probably recommend something like *Ron Padgett: The Foot Comes Down*. But you wouldn't get any of the really juicy facts there. If you wanted that, you'd have to write to my friend at Box 141, Station F, Toronto, Ontario M4Y 2L4 and ask him for a copy of his book *Ladies & Gentlemen, Mr. Ron Padgett*. That's assuming that my friend isn't on a six-month worldwide book tour, and that his agent, bathing in gin, high living, and the Toronto literary scene, remembers to forward him his mail, which he probably wouldn't answer anyway, since it can be hard to find the correct postage off the coast of Spitsbergen. So I guess you're just going to have to keep reading here if you want to know more about Mr. Ron Padgett. Perhaps you'll find out about the certain angle he tilts his head when he's thinking up a poem, or when he's about to answer a particularly difficult question from Allen Ginsberg. Perhaps you'll find out his wife's real name, and why, if you asked her, she wouldn't recommend *Ron Padgett: The Foot Comes Down*. Or maybe I'll tell you what all the Padgetts think about the insinuations in *Ladies & Gentlemen, Mr. Ron Padgett*, that is, if their copies didn't get lost in the mail.

Because it's certainly possible that someone, say, in Columbus, Ohio, read the Padgetts' copy and is going to tell you about it right now. I wonder what they're saying? It must be pretty absorbing, since you don't seem to be listening to me. I knew I should have brought in the string section on this one.

I mean perhaps these Ohioans are telling you completely wild lies. Maybe they're telling you that Ron Padgett has only one child and that he was born in the Tulsa General Hospital. And maybe they say they have the birth records to prove it and you're wondering how I think I can get away with saying that Ron Padgett became a father on a bus in Toronto. Well, if you'll just give me a moment to explain, you'll see that I'm telling the truth:

It was the Keele Street bus and it was heading north. There were only a few passengers travelling home that late night. Ron Padgett was sitting quite near the front of the bus, wearing a large blue parka, when suddenly a child was born to him. There were no particular astrological phenomena to accompany this event, as there likewise have not been any string sections to accompany certain of my phrases.

Ron Padgett just got off the bus at the first convenient stop and called long-distance collect to the Tulsa General Hospital. Only he dialled the wrong number by accident. I know what you're thinking. You're thinking that he dialled Columbus, Ohio. You're thinking that he dialled the telephone number of the author of *Ladies & Gentlemen, Mr. Ron Padgett*. You're thinking that he dialled my number and I spoke with him and he suggested that I read *Ladies & Gentlemen, Mr. Ron Padgett*. You're thinking that he dialled the number of the author of *The Foot Comes Down*. But the truth is, he dialled your number, but you weren't home. I don't know where you were but a woman answered and explained that she, along with the rest of the string section of the Tulsa Civic Orchestra, was in the process of looting your home. Bet you wondered why all your favourite Nat King Cole records were out of order? Anyway, the string section ended up renouncing their life of crime and instead played Mr. Ron Padgett an excerpt from a concerto grosso by Corelli. Mr. Ron Padgett hung up the phone, redialled, and eventually a phone rang in a certain maternity ward in the Tulsa General Hospital.

Mr. Ron Padgett: Hello, honey, is that you?

Mrs. Ron Padgett: Yes, dear, it is. Where are you?

Mr. Ron Padgett: I'm—I'm in Toronto, but that's not important now. How are you feeling?

Mrs. Ron Padgett: Well, I'm feeling fine, just fine, and our new baby boy is feeling pretty fine too.

Mr. Ron Padgett: Oh, honey, that's great! That's just great.

What? You want me to check this in *Ladies & Gentlemen, Mr. Ron Padgett*? All right, if you want to be that way, I will. But just wait a moment while I find the right page.

Okay, okay—so Mr. Ron Padgett has only one child and it's a girl. So I've made a complete mess. I don't even think a string section would have made any difference. It's just that there are too many things that I don't know, too many things that I just don't understand. I can't believe that I've come this far and it's going to end like this. But I hope that you'll be able to see past the inconsequential mistakes, the petty lies, the attempt to appear as knowledgeable as the authors of those excellent books *Ron Padgett: The Foot Comes Down* and *Ladies & Gentlemen, Mr. Ron Padgett*.

Because I think you'll see that there's a kind of plaintive truth to my voice. A kind of wide-eyed sincerity and frankness that never quite became accustomed to airplanes, chewing gum, tickertape. And so here I am, in an open field, looking up at the blue, blue sky, the only movement around me the slowly waving wheat and the steady steps of the horses pulling surreys back from town. All the surreys have fringes on top. Oklahoma. Did I tell you that Ron Padgett was from Oklahoma? If nothing else, you can trust me on that. I know it's true. I'm really a simple man and do not seek to deceive. I ride the bus each day and earn an honest living. Sometimes I run into someone I know on the bus, and sometimes the possibility occurs to me that a famous American poet may step on me and not know it.

✦

OPERA

She walks onto the stage in her powdered wig and says, "La." The scene changes. Suddenly the stage is filled with shepherds and the lazy rays of the summer sun are slanting across the rolling fields. "Oh remember," the shepherds sing.

Enter the dogs and horses. We hear hunting horns sounding in the distance. "It cannot be," the chorus says. "It must be," the hero says. "It cannot be," the chorus says. "Oh remember, remember," the shepherds sing.

A room overlooking the estate. "La," she says, and falls into his arms. "No," he says, and writes a letter. "Oh remember, remember," the serving girls sing. "It must be," the chorus says. "It shall be," her father says. "It cannot cannot be," her mother says. "It must, it cannot, it shall, oh remember, remember. La," they sing together.

Scene change. We are surrounded by woodland nymphs. From the orchestra pit, a flute plays a pastorale. There is the sound of thunder. Three trumpets and a horn sound a fanfare. A flash of lightning and a Greek god whom we cannot identify appears onstage. "This is why," he sings. The chorus sings the words "muscular thighs" in Italian. The orchestra holds a chord. A chariot rushes into centre stage but is overtaken by a cloud. More lightning. The sounds of horses, Roman soldiers, sheep.

"I have lost him forever," she sings. "Though I am consoled by maidens, though my father, the king, though there are the heavenly sounds." "She has lost him forever," they sing. "I have lost him forever," she sings. "She has lost him," they sing. "I am here," he says. "She has lost him," they sing. "He is here," she sings. "I am here," he sings. "He is here," the king, her father, sings. "I am he is I am he is here," they sing. End of act one.

The curtain rises. A large fountain in the centre of a large square. The people are going about their business. Children are playing, chasing each other, throwing balls, and singing. The orchestra is busily playing. From the far right of the square a group of young men appears, talking excitedly. There is a clap of thunder. The scene changes. We are overlooking a brook in a wooded glade. A flute plays a cheerful tune. A young couple appears sporting amidst the trees. The chorus sings, "Remember"; the woman sings, "La." The scene changes and suddenly we are surrounded by sheep.

The clouds shoot across the summer sky like children across the square. In the distance we hear the sounds of horses, dogs, the call of hunting horns. The sound of a drum. A group of hunters appears. The sounds of harp like a waterfall. A flute. A drum. The king appears reunited with his brother. A messenger runs across the stage. "At last," the king's brother sings. "At last," the chorus says. "Forevermore, it shall be so," the king sings. "This is why," the Greek god says. The curtain falls.

✦

OVER 2.7 MILLION DOLLARS

One son is smearing yogurt and blueberries all over his thighs, the other is driving a Lego car through a plate of Parmesan cheese. The dog is barking by the door, not itself sure whether it wants food or to be let outside into the cold. Some music—or was it talking?—on the radio, barely audible over the sound of the dishwasher taking in water for the pots/pans cycle. I was standing in my pyjamas drinking a half cup of reheated coffee, washing down some raisin toast, reading, against my better judgment, the list of the week's top-grossing Hollywood films, when I looked up and there you were downstairs after sleeping in, beautiful in your bright floral dress as if someone had just turned on the wall switch for summer, along with a few of the other switches nearby.

FACT

FACT: a fish bit my father's nipple.
FACT: a small fish.
FACT: his right nipple.
FACT: swimming at night in Lake Ontario.
FACT: not a rhino's tender motions at chest level.
FACT: not grey lips moist, wistful eyes.
FACT: not Lake Huron.
QUESTION: and me? swimming beside him, not thinking.

FACTS to date: 7. QUESTIONS: 1.

It became my job to write this down, to write a report, a novel, a journal entry, an account in simple terms.

FACT: there was no swelling.
FACT: also no pain.
QUESTION: has this happened before?

Once, with forceps, he had to remove a key that somehow dropped inside my cello, late at night, my mother watching, he just back from the hospital.

FACT: I paid cash for my son's circumcision.

FACT: the procedure was later explained with the aid of a fist and a shirt sleeve.

FACT: multiple interpretations of the fish bite are possible.

QUESTION: was my father Jesus, the fish the Catholic Church? can his nipple be construed as the source of my troubles?

CLARIFICATION: here I do not refer to the nipple of Jesus.

FACT: the drywall finally giving way, an electric eel burst from the blue wall above us at the exact moment when, naked, my wife and I were about to reach the last page of Russell Hoban's *Turtle Diary*.

FACT: that book begins with a dream of an octopus.

FACT: we were soaked by the water that gushed with the eel from the wall.

FACT: after that experience, I shall have to think about having children.

I don't really know whether it was his right or his left nipple. It is my duty to record the event. If it had been a rhino, it would not have been under water. It would not have burst forth from the wall; a shared instant of understanding, my father and the rhino on the short scrub of the plain. If it had been my mother, every-thing would have been different.

FACT: a fish bit my mother's nipple.

FACT: a small fish.

FACT: we needn't go on. For that, see "The Rocks at the Bottom of the Lake" by David McFadden. And I too have lived in Hamilton, Ontario, but do not confuse autobiographical details with the author.

—right, Mom?—

FACT: in the past I've written many haiku.

FACT: that night a frog jumped into Lake Ontario.

FACT: not, however, making any contact with my father, save for the mutual perception of the ambient plash, the mutual perception of the moment when the frog falls into the water's jaws, the fish bites my father, the eel lands on my wife's legs and she realizes that she will be unable to finish *Turtle Diary*.

FACT: as found as graffiti on a bathroom wall.

SUMMARY: my father's nipple made me responsible.

FACTS: 23. QUESTIONS: 4.

FROM *CRUELTY TO FABULOUS ANIMALS* (1995)

◆

DOWN INTO THE STREETS

Have you ever been outside on a summer evening when it is cool and the stars are out and you perhaps are walking beside a hedge of tiny leaves and you feel a cool breeze on your face, and the leaves begin to rustle? Perhaps in the distance, a car drives by and you hear a frog in the grass, maybe the sound of crickets. And perhaps you are walking beside a beautiful woman in a floral skirt who tells you that there is a purpose to life, but that only certain people may know what it is. And suppose you reach into the sky with your mile-long arms and move the stars aside a bit and, with your tongue that is longer than your arms, lick the vault of heaven until in one spot, a little of the colour comes off and light comes bursting through and both of your bodies are instantly bronzed with perfect tans and the beautiful woman snaps her fingers and causes the flowers in her skirt to suddenly bloom and all around you there are strange gentle-eyed animals that you have never seen before. As you dive into the summer air, floating far above crowds in the city, you release thousands of your business cards that fall like identical snowflakes down into the streets.

✦

A RABBI, A SCHOOLBOY, AND A TAILOR

A rabbi, a schoolboy, and a tailor walk into a bar. Both the rabbi and the tailor order a drink, but the schoolboy tells this story.

He says, Imagine yourself to be a leaf, imagine yourself to be turning gold. The sound of your hands as they move through water, the sound of your feet walking on dry land. Once when I was seventeen, I did not do my homework, I became a leaf on a tree in a shopping centre, I became a discount store.

On Tuesday I was selling shoes, videotapes, German sausage, when a tall blue bird was born from my shoulder blades. I became light as a five or a six, carried by air. I was a leaf turning onto a highway from a street in the suburbs, I was a blood cell spinning in the veins of my tongue. I read the menu out loud, pronouncing each word. The wind picked up signals from Jupiter and a rock that was on my chest became a family of four, then a group of stars in the constellation Orion.

I never wanted to become immortal, but it came to me so clearly. I parked my car behind Loblaws and knew I would never die.

✦

NAILS

O nce every week, my father would go upstairs to cut his fingernails and I would follow after him, asking for cuttings to add to my collection that I stored in jars. I do not know when he cut his toenails. Perhaps in bed before my mother turned out the light. Anyway, it was his fingernails that I was after, for late at night, when my parents were asleep, I would creep downstairs into the dining room—the dining room table was the only one large enough—and arrange clippings in patterns on the table. I'd cut my fingernails and put them in the centre of a circle of my father's fingernails and then, speaking strange words, I would mix them into one great circle of nails, my nails and my father's intermingling. And in a small voice I would sing. I would sing my song of nails. I would sing it as I crept back upstairs with the nails. And I would sing it as I slipped into bed, into my bed of nails where I would dream of thousands of fingers holding me, passing me through a sea of strangers' hands, down a line of unfamiliar arms, waving at me and telling me that I would soon be home.

THE END OF A CUE

'**ve** seen him sink an eight ball on a pool table so large it was the colour green. I don't mean it was coloured green, I mean it was green, it was the idea of green. And I myself have played on this table, my face twisted in concentration, my hands like the wings of a small bird. And when I tapped the cue ball into the triangle of other balls they moved like tiny clouds across a green sky and perhaps someone on earth got lucky, or was rained on.

And though I've been close, he has never let me win, has never let anyone win, except once there was a movie where he let himself be hustled. When you try to sink a ball on the table, he tricks you, turns the ball into the slightest hint of nutmeg, and you add another pinch and give the whole thing a stir, then perhaps decide to throw in a stick or two of cinnamon for good measure. Once I spent an entire decade perfecting a delightful vegetable soup until I realized that he was 300,000 points ahead of me.

Sometimes others of us play, but we're only allowed one ball, which, in any case, has only three sides, and that more or less settles the matter right there. So we try to watch every game that we can, often placing bets among ourselves. And though we're not allowed to intervene, I will admit that I have appeared as a vision to a few players who I wished to distract.

They have a difficult shot to make, and so I appear before them, terrible in aspect. They don't understand why I'm there—they think I'm Death, hovering over the table, flickering in the light, holding their breath in my right hand. Think of it. There they are, their smooth backs bent over the table, their arms stretched out, Death waiting for them to make a shot. At this point, they usually forget to aim.

At some games where the stakes are high, we all appear as visions and there are so many of us that the pool hall becomes dark with the beating of wings. Sometimes, just to be sarcastic, a bunch of us dance on the end of a cue. Once I tried to appear as a parallel universe to some guy about to clean up, but he didn't notice and I lost all my money. And as I said, we're not allowed to intervene, not under any circumstances. We may appear in a mighty chariot, the bones of the dead as spokes, but we may not create a single wrinkle in a pool table, nor turn a cue to ash.

If only I could play a game where there was some chance that I might win, or some chance that I might lose without thunderbolts or fire. I'd be able to make a shot without anyone winning a million dollars or having a heart attack. And when he'd call me to play, perhaps I'd look right into his lidless eyes and tell him that though I'd hardly played the game, I was willing to wager a little. I'd let him win a few times, and then, when he was feeling confident and we'd doubled the stakes, I'd begin to play in earnest. Before he knew it, there would be nothing but a single ball like a blind eye on the endless green. And until the end of time, he would believe that its directionless gaze was fixed on him.

BLAMELESS ANGELS

Every time two angels make love, a sin is committed here on earth. The angels remain blameless, comb the fine hairs on each other's wings, promise each other new shoes. Dark days when I look at the sky, knowing what the angels are doing, not able to help myself, stealing from Simpsons, parking illegally, committing murder. Angels with no luggage in one-night hotels, angels skateboarding to each other's houses, angels in drugstores buying gum, toothpicks, but no birth control: the War of the Roses, the Franco-Prussian war, Nicaragua. There should be no heaven until the angels, flying together ruthlessly across the sky, become responsible for their actions.

✦

THE LICE OF MONARCHY

1.

It could have been anyone at all, but it was Reno Violin.

Reno of the pitchfork, of the day before yesterday, Reno of the Medicine Hat Fidelity Society, of basketball freefall, Reno of construction paper happy dolls. Reno standing on the pier, playing harmonica for the seagulls.

I like his codpiece and ruby birthstone ring. I like the way he and Sir Walter Raleigh get along. I like his mood steak, his tonsil car, the way his knees bristle when you mention Cordoba. But who would have thought, all those years ago, that Reno could have done such a thing.

"Oh Reno!" I said. But Reno wasn't listening. He was too busy painting the sign for his new restaurant: *Reno's Windowpane Sandwiches, tinted or not tinted*. He spent weeks biking his cart up and down the coast, ringing that little bell. His slogan was "More than you can chew!" and he did well and soon he was living the good life, awkward blond kids driving his carts through the local tourist spots, wearing their trademark Reno uniforms. Windows from the nurseries of decent homes, windshields from the pale limousines of widower farmers.

Reno cycling along the beach, drinking too much, shouting at people in the fast-food drive-throughs, Reno shaking his fist at the sky, saying, "God but I love you." This guy on a bridge thinks Reno's talking about him.

But maybe if Reno had seen this guy, he would have loved him, would have fed him, clothed him, bathed him, offered him his seat in the life raft. That is if Reno had taken time to get to know him. If Reno had invited him to dinner, met his mom, his sister, talked to his accountant.

Reno and this guy playing chess by the pool, watching their children age together, imagining the little corpuscles of their blood filling with oxygen every time they open their mouths to breathe. Reno and this guy camping with their families, waking to the sound of a bear, each reaching to put his teeth in, each accidently putting in the other guy's set. "Oh," Reno says, "Your bite is worse than your bark."

"Oh," the other guy says. "Think I'm biting with more than I can chew."

They get out their guns, they shoot the bear. Reno takes the left side home with him, the other guy takes the right. Reno makes a kind of purse from the heart. Each of them makes a half-bear tent in his backyard.

Reno showing up at my place, reaching into his bear heart, saying, "Here. Like a light?" A pale green flame comes out of the long yellow bear tooth that he holds up to my face. But I show him. I rub two children together, produce a spark that I tinder and make into a thriving fire. We talk long into the night, throw Scrabble letters, one by one, into the fire. We spell out Paganini, Heifetz, Arcangelo Corelli, all in little burning tiles. We keep no score, though it's clear that I'm in the lead. Around dawn, we watch as the board burns. We go for a long walk on the beach, play poker until lunch. Reno insists we go for a swim at his place. "Welcome to the Glass Reuben," he says as we get out of the car.

2.

It wasn't Reno's fault. I knew that from the beginning, no matter what they said. I watched him pulling out his veins, lining them up like a long blue crack along the ground. He wanted them to reach to the television station. It's too late to say this, but if only he hadn't lived in the suburbs, if only he'd lived in an apartment downtown, then they'd have reached. They'd have reached all the way to KLAM! TV instead of stopping right outside that squalid little futon shop. It was shameless the way they capitalized on it: "The river of blood runs to Hernando's Futon Hacienda." Tinted or not tinted. Oh, my dear friend Reno. Thanks for letting me sleep in the half-bear tent, if but for a single night.

They raced beetles in the tunnels where Reno's veins had been, placing bets on whose beetle could run from Reno's foot to his ear. They gathered around him on their knees. The man in the black hat started his beetle from Reno's left foot, the guy in the sports coat pushed his into Reno's right. And sometimes it took hours for the beetles to emerge, lost in the labyrinth of Reno's brain. For days on end, men—and it was mostly men—clustered around Reno's fallen body. Crowds collected and police had to cordon off the area. KLAM! TV produced exclusive news specials, a Reno vein-runner king and queen were crowned, hotel bars created subcutaneous beetle drinks, and all the while Reno lay half-asleep, only vaguely aware of the marketing schemes and franchise agreements his body was eliciting, only vaguely aware of the marathon triumphs and ear-to-ear victories of the trained insects teeming inside him.

I sat on the ochre couch in Reno's bedroom. I watched it on TV, turning it on, then off, unable to look but unable to look away. I sorted through his medicine cabinet, I rifled through the papers under his bed, I tried on all of his clothes. His satin dressing gown was terrific, his collection of Elizabethan fans was certainly the

best in the region. And oh, his ruby ring! I wore it with his opalescent gloves and bear-tongue headband. I dove into his pool, a
martini in one hand, sandalwood wire clippers in the other. There
was no sound when I broke the surface except for the voice of
Reno Violin.

I heard him calling from the bedroom television, across the
exercise room, down the quartz-lit hall, down the ebony bannis-
ters and through the twisted copper screen door of the marble
kitchen. I was a metre below the surface before I realized that it
was him. I had stripped naked, had hauled myself out of the pool,
and was running toward his car before the screaming stopped.

3.

Perhaps you won't believe me when I tell you this, but I am not
a well man. I know what you're thinking: you're thinking that I
contracted some kind of rare ursine disease the night I spent in
Reno's tent because maybe he didn't clean the bear's skin properly. I mean, considering the plagues that summer, the rodents,
lice, the monarchy. Maybe he should have picked up the tab at
the Grizzly Bar & Grill when those forest rangers were drinking
cocktails. They were in town for the big plague conference and
had just finished a stormy session on beetles, some arguing that
no coherent moral structure could be founded on iridescence
and a life in the dampness beneath stone. Surely the government
would soon fall, the estates of the rich would be sacked, and the
public libraries would be turned over to the rangers.

Yes, they said, such pestilence was upon the country, if only
control of the libraries were given to the rangers. There would
be new carpeting, the American presidents' reading room would
be used as a bunkhouse. Books would be hurled from the roof
into the streets, then collected again. Wide shiny belts would be

given to the clergy. And the plagues would stop. Perhaps rain would fall and the blades of dull grass would return to their sturdy green. Bears would once again be free to roam the streets, ride the bus for a reduced fare. In the great public squares of our cities, the universities would reopen, and the students would eat their sandwiches in the sun's bleached light. We rangers, they said, would live our lives free from rodents, free from the lice of monarchy.

4.

I was not with Reno the first night of the plagues. The streets were filled with the skin of snakes, and dogs' teeth filled the lanes. My shoes overflowed with them and my body became covered with the yellow spit of insects. The sky was a khaki green and bursts of fire shot out from store windows. The crowds ran with open mouths as if to call out, but I could distinguish no single sound above the ubiquitous roar. Over by city hall, I saw Reno's chess set, most of the pieces overturned. Still, I could tell that it would have been mate in six had the players persevered. I saw the gold legs and pewter arm of Reno's brother. Reno must have grabbed him when the chaos began, only had time to take his metal heart, his Plexiglas tongue. When he spoke or ate ordinary food, Reno's brother would refract light into many colours with his tongue, make them appear on the table before us. But Reno and his brother were gone now. They were probably on a beach somewhere, darkening in the sun, Reno counting the waves, the wave troughs, the fallen surfers, listening for every time some mother called out, "Johnny." The trick was not in building elaborate sandcastles, Reno would say, but in waiting until that certain moment when the grains of the sky collapsed in on one's tanned abdomen and one's arms became minarets of

water. Blue-muscled sharks would begin to frequent the conces-
sion stand near the road, not once mentioning what they'd like
to drink.

5.

When I watched the television that night, I saw them weave
Reno's veins into a blanket, saw them wrap it around the shoulders of his ex-wife. At one end where there was an opening, they
attached a tube draining from his swimming pool. The blanket
became fat with water, enclosing his ex-wife in his blue varicose
fist. She wasn't calling Reno's name, she was calling his brother's name. She called out the measurements of the bedroom, she
called out the postal rates for overseas parcels. And then she
called out my name.

She said, "Stop watching. Get off the ochre couch. Put the papers
back under the bed, take off the codpiece. I need you. I need you the
way Queen Elizabeth needs Sir Walter Raleigh, the way a surfboard
needs to exist independent of the word *vroom*, the way the house
I have made for you of Reno's skin needs you. I will give you the
address, come through the front door. I have had liposuction and
the excess flesh of my thick thighs and heavy belly are in a display
case in the front hall. Do not be afraid. Though you wear Reno's
bear-tongue headband and opalescent gloves, you are otherwise
naked and your frail body pleases me. I have heard how the small
hairs of your back curl like fingernail clippings, how the hairs of
your head are stout and clean. I have heard of your triumphs, though
they were long ago. I know of the weak tango of your limbs, and
of the brazen hammer of your mind as it tries to speak. Soon I will
be released from this bloated blanket of veins. It is like a map of
the lost city of Reno's broken body. It is four o'clock now. In an
hour the traffic will spill into the suburbs and I shall be free. We

shall meet for a drink at my place, tear photographs of ships from our family albums, place them in the mouths of hungry sailors, tied arm to arm in a single great circle in my garage."

I remained on the ochre couch. I did not move until long after she had spoken, until after the sports, the weather, the story of a man who had taught his pet rat to pray. It knelt as he said the Lord's Prayer, pointing at Mecca. It rocked back and forth as he chanted, its pink eyes closed in devotion. It did not gnaw on the tassels of its prayer mat and, despite elaborate temptations arranged by its trainer, it had remained celibate. When I finally left the ochre couch, I walked straight over to a travel agent and reserved a berth on the *QE II*. Not even Reno knew where I was going. I sent him a postcard with a picture of an anthill on it, though of course I did not sign it.

6.

The waters around Bermuda are calm as glass. I look up. "Would sir care to see our dessert trolly?" "No, thanks," I say, and go back to my list.

> *iii. Manacle.* I have two feet to stand on and my own abacus.
> *iv. Magnificent.* The intestines weave their way round the embellished belly, follow the sword's route through the burnished air.
> *v. Minotaur.* I am bowling with soft-soled shoes in the lanes of sleep. I take small steps over the hard-wood floor, whistle softly when I am ready to speak.
> *vi. Milk duct.* Please, nobody tell the captain, I am not well.

I play shuffleboard with squids, achieve remarkably good scores. I take many photographs of ships that are afloat in the waters around us, and several of our own vessel. Dance classes are held in the mornings and I enrol in the bunny hop. I spend the after-noons learning how to tan leather, take a special interest in two small children abandoned by their fathers. I teach them how to imitate the facial expressions of the dead, how to play harmonica the way Reno taught me. The seagulls reel around me, land on my shoulders. At midnight, I swim naked and alone in the pool, drink wine coolers on the lower deck. Far from the city of my birth, I am Reno Violin. My sins are numerous and they are thin.

MARTIN'S IDEA

Martin's Dream

We have a dog. His name is Martin.

One day Martin walked over to my wife and said, You should have a baby. Then Martin walked over to his dish of water and drank from it. Then he walked over to the fireplace, lay down on the rug, and went to sleep. Martin was asleep for a long time. This is what he dreamed:

He was walking across a field without end, a field the colour of his blond hair. At one end of the field was a large red house. Out of its chimney came puffs of smoke the shape of dogs. The sun lay low on the horizon, and all about him he heard the arfs of small dogs, calling.

He turned around. At the other end of the field there was also a red house. Puppies spilled from its windows and doors onto the soft grass of the lawn. They looked silvery and mysterious by the moon's pale light. He tried to call to them, but his barks fell to the field without sound.

It seemed he had been walking for days, the moon never rising, the sun never sinking, when suddenly he heard a voice, my voice, talking on the phone. I was saying, I think we will call him Martin, and yes, we can hardly wait.

Martin's Idea

My wife phoned me at the neighbours' and said, Martin has suggested that we have a baby. I went first to the corner store, then
straight home. I had bought two dozen roses, which I placed in
a jug on the kitchen table.

We sat down. My wife poured some coffee, we began to discuss what Martin had said.

He just walked over to me and said, You should have a baby,
my wife explained.

This is a difficult situation, I said. Perhaps I should talk to him.

I don't know, my wife said. He isn't what you would call a
reasonable dog.

Considering Martin's Idea

We talked long into the night, my wife and I at the kitchen table,
Martin asleep on the rug.

We considered Martin's idea carefully, and in the end, just as
we'd finished the last of the coffee, came to a decision.

Do you think we should tell him? my wife asked at breakfast.

I looked at Martin, still asleep on the rug. His chest moved up
and down with each of his small breaths. Not unless he asks, I
finally replied.

Martin Wakes

That night, Martin woke from his long sleep. I was in my chair,
reading the evening paper, when Martin stood up and walked
straight over to me.

I usually get that for you, he said.

Yes, I said, but you were sleeping. You have had a long sleep.

Right, said Martin, a bit embarrassed.

Martin Tells of His Dream

It was only later that Martin told me of his dream, of the endless days on the blond field, of the streams of silver dogs, of the two red houses, and of the smoke.

It was strange, he said. The sounds of dog were all around me, but I could smell nothing.

Martin in his favourite spot, curled by the fire, recounting his dream.

The whole time, I neither ate nor lifted a leg.

I tried to call them, he said, but my barks fell to the field without sound.

Both the sun and the moon remained fixed in the sky. I walked for days, it seemed, never moving.

Martin Asks

The next morning, Martin asked. We heard him on the stairs, heard him at our bedroom door, heard him by our bed. We heard Martin jump, then land on us.

Have you something to tell me? Martin asked.

The Dream

It was my turn to have a dream. It was early Sunday morning. I tried to get up, but I was beneath many blankets and their weight prevented me. Through the window I could see the first blond traces of dawn breaking across the sky. I could hear the small birds barking, the arfs of the dew worm.

I turned over on my side. My wife was gone. In her place

was a blue river flowing. Small dogs bobbed in the current like whitecaps, disappeared behind the dresser. I thought I heard a baby's cry from my sock drawer, but it was only the embers of a fire, crackling.

My wife said, Do you think we should tell him? And Martin said, No.

I was in the red house at the far end of the field. My wife was in the kitchen of the other red house, making coffee. I reached for the phone beside the bed and dialled her number.

Hello, she said.

Honey, is that you? I asked.

Yes, she said. I was just making coffee.

Oh, I said. I'm still in bed. Is Martin there?

Martin came to the phone.

Hello, he said, I think we've finally decided. We will call him Martin. And yes, we can hardly wait.

I tried to speak, but my words fell to the carpet without sound. All around me were the sounds of dog and just then I heard Martin ordering cigars.

A Few Months Later

A few months later, we drove over to my parents' house, parked by the elm tree. The wind had blown the front door open and so we stepped onto the veranda and called out, but there was no answer. We eventually found my parents, side by side on the sofa, their mouths open and sighing, their closed eyes rolling in circles, following the paths of plaster in the stuccoed ceiling.

I sat down in a chair to wait for them. Martin found his usual place on the rug and fell asleep. My wife went into the kitchen to make some coffee.

When she returned, Martin, still asleep, began to speak:

The moon's path is the circular path of the ceiling's plaster, he says.

The child is rising, my parents' sighing mouths intone.

The plaster's path is the sun's route from evening until evening, Martin says.

The child is rising, my parents' trembling voices call.

As the cool stream falls from the cleft of mountain, in the day's blond light, you shall return from the house of your birth, Martin says.

The child is rising, my parents chant.

And he shall be known as Martin, they sing together.

The Identical Dream

When we returned home and went to sleep that night, my wife and I had the identical dream.

We had taken off our sandals and were wading through a river. Whitecaps rose and fell about us like flames. On the far shore, we could see a dog walking the length of an almost endless field, walking from one red house to another. Puffs of blond smoke rose from a large cigar in the dog's mouth. Beads of silver, the shape of tiny puppies, spilled from the dog's furrowed brow as it strained through the swaying grass. A smooth-skinned baby rode on its back, bobbing up and down with each of the dog's steps. Over the rustle of the swaying field, we could hear the piercing bark of the riding baby and the steady reassuring voice of the dog.

My wife turned toward me. I think I felt the baby kick, she said, a little kick for each of Emily's soft paws.

SHEPHERDS IN THE PARKING LOT

There were no sheep anywhere and yet there the shepherds stood, between the Hondas and the late-model Fords, each in flowing robes, sometimes weeping, sometimes singing, sometimes gazing down the long road. I asked them what they were doing. They said they were waiting for their sheep to return from the restaurant across the street. The sheep had needed to use the restroom and one of the older shepherds, named Lou, had taken them. But now that they thought of it, he'd been gone quite a while and they hoped that everything was all right. I told them I was going for lunch at the restaurant, promised to check on their sheep.

As I started to leave, one of the shepherds walked over to me, placed his hand on my shoulder. He said that there were no sheep and Lou was fiction. He explained that they had lied to me: they were really a college football team that had left the high-pressure world of sports in order to lead a simpler life.

He explained that the expectations of their families, coaches, and schoolmates had been just too high and that as a result the quality of their life had suffered. He said they preferred to live on the high ground, far away from the village, where at night, when the moon was large, they told the same stories their fathers told, soft summer breezes rippling their berry-dyed cloaks. They preferred, he said, to spend their long days looking out over the dry valleys, shaping crooks from olive wood and listening to the cries of broad-winged birds. And, more than the attention of crowds, he said, they preferred the patient gaze of sheep, their eyes like smooth stones.

I said if that were the case, then what were they doing without sheep and in a parking lot in the city. He explained that they had no more money for bus fare. They had decided to become shepherds in the third down of a college championship in Calgary and had made it this far—to Toronto—before their money ran out. They would have to stay until they'd earned enough to move on.

I was not sure what to say, so I said that I was glad that they had told me the truth. Truth, I said, is an important virtue. One should always strive to be truthful. The shepherds looked earnestly at me as I spoke, listening carefully to each word. I gave them five dollars and wished them luck. I crossed the street, continuing on my way to lunch.

KING

I was sitting in my backyard when a group of young women came walking up the path, totally naked and desiring me. I finished my coffee, wrote a short story, and read an article about gardening while they waited at the gate. They began to call to me, and I answered each one of them in song:

> If I sigh deeply and sob quietly to myself, it is simply, dear ladies, when I cannot feast my eyes on your loveliness. The suffering I secretly endure is greater than any other, but I accept it willingly. All I ask is that by granting my one wish, you might ease my burden a little. Then my life would be happy as any king's.

When I finished singing, I noticed a strange look come into their otherwise clear eyes. Then one of the women turned into Volume 15 of the *Britannica*. Another became an Alfa Romeo, and yet another, Ernest Borgnine. Before it was over, I had a complete set of encyclopedias, three sports cars, and a small gathering of Hollywood celebrities. As I seemed to have no choice, I went inside for some Chardonnay.

I returned to find the garden furniture rearranged—a game of Australian rules football had broken out. One of the young women was revving her motor, and I must say, I was not unimpressed. I spent the afternoon quizzing Mr. Ed the horse about the Indian subcontinent, checking his answers in the encyclopedia. We had an argument over the meaning of the word *ghat*, which was finally resolved through a clarification on the door of a Maserati.

A modest buffet was set out on the lawn and a string trio played selections by Brahms. I enjoyed myself immensely, went for a dip in the pool. It is my impression that time stood still that day as if it were a giant dog in a doghouse the size of itself, each of us moving like tiny fleas amidst the bristling days.

"If I sigh deeply and sob quietly to myself, it is simply when I cannot feast my eyes on your loveliness. Your sweet and gentle disposition, your elegant bearing, and your candour have so captivated me that I willingly make you a loving gift of this heart of mine which far from you knows neither joy nor pleasure."

THE FOOT COMES DOWN

I n the clouds, the eggs of angels wait for the briskly swimming sperm of other angels to appear like stars. Later, you can hear the rustling as the unearthly zygote are nudged toward heaven's uterine wall.

It is the Queen's birthday. A worm begins to move across the sidewalk but is crushed by the foot of little Christopher Hoover, age eight, walking unattended toward Mapleview Public School. I can't say that I'm a particularly handsome man, but I know that I was conceived on a plane. We—I should say, they—were flying over Madagascar. The *No Smoking* sign was not illuminated. Breakfast was being served. Angels were playing golf, attending committee meetings, preparing their bodies for sex: You, you be the male. This time, I feel like being a girl.

Angels make love in about the time it took us to discover the dinosaur, bend a paperclip, or clean up after a game of solitaire. I was conceived before the stewardess spilled the coffee, but after the man behind us read the article on wine in the in-flight magazine; there is no music of the spheres, only the clangorous sounds of blastocysts becoming celestial babies, the sound of washable wallpaper being pasted throughout heaven.

By the time my parents arrived at the Ugandan International Airport, their baggage had been examined by the nimble fingers

of marmosets and by the lemur's slender tongue. You can understand my consternation when they had to sleep on chairs, my
father remaining unshaven. But still, I persevered and was opti-
mistic. I divided rapidly. The moon loomed large through the
airport window and when dawn came, they brought out the flags.

The army arrives, marching up the runway, firing bullets at the
sky. A tall man gives orders to the band and they play without
music. At Mapleview Public School in St. Catharines, Ontario, the
national anthem is sung. It is the Queen's birthday and the foot of
Christopher Hoover comes down. There are twice as many angel
cells as before, and soon, over the roar of cannons, the Queen will
blow out another candle as her grandkids flub the words.

he isn't able to stop building the alphorn:
across snowfields and meadows
through villages and between goats
it finally reaches the ocean's lowest zone

to play the horn is to send
lungfulls of alpine air to deep-sea fish
the scent of bluebells through dark liquid
until it reaches the noses of sharks

he builds and builds and the alphorn is everything
the long song that is home

ACKNOWLEDGEMENTS

This book originated when the clouds parted, the sky was rent, and I got a message (written in beautifully crafted yet concise lightning) from a committee comprised of Franz Kafka, Lydia Davis, Donald Bartheleme, and Italo Calvino, who did charge me with binding these fictions as one. Actually, it was Alessandro Porco—he'd edited my selected poems (*For It Is a Pleasure and a Surprise to Breathe*, Wolsak & Wynn)—who had the idea for a selected short fiction collection and did a lot of work beginning the selection. I am immensely grateful for his engagement, enthusiasm, and commitment to my work. Every writer should be so lucky as to have a friend and scholar like Alex Porco in their life.

My old friend Stuart Ross has been a huge influence on my writing, publishing, and life in literary community. His work, enthusiasms, and introduction to writing I didn't know have been of absolutely seminal importance. Thanks, Stu.

I am very thankful to the editors and publishers of the books, chapbooks, and journals where some of this work first appeared. Without their support, advice, and general literary heroism, this work wouldn't be here or, actually, anywhere.

Kevin Connolly published my first non-self-published chapbook, *I Parked My Car behind Loblaws and Knew I Would Never Die* with his Pink Dog Press with great editorial care and insight. Peter Baltensperger published *Cruelty to Fabulous Animals*, my first full book. I remember calling my mother from the post office, thrilled out of my mind when it arrived. Bev Daurio (The Mercury Press) has been a huge supporter and a thoughtful editor, publishing several of my books. Brian Kaufman and Karen Green (Anvil Press) made the beautiful *I, Dr. Greenblatt, Orthodontist, 251-1457,* and because of this, I continue to get emails from dental supply outlets.

Some of these fictions have appeared in the late great *Taddle Creek* (ed. Conan Tobias), *Best Canadian Stories 2024* (ed. Lisa Moore), *The Ampersand Review* (ed. Paul Vermeersch), *The Humber Review* (particular gratitude to the tremendous suggestions of Sarah Feldbloom), *Canadian Literature*, and *Me Then You Then Me* (a collaboration with Kathryn Mocker published by Kirby's beautiful Knife Fork Book), and *Devouring Tomorrow* (ed. A. G. Pasquella and Jeffrey Dupuis, Dundurn Press).

Some of these fictions also appeared as poems in my book of selected poems. Thanks to Noelle Allen at Wolsak & Wynn, for this and for all she does for literary community in our city. A. G. Pasquella's various hairbrained (hairchinned?) yet brilliant prompt-driven publications provided the occasion for several stories. Several of these fictions originated in media or literary collaborations with Donna Szöke, Dona Mayoora, Peter Chin, Mike Sikkema, and Kathryn Mocker.

Thanks to those who have kindly blurbed this book, all writers and people who I admire: Pasha Malla, Alessandro Porco, and Anuja Varghese. Your briefcase filled with unmarked rare first editions will be left under the bridge as per our agreement.

"From *Folktales from the Library of New Planets*" was written for *The Library of Known Planets*, an exhibition with work by Stephanie Vegh, Laine Groeneweg, and Steve Mazza at the Assembly Gallery (Hamilton).

I'm so glad that I had the opportunity to work with the insightful, rigorous, and imaginative editor Leigh Nash as well as other Assemblers Andrew Faulkner and Debby de Groot. And for the striking cover design that allowed us to cross the rubicund in style, thank you to Greg Tabor. My gratitude to my agents, Evan Brown and Samantha Haywood of Transatlantic Literary Agency, for their manifold assistance.

There are too many additional invaluable literary and artistic colleagues and friends to name (forty years' worth of thanks are due), but let me give a shout-out to ongoing discussions and collaborations with Derek Beaulieu, Gregory Betts, Elee Kraljii Gardiner, Tom Prime, Kathryn Mockler, Tor Lukasik-Foss, and Lillian Nećakov.

I am grateful to supporters of public funding for the arts through the Canada Council for the Arts, the Ontario Arts Council, and the City Enrichment Fund (Hamilton) for assistance over the years.

My parents made it possible for me to become a writer through their support, belief in books, the arts, education, and their belief in me. My children have also been an essential source of inspiration, discussion, great lines, and critical acumen for all their lives. It was indeed one of them who said, "Mommy makes the paper money. And Daddy makes the change."

Finally, absolutely elemental gratitude to my wife, Beth Bromberg. It turns out that the forty years represented by this book overlaps with the forty-two years I've known her. Why wasn't I writing those first two years? But it is a certainty that this book would be impossible without her.

Gary Barwin is the author of thirty-one books, including *Nothing the Same, Everything Haunted: The Ballad of Motl the Cowboy*, which won the Canadian Jewish Literary Award and was chosen for Hamilton Reads, and *Imagining Imagining: Essays on Language, Identity and Infinity*. His bestselling novel *Yiddish for Pirates* won the Leacock Medal for Humour and the Canadian Jewish Literary Award, and was a finalist for the Governor General's Award for Fiction and the Scotiabank Giller Prize. Barwin lives in Hamilton, Ontario.